TR(THE)OPE

STELLA STEVENSON

COPYRIGHT © 2022 by Stella Stevenson

All rights reserved.

Cover art by Stella Stevenson

No part of this book may be reproduced in any form or by any electronic or mechanical means, including information storage and retrieval systems, without written permission from the author, except for the use of brief quotations in a book review.

The scanning, uploading, and distribution of this book without permission is a theft of the author's intellectual property. If you would like permission to use material from the book (other than for review purposes), please contact stellaleestevenson@gmail.com. Thank you for your support of the author's rights.

This is a work of fiction. Names, characters, places, and incidents either are the product of the author's imagination or are used fictitiously, and any resemblance to actual persons, living or dead, business establishments, events, or locales is entirely coincidental.

This book is for anyone who has ever felt too whiny, too needy, or too clueless. For anyone who has been made to feel as if their differences make them too much work for others.

You aren't any of those things.
&
We deserve our happily ever after, too

CONTENT NOTES

includes possible spoilers

This is an open door romance that portrays on-page consensual sexual intimacy, suitable for readers ages 18+.

This story includes a main character who has diagnosed General Anxiety and Panic Disorders. The purpose of this story is not to show how Maggie overcomes her anxiety, but rather to share an experience that not everyone is familiar with and that those of us who are, would love to see represented more often.

Chapter 7 includes some potentially triggering misgendering and phobic comments directed towards one of the side characters. These thoughts are not the ones held by the main characters or the author and are immediately corrected on the page, but this may be distressing for some readers. This chapter can be skipped.

Through my own experiences, research, and the guidance of authenticity and beta readers, I hope I have given these subjects the care and respect that they deserve.

Please see my website www.authorstellastevenson.com for a full list of content warnings.

> "Confidence is not 'they will like me.'
> Confidence instead is 'I'll be fine if they don't.'"
> -Christina Grimmie

PROLOGUE

On the first day of kindergarten, Maggie Babbitt stood in front of twenty-four of her peers and told them she was going to be an author. She didn't use that word, author, because she didn't know it yet, but she got her point across just the same when she said she wanted to write stories. Two dozen pairs of eyes looked on with confusion and approval until one little boy, with his bowl haircut and glare, said, "You can't write stories. You can't read."

To her teacher's horror, Maggie had used all of her rage to kick Grayson right in his bony shin. For a moment, she'd felt weightless, a grin curling the corners of her mouth. Then Grayson had cried loud, sloppy tears, and she'd thought about throwing up everything she'd eaten since she was born.

"Margaret Ann," her mother had said in her you-are-in-trouble-young-lady voice when she picked her up from the nurse's office, "what on earth has gotten into you?"

Maggie tried to pull air into her tight lungs, feeling pressure sit on her chest like a dumbbell. She crossed her skinny arms across her skinnier chest and sat in the backseat, barely able to hear her mother's voice over the sound of water rushing through her ears. Spots danced in the corners of her vision. The stained backseat of her mother's sedan faded into almost nothing. Then a pair of cool hands wrapped around her upper arms and dragged her from the car. Her mother held her tight, the heat from the driveway soaking into her skin, her mother's pulse beating a pounding rhythm against her ear as her crisp voice helped Maggie list the colors of the mums lining the walkway.

"What happened, baby?" her mother asked, as Maggie's lungs loosened fraction by fraction.

"He said I couldn't be a writer."

"Well sweetling," Maggie's mother said, cuddling her closer, "can he see the future? You're the only one who knows if you can do that. Prove him wrong."

CHAPTER ONE

Maggie hit send on her email and listened to the *whoosh* as her first finished manuscript jettisoned into the ether and to her first round of readers. Since declaring her intentions at five, it had taken her twenty years, four months, and eighteen days to get to this point. Not that she'd been writing the same story that entire time, but this was the first full-length novel she'd completed, and tears had welled in her eyes as she'd typed the words "The End."

For a moment after the email sent, she felt that same weightless euphoria she'd experienced after kicking a kindergarten bully. Then she pillowed her head on her hands, fine strands of ash-brown hair splayed across her pock-marked desk, and breathed through the nausea.

Oh god, she thought as the inhalations shook her narrow body. *I did it. Now what?*

The idea that strangers were going to open her draft and sift through her words tugged on the unraveling seams of her anxiety. No one had ever read Maggie's stories before. They'd asked, demanded, pleaded, but Maggie had held firm. As long as no one read what she wrote, no one would know if it was good or terrible. Her publishing dreams were still there, in the distance, still her future. Not crushed under critique and criticism.

The only problem was if she wanted to publish her book, she had to let it out into the world. If Maggie's weekly therapy appointments had taught her anything, it was that it was okay to protect herself, but that didn't mean she could let her disorder rule her daily life. If her goal was to be an author, she had to do more than just write a book. She had to let people read it. Maggie and her therapist had worked up to this moment together—the moment when she sent the email—and they would no doubt talk again when the feedback started rolling in.

Head still down, Maggie's hand reached for her phone. She found it between two piles of half-used notebooks and under a crumpled purple sticky note. If her novel was done, should she clean her desk? Probably not. There was a certain familiar safety in the chaos, and even if she took a day and organized her apartment like Marie Kondo, it would be back to its basic level of mess within 24 hours. At the most. The phone buzzed in her hand, and Maggie swiped her finger along the cracked glass to unlock it, wincing as the sharp edges snagged on her skin.

THE TROPE

> **Audrey:**
> *This is our agreed-upon check in to make sure you sent your book out. Since I have full-faith that you did, drinks are on me tonight.*

> **Maggie:**
> *It's not a big deal. You don't have to go out of your way.*

It *was* a big deal, actually. Maggie had been working up to this moment for almost six months, and it was so gratifying to hear praise for accomplishing one of her mini goals instead of another set of rolled eyes and questions about why these little steps mattered in the grand scheme of things. Maggie was all about the little steps. Her anxiety often made those little steps monumental, like she was standing at the base of a boulder without any climbing equipment, watching everyone else hop up and over with ease.

> **Audrey:**
> *It's a huge deal, Maggie. I'll see you at 8.*

Maggie should have guessed that "drinks" in Audrey's world meant "party," but the noise when she pushed open the front door almost flattened her to the refinished hardwoods. Her friend was nowhere to be seen in the crush of people packed into the small house's living room. Red cups littered every available surface, and the walls pulsed with the bass line thundering out of the stereo.

The noise and the press of bodies had Maggie's heart pounding against her ribs and sweat beading under her arms. She'd have preferred a few drinks and a board game or a movie marathon with her close friends. Smaller crowds and familiar faces put her more at ease, but she could handle a party for one night, especially when it was meant for her. Audrey always left her an escape route in the kitchen or out back—somewhere she could find a quiet corner when the sound and the crowd overwhelmed her. Maggie didn't need it often, but it was nice to have the option.

"Audrey doesn't need an excuse to party, she just prefers one," she reminded herself before shouldering her way through the crowd to find a drink.

The kitchen was empty. No one seemed to venture towards the back of the house when the music and dancing were all at the front. Bottles of liquor covered the small counter space with a few stacks of cups and some napkins. A pile of pizza boxes from Sorento's, down the street, listed sideways, in danger of toppling to the floor.

The dated kitchen still had its original dark brown cabinets with ornate brass pulls that reminded Maggie of her nana's old home. Audrey's boyfriend Cal and his brother Tyler had inherited the place from their grandmother about a year before. The men had switched the yellow countertops out for a newer Formica, and they'd laid vinyl tiles over the old orange paisley ones. They'd even added a small peninsula with a handful of mismatched stools. Cal and his brother left the original lace curtains hanging from the scalloped valance over the sink. Audrey had tried to replace the curtains when she moved in a few months later, assuming the men just didn't know what to pick, and Tyler had almost thrown her out, citing sentimental value.

Maggie peeked under the open lid of one of the pizza boxes. A few leftover slices overlapped inside, grease creating a dark, expanding ring against the cardboard. They were all pepperoni. Not a good choice for a vegetarian. Maggie had eaten a sandwich a few hours earlier at the store, but if she was going to drink, she needed more food in her belly. Cal would eat cereal for three meals a day, if Audrey would let him, so it wouldn't be too much trouble to source a bowl of Cocoa Puffs before heading back to the party.

"There's some plain pizza in the fridge." The voice startled her like a cattle prod to the rear and Maggie jolted, a hand pressing to the center of her chest. She hadn't seen him standing there, too distracted by the mess, the memories, and the throb of the music. Tyler's back faced Maggie as he rinsed out one side of the double sink.

"Thanks, Mac." She opened the fridge to grab a slice.

"I put the butterscotch schnapps in the freezer." Mac turned off the water and grabbed a fluffy yellow dish towel. "Some of the other guests were eyeing the bottle, and I wanted to make sure there was still some left for you."

Tyler, "Mac" as his friends called him, wasn't as social as his younger brother. He had sharp umber eyes, a dark beard, and some enviable biceps thanks to the blacksmithing he did in the detached garage-turned-forge. He was a little quiet and a lot prickly, but he didn't seem to mind the crazy festivities his brother's girl liked to host.

"Thanks," Maggie said again. Almost everyone she knew made fun of her drink of choice, but not Mac.

Maggie and Mac only crossed paths at the house. He had the uncanny ability to show up when they needed to even out the players during game night. He'd single-handedly taught Maggie how to work the controllers on the Switch when she'd said she wanted to learn to play Mario. He'd shown her the buttons and kept a straight face when her longest survival time didn't break eight seconds. Cal had laughed so hard he'd fallen off the couch.

"I can heat that up for you." Mac leaned his compact body back against the counter, and Maggie mirrored him as she lifted her pizza to her mouth.

"Not necessary," she said around a healthy bite. "It defies all laws known to humankind, but cold pizza tastes better than warm pizza."

Mac nodded. Maggie took another mouthful. Sorento's had the perfect sauce to cheese to crust ratio, which meant Maggie didn't end up staining her clothes with grease or tomatoes. Maggie was technically an adult, but she still lacked the magic of stain-removal knowledge.

"I'm surprised you didn't come to the shop tonight for the tournament," she said. Mac was a pretty regular customer at The Tattered Cover, the comic-book-lover and gamer's paradise where she worked. In the last year he'd started selling some of his blades to collectors through Gary, the owner. Most of the weapons he sold were replicas of movie props or plucked from the pages of different comics. They were intricate and beautiful, and nothing stayed in stock long.

Mac met her eyes for a moment then turned away to clean his glass. "I don't play a lot of the booster draft format for Magic. I prefer to play commander."

"Mac, you know I have no idea what that means."

He turned to stare. "The tournament tonight is a draft format. You work at a comic book store and don't understand basic Magic: The Gathering formats? That's criminal, Maggie."

"Gary says the same thing, but he hasn't fired me yet."

Gary would never fire her. She was dependable, drama-free, and the only employee with handwriting legible enough to write the window displays. She occasionally felt the bite of anxiety when she had to help large groups or deal with angry customers, but her coworker was great at helping step in when she floundered. It also helped that Gary's mom was Maggie's second cousin. Sometimes nepotism had its perks.

"You played in the last three tournaments." Maggie fought down a blush at her blurted words. She didn't want to seem like she was stalking him. Mac frowned at her. He wasn't as tall as his brother, at least a few inches under six feet, but even with a smaller difference in their heights, Mac still looked down into her face.

"Just because it isn't my preferred format doesn't mean I don't play, but I had stuff that was more important tonight."

Of course he did. Several years older than Maggie, Mac taught history at the local college. He probably had papers to grade or lecture notes to prepare.

Mac pulled the schnapps bottle out of the freezer and poured a healthy slug into a cup. He pushed it into Maggie's hands, and she took it with a smile. Even schnapps burned on the way down, but the syrupy sweetness made it tolerable. Maggie grimaced as she downed the shot. Fruity blended drinks or cheap moscato were about all she could handle. And the occasional schnapps when she wanted a deeper buzz.

"I can make you something different," Mac said, eyes on her mouth. "You don't need to drink if you don't want to."

"You're sweet to offer," Maggie said.

"I'm not sweet."

"I'm good with schnapps. I might be a homebody, but I promise I'm not doing anything I don't want to do."

Tension seemed to seep out of Mac's broad shoulders. He raised the bottle, and Maggie held out her cup for another shot. He poured and then turned to put the bottle back in the freezer and Maggie let her eyes slip from his shoulders down to his butt in dark denim. She tried to blame her wandering eyes on the double shot she'd downed. She definitely blamed the heat in her cheeks on the alcohol. It definitely wasn't Mac himself.

"I'll be out back," Mac said. "Feel free to join me if you need a break from everything." He pushed his way out the back door.

Maggie finished her pizza and her second drink and then straightened her shoulders—good posture made people appear more confident—and made her way back into the party. She found Audrey in the middle of the living room, her arms wrapped around her boyfriend's neck as she sucked on his tongue. That wasn't anything new. Neither was the hand Cal had shoved up the front of Audrey's shirt. No one was paying the couple any attention, so Maggie turned away to look for other familiar faces. She could say hi to her friend when she disentangled. Or maybe even tomorrow. Given how tightly the two pressed against each other, it was plausible that they'd be disappearing sooner rather than later.

"How much would I have to pay you to blind me?" A husky voice said, and Maggie almost swallowed her own tongue. "I like Cal, but they could aim for a lower profile, don't you think? Or just not invite me."

Maggie's heart rate tripled its beat beneath her sternum. A faint ringing had started up in her ears, but she wasn't sure if that was because of the loud music or Dean's proximity. He had the same green eyes and sandy blonde hair as her best friend. Same wide smile with perfect white teeth. Audrey was tall, and Dean was taller. He had to bend almost in half to place his mouth next to her ear, but Maggie's height was below average. She turned towards his voice, and only inches separated their mouths.

"I—" Maggie wet her lips to try again, "Dean, hi."

"Hey, Babs." Dean said.

He'd always called her that ever since she first met Audrey on the bus to kindergarten. As a third grader, Dean had named himself their protector. He never seemed to mind having two pipsqueaks chasing him around. Dean smiled, eyes twinkling in the dim light, and he slung an arm around Maggie's shoulders to pull her into his body. He'd always been quick with a hug, doling out easy affection. He'd been Maggie's first kiss, although she was pretty sure he didn't know that she counted the quick touch of their lips at his high school graduation party as her first.

"I hear congratulations are in order. You finished your book." He pressed his mouth to the top of her head.

"I didn't know you'd be here," Maggie said, the words coming out breathy like she'd just run up and down the stairs a few times. She wondered if Dean could see the pulsing neon hearts in her eyes.

"I wouldn't miss your day for the world, Babs, even if I have to brave my sister's public displays of canoodling." He tightened his arm around her for a quick squeeze and then released her.

"I only finished the first draft," Maggie said. "I sent it off for some feedback today, but there's still editing and rewriting and a lot more to do before it's *done*, done."

"Still counts," Dean said. "When do I get to read it?"

Maggie thought of her sandy blonde hero with green eyes and a laughing smile. The one who traded grins and hugs like candy while fiercely protecting those he loved. She thought about chapter sixteen when the hero boosted the heroine up onto the kitchen counter as his hands wandered up her thighs.

"Never."

"You writing one of those spicy books, Babs?"

Maggie felt the flush start low on her chest and spread up her throat. Her face flamed the same red as the cups littering the living room. Her voice was gone, nonexistent, and she tried to squeak out a reply, but nothing happened. Sweat beaded along her fingers and palms, and she tried to wipe them against the denim of her black jeans.

"Hey," Dean leaned forward to lock their eyes again, "I was just teasing. I didn't mean to embarrass you." He ruffled the hair at the crown of her head.

Was it hot in here? It was definitely too hot.

"No. It's fine." Maggie forced her body to relax and smile. "I just don't like to talk about my writing." Especially not with her walking, talking inspiration. Or with anyone she knew, because what if they hated it? Or worse, what if they lied to her so she wouldn't know they hated it? What if she sucked and the last two decades had been an epic waste of time? What if her whole life had been a...

No. She would not spiral down again. Maggie was ready to take risks and believe in her book, in her storytelling. She would not let her anxiety steal this from her. Everyone said, "write what you know," and sure, Maggie had steered clear of most relationships for most of her adult life because she didn't have the time and energy to pour her little introverted heart into one, but she'd read enough romance novels to even the score. Maggie had no problem losing herself in romance novels, and she was shy, yes, but also proud of the one she'd written.

"I'm sorry," Maggie said, her eyes searching Dean's for the short time she could maintain the contact. She didn't apologize because she'd done something wrong, but because she recognized the tension thrumming under her skin, and she could feel how shallow her breathing was getting, and she was pretty sure he thought she was acting like a complete freak. So apologizing was a good idea. Apologizing was a necessity. No matter what her therapist said.

"Don't say sorry, Babs." Dean framed her face in his enormous hands, and there went all the air in the room again. "We all have things we want and need to keep private. You do not need to apologize for holding boundaries. I will love you either way."

He would love her either way.

Love her.

Holy shit.

This was the best day of Maggie's life.

CHAPTER TWO

The first comments from her readers hit Maggie's email about a week later while she was working. She'd carried her phone on her, on silent, since the moment she'd sent the book off. Gary didn't care if she or Shay, the other daytime Tattered Cover employee, had their phones behind the counter as long as they were attentive and helpful and got their work done. When the subtle vibration from her pocket alerted her to a new email, and her reader's name was on the sender line, Maggie almost bowed out of work early to go home and look at it in private.

She desperately wanted to read the message and the comments, but she knew better than to do so at work even if the shop was empty, and she wasn't sure her heart would take the strain of seeing what her reader had to say anywhere but in the privacy of her own bed.

In her bed, she could cry and rage and wrap herself up in her blankets if the comments were too much. In the store, she had to tamp down her reactions and avoid a scene. Maggie would be hard-pressed to admit it, but she enjoyed these last few moments of peace before she had to read what they thought.

She expected some negative reactions—the aim of sending it out was for constructive feedback—but suddenly she was lightheaded considering the idea that people had actually read her words and probably hated them. She'd prefer to confine any anxiety-induced panic to the privacy of her own home with her therapist on speed dial. The only problem was that even the thought of reading the feedback was tightening her chest.

"Are you okay?" Shay asked. They held a cardboard box full of recent issues of one of their newer comics ready to be shelved. "You're super jittery."

Maggie's hands trembled no matter how still she tried to hold them. Despite her hair being both fine and pin straight, the sweat on her palms kept causing her hands to snag as she dragged her fingers through the waist-length layers.

"Sorry," Maggie said and tangled her fingers together to still them. "I got my first feedback, so I'm a little out of it."

Shay slammed the box down on the glass counter. "It's good, isn't it! I knew it."

Maggie shook her head. "I haven't looked yet." She gestured around the shop. "I'm working, remember? So are you."

Shay rolled their eyes back into their head. "The store is basically dead. Go read the email, and I'll cover you."

"No," Maggie said. "I don't even know if I can read it at all, but definitely not in public."

"There's no one here. Go to the break room and read the damn email so we can squeal and jump around together when it's all glowing and shit."

Maggie stared at her friend. She would have to read the email eventually, even though the thought made her break into a cold sweat. It might be better to get it over with, especially in a comfortable, but neutral, environment. Hell, if she read the damn email at home, and it was awful, she wouldn't have anywhere to go to escape the crushing weight of failure. But if she read it at work and it was awful, she'd have to suffer through the rest of her shift and the commute home.

"I'm scared to look at it," she said to Shay. "I'm not sure I can physically make myself open the email, let alone decipher the words."

"I can read it for you. If you think it would help."

"Absolutely not." Maggie shook her head. "We're friends." Shay would have to lie to her, and Maggie would know and there would go three years of friendship, and as if that wasn't bad enough, who on earth would Maggie look forward to seeing at work every day?

"You aren't making any sense with that one, but—" Shay's eyes scanned the empty racks of comic books and playing cards. They paused at the man standing in front of some of their mystery boxes, the ones stuffed with old comic books. Mac was wearing a dark green sweater over dark denim pants, square-rimmed glasses sitting low on his nose as he checked something on his phone. "Have Mac read it to you."

Maggie struggled to hold in her snort of laughter but studied Mac, too. Shay could be on to something. Mac was *almost* a friend but not quite. They spent time together, sure, but they didn't hang out. He was polite whenever they spoke, and if he wasn't friendly, well, he wasn't a guy who was super friendly with anyone. The romance world would categorize him as a "Grumpy" if he were a main character. Mac would probably read the email for her and not spare another thought to what it said. He also wouldn't care that she was too chicken shit scared to read it herself. He'd go right back to his regular life as if nothing had happened.

"Mac," Shay said, their voice carrying in the small store.

His head lifted from the phone, glancing at Maggie and Shay standing behind the counter. Maggie watched his thumb turn off his screen, and he shoved the phone into the back pocket of his jeans. He walked over to the counter, stopping to lean his forearms on the glass. He spread his hands apart in a "what" gesture.

"Do you read?" Shay asked. They hoisted the cardboard box back off the counter.

"Of course he reads. He's a professor." Maggie blushed. She hoped Shay would correctly interpret the do-it-and-die look she was sending their way.

"Do you read romance?" Shay was apparently unaffected by eye threats.

"No," Mac said, dark eyes moving from Shay to Maggie. "Why?"

"Perfect. Maggie needs help with something." Shay winked at Maggie's red face, shifted the box to one hip, and walked away as if they hadn't tried to destroy Maggie's life.

Now, whether she wanted to or not, Maggie had to ask Mac for help. Okay, so she had planned to ask Mac for help, anyway. She'd have taken a lot more time to do so, but she would have asked. Something Shay obviously knew. Mac looked at her with interest. Dark hair peppered his forearms except for a puckered pink patch of skin above his left wrist. A burn from his forge, no doubt.

"I saw the blades you dropped off," Maggie said, and Mac blinked slowly, dark lashes brushing his tanned cheeks. "I really like those Ñoldorin daggers Galadriel gave Merry and Pippin. Even if they're from the movies, not the book. I may treat myself to one if they're still here by Friday." Payday.

"What do you need my help with?"

"It's nothing," Maggie said. "An email. And I was serious about the daggers."

"Don't waste your money," Mac said. "Tell me about the email."

"It's not a waste." Maggie put her hands on her hips. "I think you are supremely talented, and I love *The Lord of the Rings*, and even if I'm a teensy bit intimidated by weapons, they're still gorgeous art pieces." She expected him to wince at the word 'art,' but Mac did nothing. Maggie wondered if he'd even heard her.

"If you want a blade, I'll make you a blade. Tell me about the email."

"Don't be ridiculous, Mac. That's a lot of work and time—"

"Maggie." One hand lifted to pinch the bridge of his nose and he let out a rough breath. "Do you need me to read an email? Or write an email?"

Maggie sucked in a breath, her nerves swirling in a dizzying rush, even as the tension left her shoulders. Her voice, when she found it, came out in a whisper. "Read it, please."

"Okay." Mac opened his eyes and held his calloused hand out for her phone. "Do you want to do it here or somewhere more private?" Maggie blinked up at him and Mac cursed. He moved his outstretched hand to run through his shaggy hair, leaving the thick strands standing straight up. "I didn't mean…. Never mind." He held his hand out again and opened and closed his fingers a few times to get her moving.

"We can go to the break room," Maggie said. "Don't tell Gary, although you're basically an employee."

She stepped away from the counter and pushed her phone into Mac's hand as she passed him. His palm was a little sweaty against hers, or maybe her palm was sweaty against his. She smiled at Mac, a smile he didn't return, but his eyes didn't leave her face as he curled his fingers around her cracked iPhone. Maggie gestured for Mac to follow her down the far wall, studded with Pokémon paraphernalia, to the break room at the back of the shop. She let the door click closed behind them, knowing Shay would watch the front. Her heart pounded in her chest.

Mac held her phone up.

"You should probably pull the email up yourself and give me a little context. Have you read it yet?"

Maggie typed in her passcode—her thumbprint had stopped working months ago—and pulled up her Gmail account. She ignored the three-hundred and ten notification bubbles that assaulted her and navigated to the unread email. She handed the phone back to Mac. He was watching her, brows pulled together in the typical frown he always wore around her. Around everyone.

"It's the first feedback on my book," she said, voice low, and for a moment, his brows lifted in surprise before they settled back into his permanent scowl. "I haven't read it yet."

"Why not?"

"What if they hated it?"

Mac took a deep breath and glanced from Maggie's phone to her face. "It's their job to help you strengthen your story, right?"

Maggie nodded.

"So the feedback should be constructive, not negative."

"It could still be negative."

Mac tilted his head, his eyes warming her skin like a physical touch. "Would you quit if it was?"

"What?" Maggie asked.

"Would you abandon the book? Stop writing?"

"Of course not." Walking away from her first novel was unthinkable. She'd re-write it and re-work it if she had to, but she couldn't walk away. She'd poured her soul into the words, the story, and the characters. She'd spent hours of her life agonizing over the pages.

"Then there's nothing to be scared of." Mac reached a hand out as if to touch her. He stopped and let it fall to his side, balling the fingers into a tight fist.

Maggie's chest heaved as her breath sawed in and out of her lungs. She tangled her fingers in the hem of her cardigan. "Will you still read it for me?" Her voice cracked at the end.

"Read it out loud? Or summarize?"

"Out loud, please."

He met her eyes and the very edge of his full lips tipped into a smile. "Tell me when you're ready."

"I'm ready."

Mac looked down at the screen in his hands and tapped something, probably the email, with one blunt finger. He scanned the top and then scrolled down. His eyes flicked up to Maggie's again, deep brown colliding with cornflower blue. Mac took a deep breath, and Maggie watched his shoulders rise and fall as the air filled his lungs.

"Thank you for sharing your novel with me. I have attached a copy of your draft with my notes to this email. I wanted to say that I think you have some real potential here. Your plot is new and interesting, and your characters are lovable and have some real promise. My only real worry is that I'm not feeling any chemistry between your main characters. There are some missed opportunities to show their

emotions or how they are experiencing different situations as opposed to telling the reader.

"The result is a relationship that comes across rather forced. It reads like you focused more on what you thought should happen between your characters, as opposed to what they needed to bring them together. Write scenes that are real, not only the tropes you see in every romance novel. I've marked the places where this seemed the most problematic for me, but it was particularly noticeable at the end of chapters five and twelve. I think it's a matter of getting to know your characters better. That way they can lead you, and us, to where they need to be together. I also found some spelling and grammar errors. I marked them for you, but nothing egregious—"

Mac trailed off as he took in Maggie's blank expression. All the blood had seeped out of her face, and there was a rushing in her ears. Was the room spinning? It might be spinning. Or that flipping sensation could have been in her stomach. A pair of strong hands wrapped around her biceps, grounding her body, but her mind continued to spiral. Her book was a failure. A flop. They hated it.

"Maggie," Mac's voice cut through the panic. She focused on his face, her eyes meeting his worried ones. His fingers squeezed into the nonexistent muscles of her upper arms before he released them. "Hey," he said. "It's not bad. They see a lot of potential."

Maggie shook her head. "My characters are flat. It's unbelievable. There's no romance."

"Hey," Mac said again. "Don't start that shit. You said you weren't going to quit."

Maggie shrugged. That had been before the feedback had been negative. Before she'd felt like her soul had been torn out and trampled. In theory she knew she was overreacting, but she was having a hard time reining her brain back into compliance. "I'm not quitting, but—"

"No buts." Mac framed her face, his hands warm against her skin. "You need to get to know your characters better. How do you do that?"

"I don't know." Her voice was weak, quiet. She hated it.

"You do," he said. When had he gotten so close? "When was the last time you had a great date or fell in love? Channel that."

That was going to be a problem, wasn't it? Maggie had never been in love with someone who loved her back, so it probably didn't count. As for dating, she'd grabbed dinner with one of Cal's coworkers about a year ago. He'd left halfway through, and she'd been stuck paying for his surf 'n turf even though she didn't eat meat. Shay had laughed for thirty minutes after hearing that and informed Maggie she should have only paid for her own meal and provided her date's contact info to the restaurant for the rest of it. But yea, Maggie wouldn't have done that, ever. She was a romance writer who was basically a romance virgin.

"I—" She looked at Mac. He wasn't particularly tall, and the beard and permafrown definitely gave a distinct "back off" vibe. His lashes were the longest she'd ever seen. He was always respectful to other people. And the muscles in his arms rivaled Thor's. He was also wickedly smart but not at all condescending. Maggie was sure he had plenty of girlfriends, plenty of dates. She blushed. She couldn't admit to Mac that she was a romance-less romance writer. She couldn't tell him she was a fraud. Was she a fraud?

"Are you okay?" Mac asked, and his voice sounded like it was underwater. It burbled against her ears. "It's one person's opinion, Maggie. You sent this thing to several readers? I bet they'll all have different thoughts."

Maggie nodded. Her head felt weighed down, as if each thought were a lead ball rolling from the back of her brain to the front.

"I think you need to go home," Mac said. His eyes looked too large in his face as he peered into hers. "Maggie?"

She nodded again, and her brain did the same rolling swoop as before. Mac's voice sounded even further away.

"Sorry," Maggie said because she was probably overreacting. She was probably being dramatic. This poor man had done something nice for her, and now she was ruining it by acting like a total fool.

Maggie forced herself to take a deep breath. She dragged air into her lungs, and it cut like swallowing a sharp piece of cereal the whole way down. A quick pause, then she forced another. She could feel the sharp edges of her panic as anxiety tried to sink its talons into her. She needed to ground herself. Maggie glanced around the employee break room, cataloging five things she could see. There was the frayed hole in the green paisley couch. The staff photo of her, Gary, and Shay all standing behind the register and grinning like loons. The spot on the floor where two black squares butted up against each other on the mislaid vinyl tiles. The hot pink swirl of her no-tie shoelaces. And the warm gold glint of the chain around Mac's neck. She already felt a little better.

"Don't apologize, dammit," Mac said, his voice cracking. "Stay right here. I'll be right back."

Maggie felt the rough scrape of his fingers as he let go of her cheeks. The bumpy center of the button at the bottom of her cardigan. She slid her hands over the worn denim of her jeans. She twisted the cool silver ring on her thumb. Four things she could feel.

While she was busy collecting herself, Mac strode to the break room door and pulled it open. He ducked his head out but didn't leave the room. Maggie heard the squeak of the metal hinges protesting the force Mac used to wrench it open. She heard a ping as his phone signaled something—a text or an email. She heard his rich voice as he called out to Shay that he was going to take her home. Three things she could hear.

Wait. What? He was taking her home? Her breathing didn't hurt as much as before, but she had to finish. Getting through all five senses was necessary, or she could fall right back into her panic.

Gary had left a sweatshirt draped over the back of a chair in the break room. Maggie could smell the faint hint of the menthols he insisted he would quit. He was careful about smoking in and around the merchandise—fans could be feral—but the scent never quite left his outer layers. Mac stepped back in front of her, green sweater blocking her entire field of vision, but she wasn't on sight anymore, she was on smell. She inhaled through her nose and caught a whiff of iron and coal mixed with pine. Mac smelled smoky, too, but infinitely better than Gary's cigarette sweatshirt. Two things she could smell.

"Come on, Maggie," Mac said, and his words no longer bounced out of her ears. "I'm going to drive you home. Shay has you covered."

One more thing, something she could taste. Maggie licked her lips and tasted salt. A lone tear had tracked down her cheek to her mouth.

"Thank you, Mac." She forced a smile, letting her dimples out. "I'm okay, but thank you."

Mac scrubbed a hand down his face, his tan skin a nice contrast to his dark beard. He held out her phone, and she took it back, shoving it deep into the back pocket of her jeans.

"Okay," Mac said, his frown back in place. "I want to be clear that I don't really believe you, but I'm choosing to trust you, anyway."

Maggie's pulse tripped. She'd gotten good at pretending things were fine after an episode. She'd had to learn to fake it after a few too many breakdowns in public. In reality, they left her drained, exhausted. Her brain sluggish and her limbs heavy.

"Thank you," she said. "I'm okay. Sad, but okay. I'll figure it out."

Mac's frown deepened, his brows almost touching. "I know we aren't friends, but if there's a way I can help—"

"We aren't friends, Mac?" Maggie asked, pouting to annoy him further and because his words stung a bit. "I'm heartbroken."

"You annoy me less than most, Maggie," Mac's lips tipped up into a tiny hint of a smile, "but let's not push it."

CHAPTER THREE

"You never told me what your readers thought!" Audrey swirled her wine in her stemless glass, pinning Maggie with a knowing look over the rim.

It was tradition for Audrey and Maggie to finish each week with wine and cheese and Netflix. They'd started the practice in high school and hadn't missed a week in seven years. This week they were sitting on Audrey's couch, feet propped on the heavy wooden coffee table, eating from a labeled cheese board. A reality dating show where some guy's mother made each pick played on the television. They were five episodes deep in this dating show, having binged it the week before at Maggie's. When Maggie hosted girls' night, they still put their feet up and ate in front of the television, but they typically ate pre-sliced cheese directly from the package. Audrey always picked the wine since if it were up to Maggie, they'd only drink moscato or piña coladas.

"It wasn't great," Maggie said. "They all said the same thing. My characters don't have chemistry."

"What twats." Audrey took another sip of wine. "Your characters were so real. I'm pretty sure I've met your hero. Like in real life."

You mean your brother? Maggie used both hands to shove that thought right out of her mind.

It had taken the last four days, but after her panic attack at the store and crying herself to sleep on the couch while *Pride and Prejudice* played on repeat and rereading her current favorite book, she was ready to face the next step with her novel.

"The issue isn't the characters themselves, it's their relationship. It fell flat. The romance wasn't believable because they didn't seem drawn to each other or in love."

"And that's a bad thing?"

"For a romance novel, yes."

"So just write them into love."

"It's not that simple," Maggie said. She set her wine glass on the table, searching for the words. "I can't just tell my readers what my characters are thinking or feeling. I have to build the tension and the stakes in other ways. It needs to be in the minute interactions, the way he looks at her, the way their fingers brush, the way she puts his needs first. But somehow I'm not capturing it. My readers need to ship my characters. Right now they don't."

Audrey tapped her index finger against her pursed lips. "Okay, we can fix this."

We? Maggie wanted to ask, because only one of them was actually writing the story. Her characters, Jenna and Luke, were so much fun to write and learn. And yes, Luke had a heavy dose of golden hair and mossy green eyes, and innate protectiveness stolen directly from Audrey's brother, but she had no idea how to change the chemistry. Absolutely none. And as much as Maggie loved Audrey like family and trusted her with things nobody else knew, Audrey was not a writer. She was barely even a reader unless it was true crime or covered in gore. They'd had to settle on reality television since her previous movie night picks usually caused Maggie some extensive nightmares, and Maggie did not have extra funds for extra therapy.

"I appreciate your support, but I can handle this," Maggie said.

Audrey shook her head. "Maggie, I love you. I adore you. But you don't stress well. Please let me help." She reached for Maggie's hand, enclosing it in both of hers. "I don't say this to be mean, but your anxiety sometimes leads you to a major freak out, and I want to help get you on the 'fix it' path instead of the panic path."

Most of Maggie's anxiety stemmed from the worry that she'd failed at something or let someone down, but she could handle other pressures just fine. Sometimes. There were times when she could feel the panic coming, seeping over her skin and into her pores like cold water, chilling her down to the bone. Other times she barely recognized the grip of anxiety before she was spiraling into a tangled web of intrusive thoughts and heart palpitations. Audrey was uniquely skilled at helping bring Maggie back down when she was stuck in her own slide. As much as she loved her friend and appreciated her carefulness, sometimes Maggie felt like Audrey underestimated her.

"I already had the panic," Maggie said, and Audrey immediately pulled her into a hug. "I'm okay, I swear. Mac helped."

"Mac?"

"He was at the store when I got the first email."

"And he helped." Audrey's tone was flat. "Mac."

Audrey got along just fine with her boyfriend's brother, so Maggie was having a hard time deciphering the look on her friend's face. Mac wasn't a mean guy, he was just introverted. Extremely introverted.

"It doesn't matter." Maggie said, "It still doesn't solve my current writing issues."

Audrey was quiet for a few minutes as she chewed on a spelt cracker and a piece of Gruyère.

"I say this with love," Audrey said, "but you don't date, and maybe you should."

Maggie blinked at her best friend. She opened her mouth to protest, and Audrey cut her off. "Maybe you struggle to write chemistry because you haven't experienced it firsthand."

"I don't have time to date." Maggie's rebuff was automatic.

Audrey fixed her with a knowing smile. "Do you not have time? Or do you not have interest? It's okay if you don't have an interest in anyone or in dating or in sex."

Maggie blushed.

"What if giving it a shot would give you some insight into your book?"

Maggie was interested in people, well one in particular, but the idea of putting herself out there with strangers made her itchy and lightheaded. Was it possible to be allergic to dating? She couldn't remember the last time she'd been attracted to someone other than Dean, and men seemed to take it personally when their dates weren't attracted to them. She could recognize a good-looking man, Mac, for example, but her love for her best friend's brother kind of negated that knowledge.

"You could plan a couple of movie-worthy dates with a hot guy and then take all those mental notes you're so good at." Audrey's words were coming faster, a sure sign she was getting excited. "I'm sure Cal can find someone hot but respectful."

Dean flashed through Maggie's mind before she could censor her own thoughts. Warm green eyes and straight white teeth. Her stomach flipped. She could never ask Dean, could she?

"Cal can find what?" Audrey's boyfriend walked through the front door with his brother. Cal stopped by the couch to press a kiss to Audrey's mouth.

Mac lifted one hand in greeting and Maggie lifted hers back. He leaned his shoulder back against the door frame to the kitchen. Maggie hadn't seen him since her panic at The Tattered Cover, but her insides felt a little warm, and she also felt a lot grateful that he hadn't mentioned her panic attack to Audrey. He'd grounded her when she needed it, but he hadn't made more of the moment than it was. Mac's sweater was black with his same dark jeans and worn brown boots and the same frown permanently creasing his face.

"Someone for Maggie to date," Audrey said with a big grin. Mac's eyes snapped to Maggie.

"Sure," Cal said and jumped right in like he always did. "Jack's a good guy. Sam and Stubbs, too. I know they think she's cute."

"'She' is right here," Maggie reminded Cal, but his energy was infectious, so she was smiling too.

"I know you are, Hon. We'll get you set up in no time," Cal said.

Maggie grinned. It couldn't be all bad. Even if she didn't want to date any of the guys Cal would come up with. Not that she thought he would pick someone awful. Cal's friends were all similarly good-looking, but she wasn't sure about starting an actual relationship with someone if she was using the experience for research. It seemed dishonest.

Maggie didn't like to lie. The thought of pretending to like one of Cal's friends, just to get ahead with her writing, seemed mercenary. Cal promised his friends wouldn't care—spending time with a good-looking girl was reward enough—but what if the guy she picked was looking for more? Maggie was irrevocably in love with someone else. She didn't want to hurt anyone, and she really didn't want to tie herself to awkward dates. And the dates *would* be awkward if the guys thought she was interested and then found out she wasn't. What if she was honest from the start? Would any of Cal's friends be willing to pretend to date her?

Romance novels had always been a comfort. Maggie had picked up her first one at twelve. She'd borrowed it from her nana and been simultaneously scandalized and obsessed enough to forget to return it. She loved the romance, the tension, the heat, but most of all, Maggie loved the happily ever afters. Maggie read romance novels for the same reason she preferred to rewatch her favorite television shows and movies: she already knew how they were going to end. A guaranteed happy ending went a long way toward putting her at ease. There was no reason to worry about what was happening, even when the author ripped her guts apart, because she knew things would work out in the end. Some readers might not like the familiarity, searching for something new and different to hold their attention, but Maggie thrived on these common moments. It was refreshing to have one part of her life where things worked out the way they were supposed to.

Fake dating was common in romance novels. Usually it involved two parties signing on to a mutually beneficial pretend relationship and ended with them realizing they wanted more than just pretend romance. Maggie couldn't think of a single book she'd read where the fake dating trope didn't unearth feelings on both sides. Maybe she was looking at this all wrong. She'd live out a famous trope, have time to go on some romantic dates, and she could take some fantastic notes. No one could say her novel wasn't believable if she wrote what she lived. And if her fake date, she already knew who she could ask, recognized he had feelings for her? Even better.

"Why?" Mac's voice cut through her daydream and it took Maggie a minute to remind herself what he was asking. "Why do you need to be set up? You don't date."

Like being doused by a bucket of cold water, the doubt seeped into Maggie's bones. Fantasy wasn't real life. Romance novels weren't real life. Using a trope to jumpstart her own love life and then her book was a stupid idea. It was the idea of Mac, supportive, watchful Mac, pointing it out that made her chest ache.

"It's nothing," Maggie said, at the same time Audrey said, "Maggie's going to get a boyfriend so she can do some research on chemistry and dating for her book revision."

Mac sucked his teeth. "Do you think that will work?"

"Yes," Maggie answered, steeling her spine so she'd sound confident and certain, despite feeling anything but. "I obviously don't know enough about love and relationships to write believable ones, so I need to get some experience first."

"You're sure?" He asked, dark eyes searching her face.

Maggie nodded.

"Then don't let Cal set you up." Mac was still leaning against the door, but the way he watched her made it seem like he was standing directly in front of her. As if he were close enough to touch. Heat curled under her belly button even as her muscles felt loose and weak. It was a good thing she was still sitting down, or she may have needed some help to stay upright. Mac and his muscles could probably hold her up with his pinky finger.

"Hey." Cal said, "I know some great guys for Maggie."

"Pick someone you want," Mac said to Maggie, ignoring his brother. "You want to write about true feelings? Then pick someone who you want and who wants you." Then Mac disappeared into the kitchen and Maggie heard the slam of the back door. He'd gone out to the garage to work on a blade.

"How does he forge in those sweaters?" Maggie asked no one in particular. "They have to be a fire hazard."

"He takes them off," Cal said, and stole a cracker from the spread.

Maggie coughed as a flush of heat swept up her throat to her cheeks.

"Mac's right. Pick someone you're interested in, but I know some good guys who would be both interested and fun. Let me know if you want any introductions."

"Thanks, Cal," Maggie said, and another vision of Dean scrolled through her mind.

"Shoo." Audrey flapped her hands at her boyfriend. "We're having wine and cheese night. Go bother Mac or play Halo and I'll come find you when we're done."

Cal pressed another kiss to Audrey's mouth, waved to Maggie, and disappeared up the stairs to his and Audrey's room. Audrey studied her for a moment. Maggie tried to school her expression into a neutral mask, wanting to give nothing away.

"You could ask—" Audrey bit her lip and turned away.

"Ask who?" Maggie frowned around a mouthful of brie.

"Never mind," Audrey waved the question off and pressed start. "Ask anyone you want, Maggie. I promise no one will judge your choice."

CHAPTER FOUR

An hour later, show finished and dishes stacked in the dishwasher, Maggie said goodbye to Audrey and headed for her car. Her ancient two-door Civic could only be considered a car by the most basic of definitions. The air conditioner didn't work at all, the heater only worked occasionally, and duct tape held at least one mirror in place. But the old girl hadn't let her down once since Maggie had inherited it from her nana at sixteen.

Instead of driving home, Maggie took the less familiar roads to the snazzy apartments in the center of downtown. It was easy to pretend that she didn't know why she'd driven here, but the minute Audrey's idea had taken root in her mind, there was only one man that really fit what Maggie was looking for. Dean's face had flashed across her brain and scalded itself across the back of her retinas.

She'd spent years dreaming of him in place of her heroes. Hell, she'd written him into her book. Real life wasn't written by Tessa Bailey or Emily Henry, but Maggie could sure as hell write her own life, thank you.

Maggie put the car in park and shoved her keys into her giant messenger bag. Her car door echoed through the parking lot when she slammed it shut, and she winced. This wasn't abnormal. She'd been here to see Dean before, usually with Audrey, but still. There was no reason to be nervous and no reason to sneak. She buzzed his apartment and in true Dean fashion, he let her in without even asking who she was.

Dean's eyes went wide when he opened his door and saw her standing there, but his smile didn't slip, and he waved her inside his apartment.

"Sorry." Maggie clutched the strap of her bag tightly in her fist. "Am I interrupting anything?"

Dean glanced down the hallway as he shut the door, but he shook his head. "Kyle's stopping by later, but I'm all yours for now, Babs." He squeezed her shoulder in his hand as he walked past her into his open-concept kitchen and living room. "Can I get you anything?"

Yes, Maggie wanted to say. *You can be my fake boyfriend, and then we can go on dates, and you can realize that you've loved me as long as I've loved you, and it will be glorious.*

"I'm fine," she said.

Dean looked at her, his green eyes narrowing as he crossed his arms over his chest.

"If you're fine, Babs, then why are you here at," he checked the heavy silver watch on his wrist, "nine-thirty at night."

Maggie looked up into Dean's classically handsome face. This was the same boy who had punched fifth grader Justin Krone when he'd tried to look up her skirt on the bus. Dean was the boy who wrapped his flannel shirt around her waist when she'd bled through her pants during freshman year bio. He'd shown up at her house later that night with chocolate, Dr. Pepper, a box of pads, and romcoms to help ease her cramps and pride. This was the boy who had picked her up, just last year, at the airport in the middle of the night because her delayed flight landed after the taxis and shuttle stopped running and Audrey hadn't heard her phone ring. All she had to do was ask him, and he'd say yes.

Maggie took a deep breath to calm her nerves. Her stomach was twisting in on itself like a collapsing black hole. "Actually, I could use your help with something. Something important."

Dean unwound his arms and straightened his shoulders. "You in trouble?"

Maggie shook her head. "No. I just need help from a guy, and you're the one I trust most."

Dean blanched and his eyes swept from her head to her toes and back. They focused on her flat stomach underneath her old Led Zeppelin tee. "Is this a sex or baby thing?"

Maggie had to give Dean credit where it was due. He'd gone whiter than his couch, but he didn't let his smile drop. Maggie's blush suffused her cheeks as she shook her head.

"Neither." Her voice cracked, and Dean relaxed.

"What do you need me to do?"

Maggie looked down at her scuffed sneakers. She was wearing two different colored socks. How had she gone a whole day without noticing that?

"Babs?" Dean had stepped closer to her. His voice was soft and soothing, the same voice he used the time he talked her out from under the bleachers in middle school, or after last Halloween when Audrey insisted on watching horror movies after all the trick-or-treaters had gone home and she'd been too scared to walk to her car in the dark. "Whatever you need, I'm here."

Maggie looked up into his mossy green eyes with the brown flecks running through the irises. She looked at the soft curve of his pink lips, and the buzz of his sandy stubble along a chiseled jaw. She took a deep breath. Cool air and the spicy scent of Dean's cologne entered her lungs. This was half the reason she loved him. No questions asked. He would do anything for her. Within reason, of course.

"I need you to be my boyfriend." Maggie sent Dean a wholesome smile, trying to soften the shock that had locked down his every muscle. "Fake boyfriend," she clarified. Dean swallowed, his Adam's apple bobbing in his tanned throat.

"I think I'm going to need a drink and an explanation." Dean took a highball glass out of the cupboard. He grabbed a second one for Maggie and poured two fingers of honey-brown liquor into each glass. He turned and held one out. Maggie didn't drink whiskey, but she took the glass between her palms and held it tight. Dean took a sip, paused, then threw the rest of the alcohol back. "Let's sit down,"

With a hand on Maggie's elbow, he led her to his pristine leather couch. Maggie perched on the very end of her cushion, trying to sit as still as possible to not spill her drink. Dean sat next to her. He leaned all the way into the back of the couch and propped his ankle on the opposite thigh, keeping his gaze pinned to her face as though he could figure out her secrets just from the eye contact.

"Let's start with why you need a fake boyfriend," Dean said.

Maggie nodded and leaned forward to set her drink on the low-slung coffee table. Dean needed an explanation. Dean deserved an explanation. One other than how she hoped it would make him fall head over heels for her. She did hope that, but she also needed help with her book. Maggie explained about her characters, the reader feedback, and her need for real-world experiences. She felt like a child, bumbling through her thoughts and blush stealing up her cheeks as she admitted she'd preferred reading to dating and sex. She would forever be grateful that Dean listened with a straight face. He leaned forward, fingers steepled as he considered what she said.

"Why a fake boyfriend?" Dean asked. "Why not pick a guy you like and date them for real?"

Technically, that's what she was trying to do. Couldn't he be a little more cooperative?

Maggie shook her head. "There's no one," *other than you*, "I'm interested in, and I don't have the time to just wait for something to develop. I just need to get some of the life experiences now so I can write about them."

And, if everything went according to paperbacks, Dean would realize and confess that he loved her, too.

"I'm not the right choice for you," Dean said. He blew out a breath and leaned back in his seat. He ran one of his enormous hands through his sandy hair.

"You're the only guy I would trust with this," Maggie said. And while she wanted Dean to agree because she liked him, she also was telling the truth about trusting him. Dean would take care of her. He'd keep her body and her emotions safe. Dean would make sure she got the experiences and information she needed and make sure that she didn't get hurt.

His sigh came from deep in his chest. "What would you need your fake boyfriend to do?"

Maggie took a minute to organize her pitch. They'd need to go on dates. Public ones. That was something people did when fake dating. She could set up the dates she loved to read about. Bonus points if they came from fake dating novels. The greater the chance he would realize he loved her. And they should keep their plan a secret. Hiding the pretend part of their relationship meant they'd have to act like an actual couple. Maggie blushed just thinking about being half of a genuine couple with Dean.

"We'd need to go out," Maggie said. "I have a few ideas for dates I'd like to experience. Then I'll take some notes on my thoughts and feelings and incorporate them into my novel."

"That's it?" Dean asked, "Just a few dates?"

"And pretend like we're actually dating. Yes."

Dean chuckled and rubbed the back of his neck with one wide palm. He gave his head a little shake, as if to clear his thoughts. He muttered something under his breath, something that sounded like 'this is insane,' but Maggie decided not to take that to heart. Especially if he agreed to her proposition.

"This will help you?"

Maggie nodded.

"Damn it, Babs." Dean shook his head, but his smile was back. "How long do you need a… boyfriend?"

"Not long," Maggie said. Her heart was still pounding, but the rushing in her ears had subsided and the fluttering in her stomach wasn't nausea anymore. He was going to say yes. She knew Dean. He was going to say yes. "A few weeks. Maybe a month?" Dean's frown was back, "Or less."

"I can give you a month," Dean said, his eyes crinkling at the corners as he looked down at her. "But Babs, we have to be on the same page about this."

Maggie frowned. She'd laid out what she needed and for how long. He'd agreed. Didn't that count as being on the same page?

Dean cleared his throat. "Intimate encounters."

Maggie's blush hadn't died down, but now she felt the heat rush back to her cheeks. They burned like the time she and Audrey had gone to the beach and

Maggie had fallen asleep in the sun and forgotten to reapply sunscreen. Her skin had been the color of hot Cheetos, and everything felt tight and achy when she moved.

Dean shifted, drawing her eyes back to his. "I don't think sex would be appropriate for a fake relationship."

"Will you," she searched for the right words, "be intimate with other people? While we're—"

She couldn't remember the last time she'd seen Dean with a girlfriend or even a date. He didn't run through partners like other guys, but she knew he'd dated in high school and college. With his classic good looks, endless charm, and sweet smile, he couldn't be hurting for company if he wanted it. The thought of him sleeping with other people during their arrangement sunk like a lead weight into her stomach.

"I won't date anyone else while I'm helping you," Dean said, cutting through her devolving thoughts. "It would look a little suspicious if we said we were dating and then I slept with someone else. But I expect the same from you in return."

Maggie didn't mean to laugh. She tried to hold in the guffaw, but it found its way out.

"Dean, I think we've established that I'm asking for your help because I don't date, and my prospects are slim."

"I just figured you might have someone you, uh, exercise your libido with. But forget it, I don't want to know."

Maggie shook her head. Casual sex wasn't her style. Her last fantasy had included some steamy hand holding with the sparkling man sitting next to her. And maybe some weird tummy flutters from looking too long at Mac's chest. Both were men she knew fairly well and trusted to listen to an emphatic no if she gave it.

"Listen, if that changes, and you find someone you want to be with during our... arrangement, then we can end things with no hard feelings."

Maggie nodded. She couldn't contain her grin. Her real one that showed her gums above her top teeth and scrunched her eyes until it looked like they were closed.

"Thank you, Dean. Thank you, thank you, thank you." Without conscious will, Maggie launched herself at her best friend's older brother. She landed in his lap, her arms looped around his neck and shoulders. Her bag sat between their bodies, buffering any more intimate contact. She smiled up at the best man she'd ever known and decided that a critical review and a pesky panic attack may have been the best series of events that had ever happened to her.

"Let me know when you're free, and I'll give you a date to write home about, pun absolutely intended."

Dean let his arms circle Maggie's waist, and he smiled down at her. He shifted her on his lap, and for a moment, she thought he was going to press his mouth to hers. Maggie sucked her breath in like a prayer because she wanted a kiss. She wanted a perfect kiss in a perfect moment. A kiss that set off butterflies in her stomach and made her want more.

Maggie had had kisses before. Hell, she'd had sex, too—thank you—but her previous kisses had always felt awkward and sloppy. Her partners had never seemed to mind, but it took Maggie only a few tries to learn that she preferred her tongue to be the only one inside her mouth. It eased some of the drool issues and most of the stale breath problems her previous partners all seemed to have. Deep down, she'd always wondered if the problem was with her. Maybe she was a terrible kisser. Or maybe it would be different to share a kiss with someone she was attracted to. Someone like Dean.

Dean rested his chin on top of her head and let his fingers trail lightly up and down her arms. She broke out in goosebumps, feeling the shiver wrack her body.

"Cold?" He nestled her in closer. Maggie shook her head.

"Grateful," she said.

Dean fished his sleek, trendy phone out of the pocket of his pants and thumbed to his contacts. He typed out a message before setting the phone next to him on the couch.

"Are you telling Aud about us? Or am I?" He asked.

"I will," Maggie said. "She kind of helped me come up with the whole idea."

Dean frowned. "She told you to fake date me?"

"No. She suggested I date someone to get some insight into my characters. She didn't mention you at all." Maggie frowned, too. "Cal was going to call one of his friends, but Mac said…"

"Mac?" Dean repeated the name, his grip on her tightening the tiniest bit. Maggie searched Dean's face. As far as she knew, the two men were friendly, although their paths crossed about as often as hers and Mac's did. Maybe less. She saw Mac at the store sometimes. "You didn't want to ask him?"

"Mac said to pick someone I like and trust." Maggie widened her eyes. She hoped she looked innocent and guileless. Although it was the same face Audrey had often called her 'utter terror' face. "You're the only person who fits the description other than your sister."

"That's sad, Babs. We both know you have a lot more friends than that," Dean said, but he'd tucked her back under his chin and she could feel the steady *thump, thump* of his heart against her ear. "But I'm flattered that you want it to be me. I'll help you anyway I can. What are the brothers of our best friends for?"

CHAPTER FIVE

Maggie intended to share everything with Audrey after Dean agreed to help her. Although they weren't advertising the pretend part of their relationship, Maggie had always assumed Audrey would be privy to the truth. She had put it off to tell her friend in person, rather than over the phone, but someone had beaten her to the headline. She'd expected a surprised Audrey, an Audrey with a million questions. She hadn't expected an enraged Audrey.

"My brother." Audrey's arms crossed over her chest and her foot tapped a staccato beat when she opened the door the next morning. "You picked my goddamn brother!"

Maggie stood on the front stoop with two iced coffees—from Starbucks, too—and a bag with some chocolate croissants. She shook the bag at Audrey in offering.

"Am I allowed inside? Or are you planning to filet me right here?"

Audrey snatched the bag out of Maggie's hand and turned to head into the house, leaving the door wide open. Maggie assumed that was an invitation and followed her friend inside. Audrey continued into the kitchen and plopped the pastries into the ancient toaster oven. Maggie handed her the iced Americano, took a sip of her iced latte with enough sugar to fell a rhino, and waited.

"Explain." Audrey took a healthy gulp of coffee and sank onto one of the bar stools facing the tiny peninsula. Maggie rested her arms on the counter across from Audrey. She picked at the sticker on the side of her drink, trying to figure out how and what to share.

"It's not real." Maggie looked down at her hands and the shredded remnants of the sticker. "The dating, I mean. Dean will help me get some experience—"

"Sex?" Audrey's voice was shrill enough to shatter glass, and Maggie resisted the urge to cover her ears. She couldn't resist the wince.

"Of course not, Audrey. We're just going to date."

"Date." Audrey took another sip of caffeine. "You and Dean."

Maggie felt the ice of nerves splinter over her in the face of Audrey's anger. She knew picking Dean would be unexpected, but Audrey knew about her crush. Audrey had told her to pick whoever she wanted. Audrey told her no one would judge her. Maggie felt the heat of her temper burn away her nerves. She understood Audrey might not have wanted Dean involved in the whole scenario, but did she need to sound so horrified at the thought of them being together? Audrey had had no problem officiating weddings between Maggie and her brother for most of their childhoods. They used to plan for a future where the two of them would be sisters through marriage. Would it be so awful as a reality?

"Why are you mad at me?" Maggie asked, her voice wavering more than she would have liked. She would not be cowed on this one.

"I'm not mad at you," Audrey said. Maggie didn't believe her.

"This was not my idea." Maggie pointed her finger at her friend's chest. "The dating anyone part? That was your idea. Mac said to pick someone I trust, and you know how I feel about your brother. You know I trust him more than anyone."

"Maggie—"

"You said no judgment. If you were going to have an issue with me choosing Dean, which you should have known I would do, then you should have told me that yesterday."

"I'm not mad," Audrey said. She reached out and took Maggie's hands in both of hers, squeezing the way she usually did to help ground Maggie during an episode.

"Bullshit," Maggie said, squeezing back because she loved Audrey, even when she was acting like a judgmental know-it-all.

Audrey shook her head. "I'm not mad. I'm surprised."

Maggie raised an eyebrow, a skill Audrey had been jealous of since Maggie discovered she could do it in second grade.

"You're right. I knew you'd ask Dean, just like I knew he'd say yes. I was maybe hoping there was someone else you'd be interested in." Audrey pushed her hair back behind her ears and centered the charm bracelet on her wrist.

"Someone else?"

When had Maggie ever led Audrey to believe she was interested in anyone but Dean? She didn't hide her emotions from Audrey. She hadn't even hid her crush on Audrey's brother. Even the few times she'd been out with a man, not that she could qualify them as relationships, Maggie had only gone because Audrey had convinced her it was a good idea. Actually, this was probably new territory for Audrey. She was used to making the decisions for them both, and now Maggie had gone off script and done something just for herself.

"Never mind. Look, Dean is—" Audrey swallowed whatever she'd been about to say. "He's a wonderful brother, and he loves you so much, but he's not going to give you what you're looking for."

Maggie reared back, feeling Audrey's words like a slap to the face.

"Dean won't hurt me. I know him. I trust him more than any other man I've ever met."

"Sweetie." Audrey reached for her hand. "I know you do. And I know he'd never mean to hurt you, but the whole point of this exercise is to find chemistry with someone. Not just go on dates."

"We could have chemistry," Maggie said. How on earth did Audrey think she could just say they didn't? "Just because we're starting as friends doesn't mean it can't mean something. Unless there's something you're not telling me." Audrey searched Maggie's eyes, and it took everything Maggie had not to drop the contact. "Look, he said he'd help me. You need to trust both of us to make our own decisions," Maggie said, her voice steady.

"I don't want to see you hurt."

Maggie fought back the slap of annoyance. It bothered her that Audrey assumed she'd be the one left with a broken heart. She was a catch, dammit. Audrey frowned and shrugged her slim shoulders. She tossed her blonde hair back. Audrey chewed on her bottom lip, smearing her leftover lipstick.

"Okay then. I hope this is everything you want and need it to be, Maggie. I do. I just want you to be happy."

"I love you," Maggie said to her best friend, "but I need you to let me do this my way."

"If you need out, or he isn't what you expect, then we'll regroup."

"Thank you."

"Don't thank me. Just don't make me choose between my best friend and my brother."

If Maggie had her way, then Audrey wouldn't have to choose. They could end up sisters. She took her pinky finger and crossed it over her heart, just as they'd always done as kids.

"I promise." Maggie said, and Audrey crossed her pinky over her heart, too. Then she threw back the last of her coffee and grabbed the croissants from the oven. She placed them both on dainty white plates and slid one to Maggie.

"Oh, I almost forgot. There's something here for you!" Audrey said.

"For me?"

Ever since she'd moved out, Audrey had become a real gift giver. She'd give Maggie cookies, a special pen, Tylenol when Maggie was sick. Audrey had always been someone who shared her feelings and affection with words, but the gifts were fun and Maggie always felt a little pop of warmth in her chest when Audrey gifted her something. Especially because the gifts were always exactly what she needed and showed just how often Audrey thought of her. Maggie missed having a roommate, but she couldn't lie. Having her own place was also very freeing.

Audrey opened a cabinet and pulled out a tiny rubber duck. It had a painted blue hat sitting over a mop of brown curls, a high-necked blue and white dress—Maggie thought it was a dress—covering the duck's body, and under one wing was a brown book with the title "Pond & Prejudice." Maggie squeezed it in her hand and a wheezy honk sound came from the duck's belly.

"It's a—"

"Jane Austen Rubber Duck," Maggie said with a laugh. "Audrey, this is amazing. Where did you even find this?" She brought the duck up close to admire the tiny gold ring painted onto the duck's wing.

"Oh, you know, around. It's no secret that P&P is your favorite Austen novel, and that you watch the 1995 version on repeat when you're stressed."

"Thank you," Maggie said and clutched the little toy close and her friend waved her off.

"Okay, tell me about date number one," Audrey said and bit into the pastry. Footsteps pounded down the stairs, and Mac's dark head appeared in the doorway to the kitchen. He nodded at the women and headed straight to the coffee pot. He was wearing a long-sleeve gray t-shirt, a sure sign he'd be heading out to his forge after caffeinating. Audrey turned her attention back to Maggie. "When is it, and where are you going?"

"We agreed on Saturday," Maggie said and took a bite of her croissant, letting the sweet chocolate spread across her tongue. "But no idea where we're going yet."

"What's happening Saturday?" Mac asked, his hands wrapped around a mug the size of a soup bowl, full to the brim with steaming black coffee. Maggie froze, unsure of what to say. Mac's dark eyes bored into hers over the rim of his cup before they dipped down to the yellow duck in her hands. He lowered the mug, his lips twitching like he might say something and Maggie felt a tension squeeze against her throat, like she might cry, but without the tears. Strange.

Audrey took a slow bite of her breakfast, chewed, and swallowed. Her eyes stayed glued to Maggie the entire time.

"Maggie has a date," Audrey said.

Mac's hands froze around his coffee cup, and his throat bobbed as he swallowed. His gaze moved from Audrey back to Maggie.

"You work fast," Mac said, and Maggie blushed.

"Hey Mac," Audrey turned her devious smile on her roommate, "you're a guy."

"Thank you for noticing." Mac frowned into his mug.

"If you had a date with your dream girl, where would you take her?" Audrey twisted a strand of silky hair around her fingers. "We're trying to source some ideas for Maggie."

Mac blew on the steaming liquid in his cup, his lips forming a soft circle. He took a sip, and his eyes met Maggie's as he looked up. He held her gaze as he tilted his head, thoughts flitting behind his dark eyes.

"If I were feeling romantic, I'd take her to the county fair. It's setting up tomorrow, so perfect timing."

Audrey nodded like it was a great idea.

"Why the fair?" Maggie asked. She wasn't sure what was romantic about fried dough, farm animals, and monster trucks. It was a great idea for a movie, but sweat and crowds didn't sound all that enticing.

"Because," Mac said, "it's a family friendly event in the middle of the day. The temptation to find a spot alone, to press a kiss to her neck, or slide my hands somewhere I shouldn't would be overwhelming, impossible. I'd spend the day trying to make her smile while also keeping an eye out for a secluded corner so that I could get my hands on her. We'd trade something sweet between us, like a giant lollipop, or a cotton candy, or an ice cream and I wouldn't even notice how it tasted because I'd only taste her. Just when I thought I couldn't handle it anymore, when I'd be ready to consider public indecency charges and how they'd be worth it for a taste of her mouth, I'd take her on the Ferris wheel, and we'd sit with our thighs and hips and sides pressed to each other. I'd loop an arm around the back of her seat, and when we got stuck at the very top, with the fairgrounds spilling out below us, I'd kiss her like I'd wanted to all day. I'd kiss her until the wheel started moving and we'd have to get off. Kiss her until the other people riding with us either applauded or shot us dirty looks."

Maggie could barely hear over the sound of her pulse thudding in her ears.

"It's the perfect place to imagine a future together," Mac said. "Bringing your own kids there, while reliving the past, like high schoolers on their very first date."

"The fair, you said?" Audrey asked, her face a little flushed.

"That's what I'd do." Mac shrugged and tore his gaze away from Maggie. "I'll be out back if anyone needs me." He said and took his coffee cup with him on his way out the door.

Maggie thought she nodded, or waved, but she couldn't be sure. She was having enough trouble pulling in a breath. The butterflies in her stomach had opted for tap shoes, and they were having a field day on her internal organs, and her cheeks burned so hot it felt like they could burst into flames. Maggie pressed her hands against the cool counter, shocked to see her limbs trembling against the Formica. Not outright shaking, but wavering. She pressed her cheek to the faux-stone countertop, surprised steam didn't rise from the point of contact.

"We're going to the damn fair." Audrey said and Maggie said, "We?"

"Hell yes," Audrey said and fanned her own flaming cheeks. "I'm making Cal take me after that. They're related. If I'm lucky, Cal will have similar thoughts. About me. We'll double date."

"I'll tell Dean," Maggie said.

CHAPTER SIX

Maggie couldn't remember the last time she had visited a county fair. She'd definitely never done so on a date. Dean pulled the car into the dirt lot and parked in the sea of other vehicles. With all the dust, Maggie felt a little guilty that they hadn't brought her beater instead of Dean's Mercedes, but he'd been all in when she mentioned the fair and had picked her up that morning with a smile. He'd even held the passenger door open for her and handed her into the car.

Dean popped the passenger door and held his hand out for her. Maggie took it. His palm was warm and smooth against hers and kicked up a few tiny flutters in her belly as he pulled her out of the vehicle, her front almost smacking up against his. The dull roar of the crowded fairgrounds was a buzz in her ears, and if she looked around Dean's gigantic body the red and white tents and the fencing housing all the animals were just visible. The curve of a Ferris wheel rose above it all, calling to her.

"This was a fun idea." Dean wrapped an arm around her shoulders and steered her towards the fairground entrance. "Sweet, like you."

Maggie grinned up at Dean, wishing she could see his green eyes, but he'd hidden them behind a set of mirrored aviator sunglasses. Her own reflection stared back at her, pointed chin, upturned nose, and all.

"Hot," Maggie said.

Dean said, "That too," and pulled his t-shirt away from his body to catch a breeze. It was still spring, but the weather had turned towards summer, and while the temperature itself was only hovering around the seventies, the sun and the humidity were already closing in even at ten in the morning. "What do you want to do first?" Dean paid both of their entrance fees and the ancient man inside the booth stamped their hands with smiley faces. "Food? Rides? Animals?"

"Everything." Maggie said. She definitely wanted to go on the Ferris wheel, but not immediately. It would be the perfect end to a chapter, not the beginning. First, they could walk around, hold hands, talk about important stuff, and fall in love. Her phone buzzed from her back pocket at the same time Dean's buzzed in his shorts.

"Maggie! Dean!" Audrey fought her way through the throng of people dragging Cal right along with her. "Hi! I just texted you guys!"

Dean smiled and hugged his sister, and Maggie forced herself to smile too. She'd thought they'd have a few minutes alone before dating in front of an audience.

"Hi Audrey," Maggie waved at her best friend, who looked like she belonged on a movie set in her red gingham dress and cowboy boots. "Cal." She nodded to the man with his arm wrapped around Audrey's waist. "Mac."

What was Mac doing here? She had expected a double date, not a group encounter. He wore a pair of worn jeans, and she half expected another sweater. The man only ever dressed for lectures or for bladesmithing, but his University of Michigan shirt was a welcome surprise. He still wore his customary frown, thick brows pinched together as he took in the throngs of people.

"We didn't want to leave him home alone," Audrey said with a smile for her grumpy roommate. "It was his idea to come here."

Mac's scowl darkened. "You make it sound like I was going to pee on the carpet. I'm not a puppy."

"No, just cute like one." Audrey playfully smacked his cheek, the blow softened by Mac's facial hair.

"Hey man." Dean held a hand out for Mac to shake. "Glad you're here."

Mac stared at the offered hand. Then he shook it with two quick pumps before dropping it like an angry rattlesnake.

"Sorry for crashing your date," Mac said to Dean, his voice flat, but his eyes strayed to Maggie.

"No worries." Dean wrapped his arm back around Maggie's shoulders and pulled her into his solid frame. "The more the merrier. Right, Babs?"

Maggie flushed, but held her smile. "Yea. It was your idea to visit. You deserve a chance to enjoy it."

Hot, dark eyes searched her face.

"I want to see the baby animals," Audrey said, tugging on her boyfriend's arm, and Mac dropped his gaze. "You guys coming?"

"Lead the way." Dean said. Maggie didn't realize they were moving until the weight of Dean's arm propelled her feet forward. Mac fell into step behind them, his heavy footsteps echoing hers.

The pen to the left of the entrance held sheep and goats and one disgruntled turkey. Most of the animals were watermelon fat, their bellies swaying as they moved around the pen, nibbling at the dried corn eager guests had dropped for them. A few tiny brand new babies hopped and skipped after their mamas, unsure about the crowds.

Audrey wrinkled her nose up at the smells, but Maggie let her knees hit the dirt as she kneeled next to a tiny fluff of a lamb pressed against the fencing. It allowed her to reach through and stroke its soft back before it scampered off with a soft bleat. A little goat with nubs for horns ran up and smashed into the fence directly in front of her. With a shrieked laugh, Maggie sat back hard on her butt.

"Alright, Babs?" Dean called from a few feet away. He leaned over the fence to wiggle his fingers at one of the larger goats.

"I'm fine." Not even her bumped pride overrode the joy at seeing those tiny babies frolic.

A tanned hand with short blunt nails capping the fingers appeared in her line of sight. The hand attached to a thick arm dusted with dark hair. Mac's frowning face stood above her, dark chocolate hair falling into his eyes. He wasn't looking at her, but at something or someone just beyond her.

"Are you going to leave me hanging? Or will you take my help?" Mac scowled, his broad shoulders backlit by the bright sun.

Maggie's grin tripled in size as she slipped her hand into his larger one. His calloused palm was rough against hers. The small patches of scar tissue, where his skin healed around minor burns, were soft against her skin. Mac's fingers flexed and then he hauled her to her feet as if she weighed less than one of the baby goats. Maggie knew she was a small woman, her body flat and rectangular. Still, the ease with which Mac lifted her was a bit of a surprise. She knew forging was hard labor, but his biceps stretched the sleeves of his shirt. The flutters started up in her stomach and she ruthlessly tried to drown them. This was Mac.

"Dean?" His voice pitched low, for her ears only, and it took Maggie a moment to realize he was asking her a question, not looking for her fake boyfriend.

"You said to pick someone I trust, someone I love." Even through his beard, she saw Mac tighten his jaw.

Maggie bit back the apology that sat on her tongue like a prisoner, watchful for any opening to escape. She didn't know what she would apologize for, but the urge to soothe Mac was undeniable. Mac, who looked like someone had mixed glass shards into his morning cereal.

He took his hand back. "I didn't know."

Maggie wanted to ask if it would have mattered if she'd told him, but that seemed like an inappropriate question for her best friend's boyfriend's brother. She almost told him the relationship was fake, but something stopped those words in her throat.

An arm wrapped around her waist and pulled her back into a firm, male chest.

"Hey baby," Dean said, his voice low and against her ear. "Everything okay?" He'd called her 'baby' and not 'Babs' and she bit back a nervous giggle as her pulse increased speed. Her eyes stayed fixed on the hot depths of Mac's.

"It's all good," Mac said, "Just giving her a hand."

Dean's kiss was a warm caress against her flaming cheek, and Mac took a step back. Maggie wanted to bask in the softness of Dean's lips against her skin, but couldn't take her eyes off of Mac's hands, clenched into fists so tight the white of his knuckles pushed against his tanned skin. Then Mac shoved both hands deep into his jeans pockets and she shook her head to clear her thoughts.

"Come on." Dean pulled on the belt loops at the front of Maggie's shorts. "Let's get you some of that dried corn to feed those babies."

Maggie turned her smile back on Dean. She was here to spend time with him. It didn't matter that Mac was grumpier than usual. He could have stayed home.

Dean put some loose coins into the gumball machine and Maggie cupped her hands to catch the tumbling feed. When she approached the fence with her bounty, the sheep and goats trampled each other to get as close as possible. They hoovered the corn from her palms like little vacuums. Even the little nips of their blunt teeth tickled.

Maggie let a laugh bubble through her chest. She hadn't had this much fun in ages. She spent most of her free time curled up on her couch or draped over Audrey's with a romance novel on her Kindle or glued to her laptop screen while working on her own writing. She rarely chose to vary her plans unless Audrey kidnapped her. It wasn't that Maggie didn't like people—she just preferred fictional ones to most real ones.

After feeding the animals, they washed their hands under a nearby spigot and explored some of the other tents. There were a few with prize-winning vegetables and pies. One housed homemade quilts, another showcased competitive table setting. Maggie didn't understand any of what she was seeing, but she stuck close as Audrey peppered the women running the booths with questions. She asked about the vegetable judging criteria and the creative process that went into the quilts. Dean held Maggie's hand through each tent. Every few minutes, he'd squeeze her hand in his and send her a smile out of the corner of his eyes.

THE TROPE

The sweet looks may have kept Maggie breathless and flushed, but she still wasn't used to holding hands with anyone. While she appreciated how close Dean was staying and the attention he was giving her, her palm was sweating. She found it more annoying than sweet to have only one hand free. She still felt flushed, but the heat was the sweaty kind. Behind a tent selling hand carved walking sticks, she pulled her hand away. Dean glanced over, meeting her eyes.

"Sorry." Maggie tried to wipe her hand on the side of her shorts without him noticing.

Dean's eyes crinkled. "You don't need to be sorry, Babs. You call one hundred percent of the shots. We don't do anything you aren't sure about." He wiped his hand down his cargo shorts. "I was getting sweaty too."

Maggie looked around, but no one was listening. "I want to do this right."

"You're doing it right," Dean said. "This is the best date I have had in a while."

Maggie had to agree with him. It was the best for her, too.

For lunch, they stopped by the food carts and grabbed an assortment of "the classics" as Cal referred to them. Maggie started piling her veggie dog high with meatless chili and onions but stopped. She was still planning to take a ride on the Ferris wheel. Still hoping for a kiss at the top. The least she could do for Dean would be to avoid the extra fragrant toppings. Then Dean handed her a paper dish full of steaming, fried pickles, and she remembered he knew her inside and out and added the chili, anyway.

After the hotdogs and pickles, Audrey and Maggie split a bag of neon pink cotton candy and a funnel cake. Dean shook his head as she picked up a bright red candy apple, but he gamely handed some cash to the woman selling the treats. The same way he'd paid for everything else she'd eaten and done. All without a word of censure.

"You don't need to pay," she said, mouth sticky with sugar. "I have cash."

"It's a date." Dean tapped her on the nose. "Now tell me what else you want."

The brightly colored cars on the Ferris wheel swung as it turned, standing tall above the fairgrounds. It looked a lot bigger now that they were standing in its shadow. Maggie wasn't the most comfortable with heights, but they weren't one of her triggers. And it wasn't like she'd be up there alone. Dean would put his arm around her, snuggle her close, and her stomach would do somersaults when the wheel creaked to a stop. And then he'd kiss her. Maybe. Hopefully.

"I want to ride the Ferris wheel." Maggie's eyes snagged on Mac standing off to the side, chatting with his brother.

"Ferris wheel it is," Dean said. "Wait here. I'll go grab us tickets." Dean nudged her with his shoulder and then strode off to the booth at the base of the ride. A teenager sporting a lime green Mohawk was manning the controls, looking more bored than Maggie would have imagined possible.

"Cal," Audrey bumped her shoulder against Maggie's with a grin. "I want to ride the Ferris wheel too."

"On it." Cal jogged after Dean.

"Aren't you terrified of heights?" Audrey asked, her voice teasing. They both knew the Ferris wheel was the whole reason they'd braved the heat to enjoy the fair.

"Someone mentioned it would be romantic. Especially when we get stuck at the top."

"Ferris wheels don't always get stuck," Mac said, watching the wheel turn.

"They do in books."

"This isn't a book."

Maggie glared at Mac. This whole thing had been his idea. "I know it's not," she said, "but it's still a great way to end a wonderful date."

Mac scoffed.

"It has been a wonderful date." Maggie repeated. "Dean is attentive and kind, and he doesn't spend all day glowering at people."

Mac unfolded his arms and stepped back from the fence. "You're right."

"I'm going to get on that Ferris wheel with my boyfriend." Maggie felt a rush of heat burn through her. "And when that wheel stops at the top, I will kiss him because today has been a perfect date and it deserves a perfect end."

"Boyfriend," Mac nodded. "I thought this was your first date."

Audrey was frowning at Maggie from behind Mac's shoulder. Maggie wondered when he'd gotten so close. The burn from her anger centered low in her belly and made her stomach pitch and roll. It also stole the breath right out of her lungs. Her ribs expanded as she tried to suck in more air. Mac's chest heaved, too, his breath panting over her upturned face.

"Please don't ruin this for me," Maggie said, and Mac's throat bobbed as he swallowed. He took a step back and Maggie shivered as the cool air rushed into the space between them like a caress.

"I'm going to find the restroom," he said before he turned and jogged away.

Maggie watched him go, willing her body to relax and her breathing to return to normal. Her heart was still galloping away in her chest.

"Whatever that was," Audrey said under her breath, "Cut it out now. The boys are coming back." Maggie turned, expecting Mac, and saw Dean and Cal headed towards them.

Dean was handsome. Dean was kind. This had been a wonderful afternoon.

"Two tickets," Dean said and held his arm out for her to hold. "Ready?"

Maggie let Dean take her hand in his and lead her to the base of the ride. The mohawked kid operating the wheel opened the door to a yellow car and ushered them inside. Dean slid across the metal seat and pulled Maggie in after him. He lay his arm across the back of the car as the operator closed and latched the door.

"Have a good time," the kid moved back to the controls, body hunched under a layer of black clothes and heavily spiked hair.

The car started with a jolt, and Maggie slid into Dean's body. They were pressed together, thigh to thigh, hip to hip, just like Mac had said. Maggie shook her head. She was *not* thinking about Mac. He and his grumpy attitude had no place on this ride with her. The car lurched forward and stopped, lurched and stopped as the cars behind them filled up. Maggie turned to see where Audrey and Cal ended up and caught sight of Mac talking with the kid manning the controls. She saw Mac hand over some cash, buying his own ticket, and the kid nodded.

The sun had warmed the metal of the bench, so Maggie kept her knees raised, trying not to burn herself. She had to rest on the tips of her toes to keep her thighs up. Her legs were barely long enough to keep them off of the metal. Noticing her struggle, Dean looped an arm under her knees and propped her legs across his lap.

"Are you having a good time today?" Dean's voice was a low rumble against her chest.

Maggie smiled up at him and nodded because she was having a wonderful time, but being so close made her forget how to use her vocal cords. The car had made a full rotation by the time she found her words.

"I'm having a great time, Dean. I'm so glad I asked you to help me."

"I'm having a good time, too." Dean said, "And I'm happy to play boyfriend with you. Are you getting the stuff you need?"

Maggie nodded. "I think so."

The car swung past the controls and continued to climb up towards the top again. Maggie forced herself to look away from Dean and around at the green fairgrounds dotted with little red tents and even littler animals and people. Even if the car didn't stop, she could still write some details from this experience. The scent of popcorn and sugar mixed with the animals below, and she noted she should add that detail. Heat from the metal seats and the warmth from Dean's body made sweat bead up along her forehead and behind her knees.

When she looked down, Maggie noticed the skin of her translucent thighs, unused to so much time under the UV rays, was already inching towards the cardinal red. That was going to hurt later. But all the discomfort was worth it to see Dean's hair catch the sun like gold.

The car squealed and came to a shuddering stop, and Maggie's breath caught. They sat perched at the very top of the wheel. Whoops and squeals from some of the other cars and passengers hit her ears.

"You okay?" Dean pulled her closer. "If you don't look down, you can pretend we aren't so high up."

Maggie hadn't considered being nervous. She was too thrilled about being stuck. It helped to have Dean's solid weight pressed against her.

"I'm okay." She said and let her smile bleed across her face. She closed her eyes and tipped her head back to let the sun kiss her forehead and cheeks. *Take that, Mac*, she thought, and her smile grew. The Ferris wheel had stopped all on its own. Fate had clearly thrown her a gift.

"Hey Babs," Dean said, and she turned her face towards him but didn't open her eyes. "If this were an actual date, I'd end it with a kiss."

Maggie's eyes popped open. Her skin was stretched tight, itchy. "What?"

"Yes or no, Maggie?" Dean said.

"Yes," Maggie said, but something wasn't quite right. Her stomach pitched and twisted, saliva flooding her mouth.

Dean leaned towards her, his green eyes shuttering as he moved. Then the car lurched, and the wheel turned again, and Maggie recognized the lurching roil of her stomach. With a shove, she pushed Dean away and leaned over the side of the car, losing her dignity along with her lunch.

CHAPTER SEVEN

As she stared down at her blinking cursor, and the words still wouldn't come, Maggie had to admit dating Dean would not be a quick fix. Maggie had translated some of the warmth from when he'd held her hand or smiled at her. She'd also been able to express some flutters that had kicked off in her belly when they'd been at the very top of the wheel. But the words and feelings were so contrived on the page that she wanted to roll her own eyes when she read her words back.

Love was universal, but it was also unique. The vague descriptions she was coming up with were like looking at love through a haze of smoke she kept trying desperately to clear.

Maggie had her iPad and keyboard set up just to the left of the register. Shay was somewhere in the bowels of the store, reading the latest manga they'd stocked and shelved that morning. The store was pretty empty during the week with only the occasional customer on lunch break. Maggie had hoped a change of scenery might inspire some revisions. There were only so many hours she could stare at the divots in her wooden desk while pretending she was working.

The bell over the door tinkled as someone walked into the shop. Maggie shut her iPad and pushed her ash-brown hair behind her ears. She could worry about her misbehaving manuscript later.

"Welcome to The Tattered Cover," Maggie said with her customer service smile. "Can I help you find anything today?"

The man waved her off and headed down one row of books towards the back of the store. Shay was back there and could help him if he needed it. Maggie tucked her tablet away on the little shelf below the register and grabbed a rag and some cleaner to wipe down the glass display case. The display housed some of the more expensive playing cards for games Maggie was only tangentially familiar with, some adorable alien-eyed collectable figurines, and a few of Mac's blades. Gary liked to show off more high-cost items at the front, and the cabinet's lock was just a bonus. Did Maggie enjoy cleaning display cases? No, it wasn't a favorite work task at all. Was it better than staring at her unrevised novel? Yes.

It had been three days since the fair, and she hadn't seen Dean since he dropped her off at her apartment. Maggie knew it would take at least a few dates for him to realize she was the love of his life—especially after her gastrointestinal pyrotechnics. When the Ferris wheel had stopped, Dean had helped her off the ride and grabbed a bottle of water. Mac had propped her up against the security fence and offered a handkerchief to wipe her mouth. Neither had treated her like a leper, so she was hopeful Dean wasn't too grossed out to keep their pseudo relationship going.

Maggie knew Dean's advertising job held more traditional banker hours than her job at the shop, so she assumed their next date would be on the weekend. She had time to mine her favorite novels for ideas. Tropes were tropes for a reason. They always worked out. In books. Maggie's first date had gone a little off the rails, but the Ferris wheel still stopped at the top, despite what Mac had said. The next date would go off without a hitch. It had to.

Heavy footsteps broke Maggie's internal dialogue, and she looked up, coming face to face with the customer who'd waved her off not ten minutes before.

"Hi." He leaned on the counter, smudging the clean surface with his blunt fingertips. "Maybe you can help me. Your employee—" he sighed and gestured towards the back where Shay must have been, "She was less than helpful."

"I'd be more than happy to give you a hand." Maggie's smile stretched thin. "But I need to clarify that my coworker uses they/them pronouns, and we would both appreciate you using them going forward."

"Seriously?" A muscle in the man's jaw clenched. "Does it even matter? She isn't here right now."

"*They* aren't here right now." Maggie corrected. "And it does matter."

"Sure, I'm looking for a Mighty Morphin Power Rangers Action Figure. The Red Ranger or Megazord from '93 or '94."

"Let me check the computer, and we can head back to see what we have."

"Thank you." He pulled his body off the counter and out of her personal space.

Maggie sidestepped to the computer by the register and waited for the log-in screen to load. "This may take a few minutes. The system is pretty old."

"That's fine," the man said. "At least you're helping me. That girl just sat there reading her damn comic book while I—"

"My coworker is nonbinary." Maggie's annoyance clogged her throat. "They use they/them pronouns. I cannot help you if you cannot be respectful of them."

"This has to be a joke." The man propped his hands on his hips, teeth so tightly clenched that his words were barely recognizable. "She—" He looked at Maggie's pursed lips and flashing eyes. "They are wearing a skirt."

"The clothes someone wears do not dictate their gender identity. I'm wearing pants. That doesn't make me a man."

"What?" The man rolled his eyes. "You're telling me that's a dude in a skirt? Whatever. Just type on your computer, little girl, and tell me if you have what I want."

"No," Maggie said.

"I'm a customer." Spittle covered the glass display. "Your job is to help me."

"No."

"It's not like they hired you for your intelligence," He said, his words choppy. "Listen, bitch—"

A hand slammed down on the display counter, clanking the daggers and action figures against each other. Maggie jumped at the sudden sound, and her heart hammered inside her chest, but as she looked up into Mac's stony face, it wasn't fear that made her pulse pound. Mac stared at the other man, his face blank. He was a few inches shorter than the rude customer, but with his dark glower and menace wafting off of his broad body, he seemed to take up the entire shop. Maggie could see the vein pulsing along his temple, and his cheeks flushed with anger. His knuckles ridged white bumps underneath his tanned skin.

"Don't finish that sentence." Mac's voice was so low Maggie almost didn't understand the words. She understood the tone, though. So did the angry customer.

"Are you the damn owner?" Mr. Angry sized up Mac, smirking when he recognized his taller height. Mac's frown returned to his face, deep lines furrowing between his thick eyebrows and his nostrils flared as he took a deep breath.

"No."

"How do you think the owner would feel about this prissy thing denying a huge sale because she just had to be politically correct?"

Maggie could hear the teeth grinding together in Mac's jaw. Desperate to save some of his tooth enamel—he had a pleasant smile—she slid her hand over the top of the one Mac still splayed out on the counter. Mac took a shuddering breath and flipped his hand so their palms kissed. He laced their fingers together and squeezed. Maggie squeezed back, then slid her hand away.

"Gary supports his employees and understands that no job is worth debasing yourself for disrespectful idiots," Maggie said, pasting on a sweet smile tailored to rankle the bigot in front of her. She kept her hands behind the counter so neither man would see them shake.

"You would be the disrespectful idiot." Mac's grin erred on the side of terrifying. "Get out."

"Excuse me." Mr. Angry glared at Mac. "You don't know what happened here."

"I don't need to." Mac said. "Get out."

"You just lost a huge amount of cash," Mr. Angry turned his glare on Maggie. Mac stepped in front of her to block the other man's view. "I'll be back next week when your scrawny ass is out of a job."

That was laughable. Gary would have been the first to remove self-entitled, self-important Mr. Bigot. And he definitely wouldn't fire either her or Shay for defending themselves. Gary did not subscribe to the notion that the customer was always right.

Mac growled. At least Maggie was pretty sure it was a growl. She'd never heard one in real life. She always thought it was something romance readers just expected from broody alpha lovers, even as it defied all laws of human nature. The sound came from deep in his chest. His lips twisted together as he stared at the other man. It was thrilling, seeing staid Mac come undone like this. She could almost see him girding himself for battle like Aragorn brandishing his longsword as he faced down an army of the Uruk-Hai during the skirmish of Amon Hen. Maggie pressed her thighs together behind the counter, desperate to relieve the sudden ache pulsing through her core.

"Whatever the fuck he wanted you to find—" Mac turned his head to speak to her over the slope of his shoulder. "I'm buying it."

"You can't do that," the asshole said at the same time Maggie said, "Mac, that action figure costs several hundred dollars."

"I'll take it," Mac said to Maggie. To the other man, he said, "You don't need to come back. Ever."

With an exaggerated sigh, the other man turned toward the exit and left the shop, the bell clanging as the door closed behind him. Mac turned to face her, the two feet of counter all that separated his heaving chest from her own.

"Go get whatever it is I'm buying, Maggie." He straightened the canvas bag he wore draped across his shoulder, refusing to look at her.

"You don't need to do that."

"I do."

Maggie rolled her eyes, but she couldn't stop the smile that creased her cheeks as she left the counter and headed down the aisle where they kept the Power Rangers stock. Her hand tingled from where Mac had wrapped his fingers around hers. To dispel the feeling, she let her fingertips glide over the corners and edges of the boxes and books on the shelves. It did nothing to help the flutters in her belly or the watery weakness in her knees. Or the fire that his fury had set to her blood.

Her extensive research in the world of romance novels told her she was experiencing either attraction or capital F feelings. Except that it was *Mac* who had caused them, and she barely knew him. She was just reacting to what he'd said and done, siding with her in front of the other man. It had been a scene straight from a book. Mac could have been a complete stranger and she still would've reacted to what he said and the way he'd slammed his hand down on the counter. The way he demanded respect for Shay. For her.

She'd just re-write the scene with Dean as the defender, that was all.

Shay was sitting back against the shelves just to the right of the Power Rangers' displays. Their head was bent over a comic book, but their eyes didn't move along the page.

"I like your skirt today," Maggie said. "You look cute as hell." She stretched up towards the boxes on the shelf above her head.

"Thanks." Shay held the book open against their raised knees.

Maggie pulled a box down, checked the label and pushed it back up onto the shelf. She had to stand on the very tips of her toes and still barely got her fingertips on the boxes. Maggie didn't mind her size, but she also didn't want to go hunt down the step stool.

"He wanted the Megazord." Shay set their book to the side before standing up. "Here, I'll grab it." They snagged the box of the vintage figure and handed it to Maggie. "The idiot didn't even look for it."

The green box had the name MEGAZORD spelled out in giant yellow letters. A picture of a wide chested cyborg dressed in red, with two horn-like protrusions on either side of its head, stared up at Maggie. Unlike newer action figures with plastic windows in the cardboard, this box from the early nineties only had a picture that hinted at the toy—a collector's item—inside.

"I swear it's not for him." Maggie turned the box over in her hands, searching for blemishes. "I refused to sell it to him after what he said. It's for Mac."

"Thank you." Shay's smile was small, but noticeable. "I know Gary understands and backs me one hundred percent, but I didn't feel like engaging today. Not after he misgendered me."

"Don't thank me." Maggie reached out a hand to pat Shay's shoulder. If they didn't shudder and pretend to retch every time Maggie swooped in for a hug, she'd have put her arms around her friend. Not everyone was a hugger, and Maggie could respect that.

"I heard you correct him."

"Correcting asshats on your pronouns is the least I can do," Maggie said. "It's the bare minimum. Even when you aren't standing right there, Shay."

Shay looked away from Maggie, but the quick blinks belied the tears they were trying to contain.

"I know how confrontation makes you anxious," Shay said.

"It doesn't matter. Not like you do. I love you, idiot." Maggie tucked the box under her arm and made her way back to the front of the store.

Mac was leaning against the counter, thumbing through an Archie comic from the front display. His customary dark jeans cupped his ass, but they weren't tight. Mac had rolled the cuffs up a few times to stop them from dragging on the ground. He wore a heather gray sweater despite the warm weather. Mac almost always wore sweaters, especially on days he had class, and he wore long sleeves for working in the forge. It wasn't fair to think about him in his forge, sweating and swinging a heavy hammer, muscles bunching as he moved long pieces of heavy steel. The flutters and tingles returned with a vengeance.

His dark hair was on the wrong side of a haircut and sticking out in every direction as though he'd shoved his hands through it a few times while waiting for her. He stood angled just enough that Maggie could see the short beard he wore clipped close to his cheeks and chin. Large eyes, down-turned at the outer corner, the color of rich soil, were ringed by the thickest lashes Maggie had ever seen. He was nothing like the golden-haired, sunny Dean, but it seemed like maybe her body didn't care. Maggie couldn't deny there was a reason romance readers loved a good grumpy, dark-haired hero.

Mac must have heard her coming, because he put the book down and turned to face her. A tiny smile tipped up the corner of his full lips before he let his typical scowl take over.

"I didn't know you were a part of the Ranger Nation." Maggie set the box on the counter.

"Part of what?" Mac reached for the action figure, but his eyes were on Maggie's face.

"A Power Rangers fan."

"Oh, yeah, I like them fine." Mac pressed his knuckles to his lips, dragging them back and forth against his mouth.

"You don't have to do this," Maggie said. "I know you didn't come here intending to buy the nineteen-ninety-three Megazord. It's vintage," she winced because the figure was only a few years older than her, "so it's expensive."

"I can afford it." Oh, well then, it must be nice to drop several hundred bucks on a whim and not miss it at all. Mac leaned back over the counter to put them more eye-to-eye. "I know Gary is a good guy, but I don't want you or Shay in trouble. Besides, I bet Dean would have done the same thing."

He wouldn't have. Dean may have only been Maggie's fake boyfriend, but she'd known him her whole life. Would he have stood up for Shay? Absolutely. Would he have demanded that the jerk respect Maggie and her coworker? A million times over. But he would have done it by hauling the man out of the store, and it would not have occurred to him that Shay or Maggie could be in trouble for losing a big sale. They wouldn't have been in trouble. Gary would have sent that man packing with some strong words, but it was nice of Mac to think of them.

Maggie scanned the box, wincing at the total that appeared on the screen. Mac dug his wallet out of his back pocket and handed her a credit card before she could even read the number off.

"Can I at least pay half?" She asked, and he shook his head. Which was a mercy, really, because her bank account did not want her to pay half.

"Run the card, Maggie."

"Yes, sir," Maggie said with a mock salute. She pushed the card into the bottom of the reader and waited for it to beep. She chanced a glance up at Mac, who had frozen at her words. His pupils expanded, swallowing the dark brown of his irises. His mouth opened on a ragged inhale. Maggie's center went hot and liquid, a deep ache starting between her thighs. She rubbed her legs together, resisting the urge to either moan or giggle.

"Since I know you didn't come here for Megazord, what brought you to the shop today?" Maggie tried to wrench her wayward body back on track.

Mac stared at her, his gaze glued to her mouth. Maggie let her tongue out to wet her bottom lip. Her pulse picked up and her breath turned shallow. She was out of control. Prolonged eye contact had never made her this hot before. It must have been all the extra time spent with Dean, dating Dean, and then adding in one heroic act straight out of a romance novel, and Maggie was in heat.

Mac looked away first, and Maggie sighed in relief. She wasn't certain she would have dropped eye contact.

"I brought you something." He reached into his bag.

"Did you bring more blades?" Maggie asked, and the excitement crashing through her almost buried the tingles in her stomach. Excitement because Mac's work was exquisite.

"I brought one." Mac placed a leather wrapped dagger on the counter.

"Is that—" Maggie leaned in and looked at the wooden handle with sweeping bronze scroll work. It curved in a smooth arc, ending with a cap of bronze.

"You said you wanted one of the daggers from last week," Mac said. "I made it for you." Maggie unwrapped the leather, taking great care not to jostle the dagger. While she was staring down at the shining steel of the blade, Mac gathered up his vintage action figure and left, the bell signaling his departure.

CHAPTER EIGHT

Maggie's plan for Saturday's date involved her favorite coffee shop and a sacrifice of one of her favorite drinks. The Perk-u-Later was busy but not crowded when Maggie pulled the door open. The welcoming scents of roasted coffee beans and the buttery smell of flaky pastries wrapped around her like a hug.

There were enough people for the murmur of conversation to create a low bass line below the folk music wafting from the sound system. Chattering patrons filled half of the booths that edged the small café, but Maggie didn't need a booth for today's date. She didn't plan for them to stay in the shop that long.

Dean had left planning for each of the dates up to her and despite today's simplicity, it had still taken her two full days to put things in motion. Maggie was grateful to be in charge. In every romance book, characters fell in love over very specific and common scenes. Why not see if they'd work for her and Dean? Trying out classic tropes was also a good way to keep her nerves in check. Anxiety was a frequent companion when Maggie faced unknown scenarios and surprises, so it was better all-around if she made the plans and inserted Dean as needed.

The ending notwithstanding, their date at the fair had been as close to perfect as a fake date was possible to be. Even with the audience, she and Dean had had fun, and she'd gotten some tingles and there had been some heat when their bodies had brushed against each other. Not quite the same tingles she'd experienced during the week with Mac, but she chalked that reaction up to a high stress scenario and nothing more. It was time they had a date, just the two of them. Their eyes would meet, their hands brush, and their feelings would slip down the rocky hill into emotional entanglement. Maggie would also get a chance to see Dean maybe shirtless, after she finished dumping her coffee on him.

Maggie checked her phone for the time and saw that she was a few minutes early. Dean was one of those fashionably late people who rolled into scheduled events at least ten minutes after they started. Maggie thought it was a real testament to her feelings for Dean that his lack of punctuality didn't bother her. Usually, when people were late to meet with her, Maggie immediately assumed they weren't coming.

"Hey Maggie." Gwen waved from behind the counter, her tan apron already stained with cocoa powder and espresso grounds. Maggie waved back. "Shall I get your usual?"

"Not yet. I'm meeting someone." Her cheeks heated, and even from across the café, she heard Gwen squeal.

"A date?" Gwen wiped her hands on a striped towel before making her way around the counter to take Maggie by the arm. "Come sit. Tell me everything before they show up."

In any other situation, Maggie would have wanted the floor to open up and swallow her instead of having a bunch of strangers eavesdrop on this conversation. But Gwen was a darling. Her gray-streaked hair was piled into a messy knot on her head, and her gold rings glinted in the overhead lights as she served drinks and "nibbles" as she liked to call them. Gwen shoved Maggie down into one of the plush velvet chairs, a deep purple one, and collapsed into the seat across from her. With her chin propped in her hands, Gwen looked about ten years old, not the fifty-six she actually was.

"It's not a big deal," Maggie said, which was a lie because she went breathless, her ribs unable to expand enough, just waiting for him to show up.

Gwen raised a single arched brow. It was a move Maggie had been trying to perfect for the three years she had been frequenting the coffee shop.

"Okay, it's a big deal." Maggie buried her burning face behind her hands when Gwen whooped.

"About time." Gwen pulled Maggie's hands down, enfolding them in her own. "Now tell me everything. Who is he?"

"Dean." Maggie hid her face again. "I'm dating Dean."

"Dean?"

"What does that mean? That question? With the tone?" Maggie's mouth was dry, and the breathless feeling from before had tightened her chest.

"Nothing." Gwen patted Maggie's hand on the table. "I'm just a little surprised. I always thought... Well, it doesn't matter what I thought."

"I've loved him my whole life." Maggie cast a furtive glance around the café to be sure Dean wasn't anywhere within earshot. "I fell in love with him in second grade when we took that school field trip to the zoo, and I ended up nauseated and hyperventilating in the bathroom. Audrey wasn't there. She was having a spa day with her mother, and when my teacher did headcount—"

"I know honey," Gwen took Maggie's hand between her own and rubbed her slender fingers over Maggie's palm.

Remembering the panic in that bathroom, Maggie started gasping in air.

"Dean was the only one who noticed you didn't get back on the bus. He made sure the teachers didn't leave you there. And then he sat with you the whole way back to school."

Dean had also insisted on walking her from the bus back to class, and stayed with her until her mom came and picked her up. Even after his fifth-grade teacher had told him they'd call his parents if he didn't return to his classroom.

"I know you love him. Will always love him." It sounded like she was gearing up for a 'but,' but it never came. "If he makes you happy, then that's all I could ask for. You deserve to be happy, Maggie."

"I am happy."

A line was forming at the counter, and Gwen looked from it back at Maggie. "I have to head back over there, but chocolate croissants are on the house. I'd say everything is on the house, but it's character building to let him pay for your drink." She winked before heading back to the monster espresso machine and the hoard of thirsty customers.

The door to the shop opened to let out a little girl and her mama, and there was Dean, holding the heavy glass until they were standing on the sidewalk in the sunshine. Maggie jumped to her feet, the tension behind her breastbone easing just the slightest bit. His sandy hair was perfectly in place, wide mouth open in an amiable smile. He found her immediately, eyes skipping the crowd to lock on to hers as though drawn there by a magnet.

"Hey," Dean said, when Maggie had reached him by the door, "Did you order yet? Or do I get to buy you a coffee?"

"It's your lucky day." Maggie's whole body sagged when he threw his arm over her shoulder and pulled her into his side for a hug. This was what she'd wanted to feel, the sweet warmth of sliding into a bubble bath, when he was nearby.

Dean put his hand on her lower back and ushered her towards a smiling Gwen and her espresso machine.

There was only one other couple in front of them, and Maggie looked up into his golden face. Even with his expertly cut hair and the designer cologne, he was still that young boy who'd cared for her, protected her, and Maggie's heart lurched up to lodge into her throat. What if her stupid plan ruined them? What would she do without him?

Then Dean grinned down at her, and his lips started moving, and she remembered their lives were so intertwined that she couldn't lose him. It was impossible to cleave him entirely away from her. That sounded a lot creepier than she'd meant it to.

"Hey babies." Gwen smiled a toothy grin at them as they stepped up to the counter. "I'll get Maggie's regular started, and what do you want, Dean darling?"

Dean ducked his head at the nickname and ordered a medium coffee, black. Gwen pursed her lips and raised that eyebrow again, but her eyes still sparkled at them. Dean handed over his credit card and signed the slip when Gwen handed it to him. He also graciously slid a five-dollar bill into the tip jar.

"I knew I liked you," Gwen winked and handed over Dean's coffee and Maggie's half hot chocolate, half coffee, with three pumps of caramel sauce. "I'll bring over some nibbles once they're warmed up."

Maggie took her cup and wrapped her hands around the warm weight of it. She was grateful Gwen hadn't given her one of the heavy ceramic mugs. It would make her next move a lot easier. There wouldn't be any sharp shards to worry about littering the floor or a heavy projectile crushing either of their feet. She smiled at Gwen and took a deep breath, muscling down the nerves that tightened her chest. This was it. She just had to turn and plow directly into the front of her date's muscled chest. This worked all the time in books. Maggie closed her eyes and spun around, slamming into the solid wall of her date's body.

Dean hissed and jumped back, but the damage was done. Maggie's cup had crumpled on impact and dark brown liquid was seeping down Dean's white collared shirt. A small amount soaked down into his pants as well. Dean tugged the stained cotton away from his skin, and Maggie watched as it suctioned back against his ridged abdomen with a wet *thwap*.

Her tongue took up too much space in her mouth as she stared him down, tracing each divot his soaked shirt showcased. Gwen shoved a handful of napkins at her over the top of the counter and Maggie shook herself back together as she grabbed them. Her knees hit the concrete floor and using both hands, she pressed the napkins against Dean's belly and the waistband of his pants.

"I'm so sorry," she said, but she wasn't that sorry. Her eyes kept straying down his body. She pressed against him a little harder, and Dean shifted under her ministrations.

"Watch the hands, Babs." He reached down to help her. "We're in public."

Maggie glanced at her hands pressed just below the buckle of his belt. She flushed and dropped the napkins as if they'd caught fire, but when she finally dragged her eyes up to meet Dean's, his eyes sparkled, and his lips twitched with a barely suppressed smile.

"I'm the world's biggest klutz." She was still kneeling in front of her fake boyfriend's waist. Maggie grabbed handfuls of the scattered, coffee-stained napkins and crumpled them into her fists.

"I know you are." The corners of his eyes creased with his familiar laugh lines. He sidestepped out of the line and offered Maggie a hand to help her to her feet. One of Gwen's baristas came around the counter with a mop. "It's really okay."

Maggie let Dean take over the napkin wielding and pressed her hands to her flaming cheeks. *Now what?* In the romance books, this scenario led to a shirtless hero, and a ravished—or at least partially tumbled—heroine, but despite the copious amounts of reading research she'd done over the past few days, Maggie couldn't figure out how to get them to the next step now that she'd dumped her coffee down his front. Her mind had drawn a complete blank. It wasn't like Dean was going to strip naked in the public coffee shop. He needed a place to change.

"You can come back to my place. I live next door." Maggie pointed to the exposed brick of the wall that bordered her building.

Maggie flushed and Dean stopped mopping at his shirt to look at her. Why would he come back to her house when she didn't have clothes for him? Although she had her own washer and dryer. That was a rare gem for apartment living, but it had been a necessity since laundromats always made her itchy. She'd gone weeks between laundry loads when she and Audrey had been roommates. Once Audrey found her hand-washing her jeans in the shower, she'd taken over the laundromat trips for both of them.

"Thanks, Babs." The twinkle was gone from Dean's eyes as they flitted back and forth searching hers. He dug out his wallet and handed her his credit card. "Grab yourself another drink. I have an extra shirt in my car."

Given that she'd purposefully dumped her coffee on him, Maggie couldn't bring herself to use his money to buy a replacement. Since his hands were full of napkins, she leaned forward and tucked the card back into the pocket of his pants. She patted the denim once and then brushed past him to walk to the glass door, trying to put an extra sway in her step and a shimmy in her hips.

Dean's Mercedes had a prime parking spot in front of The Perk-u-Later. He clicked his keys and reached into the backseat, grabbing a hold of a small black duffel bag.

"Gym bag. All clean, too." He hefted the bag over his shoulder and re-locked his car. Maggie inclined her head towards the three-decker where she rented the middle floor above Mrs. Weller, who gave her a good deal on rent for help with groceries and trips to the doctor, and below Trey and Moore, a sweet couple who spent so much time jet-setting that she rarely saw them at all. Maggie set off with her exaggerated, rolling hips and Dean reached out to snag her wrist. "Hey, you don't need to be embarrassed, Babs. It was just an accident."

"I'm not embarrassed," Maggie said, because she would not tell him she doused him in coffee on purpose.

Dean frowned and rubbed the back of his neck with his free hand. "Oh, you're limping a little and I thought you were trying to escape the coffee shop because you were feeling weird or whatever." He gestured to her hips. "Are you hurt?"

"No, I'm not hurt." *Try mortified.*

Maggie left her seductress walk behind as she led Dean into the three-decker and up the stairs to her apartment. The door had barely closed behind him when Dean dropped his duffle and stripped his coffee-stained shirt off over his head. Maggie had a lifetime of memories of shirtless Dean by the pool from her childhood. She even had a secret stash of shirtless Dean memories from his high school athletics days, but both had been at least a decade in the past and did not prepare her for shirtless man Dean.

Maggie nearly swallowed her tongue seeing the acres of tanned skin. His abdomen was carved into defined muscles, his belly drum flat. A small dusting of golden chest hair grew in a little triangle between his pectorals. He used the dry part of his shirt to wipe the residual coffee off of his skin and Maggie had the urge to offer to clean him. With her tongue. Like a cat.

Dean's hands slid to his waistband and made quick work of the button on his pants. He dipped his hands inside and pushed the wet denim to his knees. Maggie almost hit the floor. He wore a pair of navy boxer briefs, and the skin of his thick thighs was the same golden color as the skin on his chest and belly. The same golden hair curled along his legs, and Maggie swore she could hear the crisp rasp as the pants slid along the hair. The sound left her almost panting. She spun to face away from him, staring at her refrigerator and trying not to imagine him sliding off the underwear too.

"Did you need anything to drink? A towel?" *A cuddle and a blow job?*

"I'm good, thanks." Dean said. Maggie heard the zipper on the duffle.

"Okay." Her voice came out at a decibel only dogs would recognize.

Dean searched through his clothes. The rustle of the vinyl bag made her wince. Suddenly, her limbs felt weighed down and heavy. Her head spun, her heart raced, and her breath came in small pants.

"I'm just going to go to the bathroom real quick." She bolted from the room on shaking legs.

Maggie locked the door behind her and sank down to sit on the lid of the toilet. Her hands were shaking as she folded them over her thighs. What was wrong with her? Why was she hiding in the bathroom after getting Dean right where she wanted him? How did she go from admiring his muscles, to being terrified of him stripping to his birthday suit? Now was the time to march out there and touch all that beautiful golden skin, and share some lingering looks, and then roll up on her toes and press their mouths together. That's what the heroine in her novels would do. She needed to take advantage of this situation. She'd already committed to it. If she missed this opportunity, she couldn't just go around dumping more drinks on him. Dean would definitely notice something like that.

Maggie took a deep breath, and willed her hands to steady. She flushed the toilet for cover and turned on the sink so he wouldn't think she had skipped washing her hands. Then she actually washed them just in case Dean noticed she didn't smell like her citrus hand soap. She grabbed one of the fluffy yellow towels off of the shower door and tucked it under her arm. She'd just take the towel out there and offer to help him dry off with it. Easy Peasy. Then he'd pull on some new clothes and she'd suggest a new Netflix show and they'd snuggle up on her tiny loveseat. For once in her life, Maggie was thankful for the tiny piece of furniture.

Except she'd taken too long. By the time Maggie made it back to her kitchen, Dean had not only pulled on fresh clothes, he'd also tossed his dirty ones into the washer that stood next to the fridge. A threadbare t-shirt and a pair of loose gray sweatpants covered all of that smooth, golden skin. But Maggie could work with gray sweatpants. Gray sweatpants in the romance world were almost better than fully naked.

"I hope you don't mind that I popped my things into your washing machine. Coffee can be a beast to get out." He was lacing up a pair of brightly colored running shoes.

"I was going to offer to wash them for you." Maggie eyed the sneakers. "Are you going somewhere? I thought we could play a board game or watch a movie or something like that."

"I'm going to go for a run." Dean straightened to his mammoth height and smiled at her, rocking in his running shoes. "I like to hit the park just a few blocks over. It's a beautiful day to be outside."

The outdoors was not Maggie's favorite place to pass the time. Exercising was even lower on the list. She'd have much preferred the indoor cuddling option, but Dean was smiling down at her and his eyes were shining again, and his butt looked damn good in his sweatpants. *A romance heroine would go for the run,* Maggie thought. She'd put on a cute set of workout pants and a sports bra, bare her perfect body, and run in the sun with the perfect hero. Either she'd impress him with her stamina, or she'd twist an ankle and he'd have to nurse her back to health.

Maggie had maybe one sports bra, not that her girls needed much support, and she had leggings even if they were regular cotton ones and not the fancy athletic kind. She did have a pair of running shoes. Yes, she'd bought them because they were purple and not because she ran or exercised at all, but sneakers were sneakers. And if she died, then at least they could star in another trope where he came to her rescue and performed mouth-to-mouth. If it came to that, Maggie hoped it worked out better than the other tropes she'd tried, because spilling coffee on him had been a bust. Yes, she'd seen Dean shirtless, but now they were headed out on a run instead of making out and having him boost her up on the washer for the spin cycle.

"Let me just change my clothes and I'll come with you," Maggie sighed, and went to dig out her sports bra, hoping it was clean and hole-free.

♡

The run had been one of the worst decisions of Maggie's life. Not only had she panted, gasped, and sweated with every step—while pretending that she wasn't—but even as she'd tried to keep step behind Dean's glorious butt, she was too tired to enjoy the view. By the time they'd stopped back at her apartment, she was too irritable to enjoy having him in her space. Dean had switched his clothes to the dryer, promised to pick them up the next day, and left her to drag her aching body to the shower. She chose not to ask him to stay, because the sweat on her skin was making her itch and the memory of him asking if she wanted to quit made her throat tight.

Maggie stood under the scalding water and tried not to think about how badly she'd messed up a simple date. She was supposed to spill coffee on him, bring him back to her place, get him shirtless, and then run her hands up his bare chest to cup the back of his neck. How hard was that? She might not have had a lot of experience seducing guys—her few partners had always done the lion's share of the work—but she loved Dean. She was attracted to Dean. She wanted to touch Dean and have him touch her. There was no logical reason she'd run off to hide in the bathroom. That wasn't her normal anxiety. She'd never run and hid from sex before.

Maybe it was the pressure of loving Dean? She wanted to get this right. She wanted him to see her as an actual romantic partner. After twenty years of friendship, that was a lot of pressure. No wonder she'd felt overwhelmed. Next time it would be easier. Next time the sight of his muscles wouldn't cause her to flee. She was attracted to him, and next time it wouldn't be a surprise. Now that she'd seen him shirtless and the pressure was off, next time she could enjoy him.

Maggie soaped up her hands and let them run across her belly and up the front of her body to her breasts. Her nipples tingled from the heat of the shower, and she let the tips of her fingers brush against them. A small shiver slid down her spine, but it wasn't unpleasant. Maggie cupped her breasts more fully and tipped her head back, letting the water flow over her neck and down her body. She slid one hand up over her neck to clutch the hair at the back of her head, not pulling, just sitting there with an obvious weight. The other hand squeezed around her breast, waiting for the heat to spread.

Dean, she thought, twisting her nipple again.
Dean, Dean, Dean.

Maggie had touched herself before. It was the only way she had sex anymore. Alone with herself. Usually it was after reading a steamy scene in a novel. Book boyfriends always did it for her. There was something safe and comfortable about loving them, as if they'd gotten to know each other better than anyone over several hundred pages. If fictional men could rev her engines, then Dean could, too. Maggie brought the hand from her breast down to her hipbone.

She could do this.

Dean's muscles had rippled as he pulled his shirt over his head.

Maggie slid her hand lower, teasing the soft skin between her thighs. It felt good. She couldn't tell if she was wet, not with the shower pounding over her, but there was a small spring coiling in her stomach as she circled her index finger around her clit. She was already hot from the shower, but an extra flush of heat climbed up her body, seeping into her limbs. She closed her eyes and thought of Dean.

His smile, even after she dumped a drink on him.

She slipped two fingers inside her heat and stroked.

The strength in his arms when he hugged her or held her.

She circled her clit again, as the tension coiled tighter

Dean's smooth voice as he said that he loved her.
She shuddered.

Dean asking if she'd hurt herself as she swung her hips.

The tension dissolved.

Dean chatting as they ran, while she sucked air in through a straw.

The heat vanished.

Dean stripping down to his skin while she grabbed a bra that she should have tossed years ago..

Maggie dropped her hands and turned off the water.

This wasn't the first time she'd lost focus while trying to get off. It was okay to not be in the mood. Her mortification over how the day had gone was enough to suffocate almost anyone's arousal. It wasn't Dean. The next date would be better. Maggie smiled at her Jane Austen duck, rubbing a hand over the smooth vinyl plastic. She grabbed a towel and stepped onto her bath mat, deciding that she was going to read a book and put the whole day out of her mind. Tomorrow would be a new start.

CHAPTER NINE

"I need a makeover." Maggie sandwiched her phone between her ear and her shoulder. She was standing in front of her closet, perusing her options for her next date with Dean. The humiliation of her decades old sports bra was sitting on her shoulders like her trusty weighted blanket. In true, main character fashion, Dean hadn't mentioned the bra. He'd given her a single grin as he looked her up and down and then politely kept his gaze off of her body.

"You don't need a makeover." Audrey's distant voice was just muffled enough that Maggie was pretty sure she was driving. "You're gorgeous, and your style is all your own."

A little fissure of warmth bloomed in Maggie's chest at Audrey's words. She would forever be grateful her photo-ready best friend saw nothing wrong with what she liked to wear, but her wardrobe needed a long-overdue update. Some version of a makeover was a standard occurrence in romance novels, films, and television. Female heroine buys new clothes, gets a new haircut, wears some makeup, and the male hero falls all over himself, picking his jaw up off the ground and seeing her as the hot and desirable woman he was overlooking before. She could get some new clothes, the first in close to a decade, and set the groundwork for another chance at slapping Dean upside the head with classic romantic tropes.

"If Cal is with you and I'm on speaker, best friend code says you have to tell me."

"You're on speaker and Cal is with me, but he's not paying attention to anything, right, baby?"

Some unintelligible conversation hit Maggie's ear and then Cal said, "Hi Maggie."

"Hi Cal,"

"Did you want me to call you back?" Audrey asked. "We'll be at the house in five."

"No, it's fine," Maggie said and resolved not to mention her underwear or the fact that her boyfriend was fake. She and Cal probably couldn't recover from that kind of sharing. "If you don't want to call it a makeover, can we agree I need a wardrobe update? Refresh? Hail Mary?"

"You're being dramatic, but if you want new clothes, then I'll drop Cal off and come grab you. I never turn down a shopping experience. I'll see you in fifteen. Be ready."

Maggie stared at her hanging t-shirts and hoodies. She grabbed the shirt she'd worn to the fair and reached for another nondescript pair of black leggings. Together they were nothing special, but a sliver of her pale stomach showed between the twist at the shirt's hem and the top of pants. The outfit was like the clothes she saw on the college students who walked past the store, so that probably counted for something. After today, she'd have a wardrobe from this decade meant to knock Dean on his bite-able butt and enough sports bras to convince him she was a regular exerciser.

Audrey pulled the car up exactly twenty minutes later—she couldn't arrive on time any more than her brother—and handed Maggie a small hair clip covered in tiny books. Maggie lifted one tiny cover with her fingernail.

"You've been pushing your hair out of your face a lot, and you've had a rough day at work this week."

Maggie turned the clip over in her hands. "Where did you even find this?"

"Oh." Audrey bit her lip and pulled the car away from the curb. "Etsy." She said and merged into traffic.

Audrey drove them both to the local mall. It was mostly dead inside, and as they walked through the multilevel atrium, a fountain burbling between two rows of massage chairs, Maggie marveled at the fact that all malls smelled exactly the same—like recycled air, vinyl, and popcorn.

"I haven't been to a mall since high school," Maggie admitted as they passed a small group of women all power-walking with their hand weights and buzzing with conversation. Maggie was pretty sure their mouths were moving faster than their legs, and they still almost knocked her flat. Audrey had the common sense to get out of their way.

"I figured it was our best bet." Audrey said and pulled her sandy blonde hair into a high ponytail. "I wasn't sure what you were actually looking for."

"Workout clothes," Maggie said.

"You don't work out."

"And some other stuff, too. I'm pretty sure most of my wardrobe came from my last mall trip."

"That's sad." Audrey pointed to the nearest shop window with headless mannequins dressed in neon Lycra. "We'll start there, and you can tell me where this idea came from. Dressing you up is usually like pulling teeth, and since you're more than your clothes, I stopped trying to change your style in eighth grade."

Audrey pulled Maggie through the store's entrance and to a rack of slippery leggings. The fluorescent lights made all the neon colors even brighter. Maggie liked color. She specifically liked black, and gray, and navy blue, and white. None of those seemed like an option in this store. She thumbed through a few of the subtler colored pants as Audrey started pulling some off the rack to hold up against Maggie's waist.

"Dean took me running," Maggie said, and Audrey almost dropped the leggings in her hands.

"Was someone chasing you?" Audrey shoved the bright fuchsia pants back into the rack to study up another. She held each pair up to the light as if they were diamonds she was inspecting for flaws or imperfections. "You don't run, Maggie."

"I know that. You know that." Maggie took the purple pair Audrey shook in her face. "And thanks to my complete lack of sporty clothes, your brother knows it, too."

Audrey paused and raised a brow at Maggie. "Why? What did you wear?"

Maggie looked down at her black cotton leggings and pinched them away from her hip. "I wore these, and my one sports bra, it only had a tiny hole near the neckline, and a t-shirt."

"That's not awful, Maggie," Audrey said. "At least you didn't wear sweatpants or jeans."

"After the third time he told me we could pick another activity, it was pretty obvious he knew I was miserable and definitely not a runner."

"Why didn't you pick something else?" Audrey moved to a table covered in sports bras.

She hadn't done that because Dean had seemed so excited to go on a run together. One thing Maggie was not good at was changing her mind after she'd agreed to something. Or saying no to people she cared about. Saying no was one of her anxiety triggers. She didn't panic at the word itself. It was the thought of disappointing whoever had asked her for something. Maggie and her therapist worked extensively on knowing and enforcing boundaries, and Maggie also had an arsenal of breathing exercises.

Not that she'd said "yes" to avoid a panic. Exercise itself wasn't a hard limit for her, and Maggie had been pretty sure Dean was going for a run with or without her, so it was better to suffer through a little extra time in his company—his company really was a good time—than to cut the date short, even as her lungs seized up and her throat stung after about five minutes. By the time she stumbled back into her apartment, her blisters had blisters, and she'd had to soak her feet in an Epsom salt bath from Mrs. Weller.

"It doesn't matter," Maggie said, "Because I may have tried to send him off my deceptive trail by saying my workout clothes were all in the wash."

"First, this is Dean." Audrey held a lime green bra up against Maggie's chest, "So I'm not really sure why it matters. You aren't trying to impress him, but at least he knows you do laundry."

Maggie rolled her eyes. "He knew I was lying, Aud. His clothes were in my washing machine and there conveniently wasn't a load of sports bras and running shorts in there because I didn't know he'd suggest running, like for fun."

A muffled snort snuck out of Audrey as she valiantly tried to hold back the rest of her laughter. She shook her head, blond wisps escaping her thick ponytail to flutter around her temples. "It's a good thing your relationship is fake," Audrey said and handed Maggie a cropped top with so many straps Maggie wasn't sure she'd be able to get it on by herself. At least it was black. "You and Dean are just too different. The only board game Dean enjoys is Chutes and Ladders, even though it's entirely luck."

"You and Cal don't share all the same interests," Maggie said. Audrey knew how she felt about Dean, so there was no reason for the tightness closing at the base of her throat, except that recently Maggie kept feeling like she had to defend her faux relationship.

"We share a lot," Audrey said and looped her arm through Maggie's, dragging her to the dressing room. "I know romance novels will convince you that opposites attract, but you're statistically more likely to be attracted to someone who is like you and shares your interests, hobbies, and values."

Maggie closed the door to the changing room and stared at her reflection in the mirror. She was sure Dean was the one for her. He showed her his love every single day. Yes, it made sense that people were attracted to others like themselves, but that wasn't true for everyone. She and Dean had things in common. They both liked to read, Dean loved Stephen King, and Maggie read romance novels. They both enjoyed trying different cuisines, although Maggie was a vegetarian who mostly lived off pasta, and Dean went keto and ate enormous slabs of meat. Maggie was sure they had enough commonalities that they would work as soon as Dean stopped seeing her as his little sister's best friend.

They both loved animals. There. That was another thing.

Maggie pulled on one pair of the pants and the less complicated of the two bras. The pants were baggy around her thighs and knees, although they fit okay on her hips. Maggie pulled the waist around to check the size. She tried on another pair of the pants and had the same fit issues. The strappy bra was a bust. She'd need someone to cut it off of her if she actually wore it.

Although, thanks to Mac, she had a shiny new knife that could handle the job.

Mac could handle the job.

What the hell was wrong with her?

"I think you're wrong about compatibility," Maggie said after she pulled her own leggings back on and left the dressing room. "If sharing interests were the most important thing, then Mac would have to wait forever for another history-loving bladesmith."

"Concerned with Mac?" Audrey arched a brow. Maggie rolled her eyes. "Maybe for Mac it would look like a partner who understood his artistry. Someone who is creative, too. Or someone who understands how he can get lost researching something for hours. Kind of like you with your writing."

"The pants were all too big," Maggie said and hung them on the clothes rack just inside the changing room door. "Let's go grab a different size or try a different store."

Audrey studied her, mouth twisted to the side. It was her concerned face, and Maggie wanted no part of it. She should have known a subject change wouldn't deter Audrey. Nothing deterred Audrey. She was a terrier masquerading as a labrador.

Audrey shoved another pair of the purple pants at her. "These are XXS, try them. I'll grab some running shorts. They'll show off your ass." Maggie took the pants and held them in her hands, thumb stroking along the smooth fabric.

"Look," Audrey said, "If you want to take up exercising then take up exercising. Don't let me tell you what you can and can't do. Don't let anyone tell you that. I just don't want to see you get hurt." Then she turned on her heel and headed back into the brightly lit aisles of the store to hunt down shorts.

Two hours later, after a stop for lingerie for Audrey and new underwear sets for Maggie, and enough cute, comfy, and trendy clothes to weigh Maggie's arms down, the pair were back in Audrey's car and blasting the radio. Maggie was unpacking her messenger bag to fill the mini pleather backpack she'd found and had to have. She transferred her two notebooks, her iPad, her wallet, her Kindle, a handful of hair ties, a bottle of iced tea, fourteen pens, a smashed pack of Oreos, and the small box she'd picked up on a whim.

"I'll bring you back to the house, and then I'll cut your hair, and we can play with some makeup if you're interested." Audrey said and flicked her turn signal on.

"Sounds good," Maggie said. "I have something for Mac, anyway."

Audrey pressed her lips together to hide a twitch, and Maggie resisted the urge to knock against her shoulder. It wouldn't be smart while Audrey was driving.

"It's just a thank you." Maggie thought about the gorgeous dagger she was using as a letter opener–although she'd never tell Mac that—and the way his palm had slammed into the top of the counter as he told off a bigoted asshole. "He made me a knife, and he stood up for Shay at the shop when he dropped it off."

"Awe. Of course he did." Audrey pulled the car into the double wide driveway and parked. "He's really the sweetest guy. He just hides it under a scowl and facial hair."

"You'd be surprised how enticing a grumpy hero can be." Maggie let herself out of the car. "There's a whole trope surrounding the grumpy hero and the heroine made of sunshine."

"Well, they haven't found Mac yet. Cal said he doesn't really date."

Maggie rolled her eyes and laughed as she hoisted her bags out of the passenger seat. "You know that just adds to his appeal, right? In romance land?"

Audrey straightened, ponytail swinging. "You should write your next book about him. Give him a happily ever after."

"I don't write about real people, Audrey," Maggie said and flushed as she thought of her tall, muscled, sandy-haired hero smiling from the pages of her rough draft. "But a grumpy sunshine story could definitely be in the future. I'll meet you inside." She shook her new backpack at her friend. "I'm going to drop off Mac's gift first."

"He's in the forge," Audrey said, as though the hum of the blower and the dings of a heavy hammer hitting metal weren't audible all the way to the driveway.

Mac's back was to Maggie as she walked down the stone path to his blacksmith's paradise. The forge was in an extra garage at the back of the property. Mac and Cal's grandparents had probably stored lawn equipment there, but Mac had added a rolling garage door and had filled the inside with medieval looking tools. He had the door open like he always did while working, and the glow from his fire pit backlit his dark hair, powerful arms, and sweat-drenched shirt.

Mac stood in front of a large, dark anvil, a pair of tongs holding the end of a glowing rectangle of metal. He swung a huge hammer down on the top edge of the heated steel. Maggie tried not to watch as the muscles in his arms and back flexed each time he brought the hammer up over his head and then down in a slicing arc. Beads of sweat clung to the back of his tanned neck and bled down to where dark wet patches of sweat soaked his shirt. Those same spots bracketed the sides of his body and the small of his back, and Maggie wondered when she started finding sweat a turn-on. Even after her run with Dean, she'd barely leaned into his side for a hug goodbye. It must be the primal core of her that wanted to press her body up against Mac's sweaty torso.

The clang of hammer on metal was loud enough to rattle Maggie's eardrums, and the boxy headphones Mac wore made the necessity of touching him seem like a more and more workable way to get his attention. She watched him swing the hammer a few more times, flinching each time the blow came. He put the hammer down and turned the billet, looking at the glowing length as he turned it left and right. The yellow was fading out of the metal, and Mac took his tongs and carried the billet to his forge before laying the whole thing inside the glowing box. He pulled one glove off and scrubbed his hand down his face and over his beard. Mac lifted his shirt to wipe the sweat from his forehead.

"Hi," Maggie said before her power of speech failed. She moved into his line of sight.

"Maggie."

Mac pulled the headphones from his ears and slammed his palm against a button on the side of the forge. The roar of the flame stopped, leaving just the sound of the blower as the light inside the structure waned.

"You don't need to stop working." Maggie clutched her backpack in front of her stomach like a shield.

"Don't want the metal to overheat or I can't use it."

"I could come back later. Audrey was going to give me a trim. I could go in and do that first so you can keep working—"

"I already turned the propane off."

Maggie bit back her apology because Mac was already frowning at her. Even without the hammer in his hands, she was still fighting against the urge to plaster herself to his damp body. Maybe she should cut back on the soy products. Clearly her hormones were having their own version of a Florida spring break vacation.

"I got you something," Maggie said and held up her backpack. "I saw it today and thought of you and how nice you were to make me that knife—"

"Dagger."

"—and that I hadn't adequately thanked you for standing up for Shay."

"So you brought me a toddler backpack?" Mac eyed the brown pleather while the corner of his mouth hitched up in a potential smile. It was lethal.

Maggie looked down at her hands, holding the bag out like an offering.

"Oh." She pulled it back to her chest before opening the top and fishing out the small box. "No, this."

The box was small and delicate in Mac's wide palms. One at a time, he wiped each hand down the legs of his jeans to rid them of sweat and turned the box over and over in his hands.

"This is—"

"It's a Lego blacksmith set." Maggie said. It was achingly hard to keep her body still when she wanted to jump up and down like a kid on Christmas morning. "See the armor and the tools? And the chicken? I'm not sure why the set included a chicken, but I thought you might like it."

"Where did you find it?" Mac asked, meeting her eyes with his dark ones.

"There was a stall in the mall. The owner uses actual Lego bricks to make their own sets, and this one made me think of you."

Mac opened the box and removed a tiny yellow figure with a brown hood draped over its plastic head. Tiny dots of black showed a stubbled beard and mustache, just like Mac's. He pulled out a tiny silver sword with divots all down the blade. Mac pushed the sword into the gloved hand of the blacksmith figurine.

"It's not super accurate, since I've never seen you forge in a sleeveless shirt," Maggie pointed to the yellow arms of the figurine.

"It's important to wear as much coverage as possible in all natural fabrics. I wear cotton or a leather apron. Non-natural fabrics can melt into your skin when hit by sparks. I have some nasty scars to prove it." He continued to turn the figure over and over in his hands. "When did you go to the mall?"

"Today. I needed some new clothes. I dress like a preteen, so Audrey and I went and depleted my bank account on new sports bras and frilly underwear." Maggie blushed when she realized what she'd said. "Anyway, I saw that and thought you'd like it. I don't even know if you like Legos, but I thought—"

"I love it." Mac said and pinned her in place with his stare. "No one's ever… I used to collect and build Lego kits all the time. This is amazing."

"I'm glad." Maggie said and looked down at her feet to avoid his eyes. "I wanted you to know I'm grateful. For the blade and for what you did the other day. It meant a lot to me. And to Shay."

She looked up again to find that Mac had stepped into her personal space, his chest centimeters from hers. Before she could move away, his thick arms came up and around her body, pulling her in flush for a hug. His chest was warm, damp from sweat, and he smelled like flame and metal and a hint of pine. Maggie let her hands come up to hug him back.

CHAPTER TEN

Maggie didn't know if it was the throngs of teenagers or the sundress that made her more anxious. She should have realized suggesting miniature golf on a sunny Saturday would include a crush of people and a breeze that threatened to flash everyone in her vicinity. Maggie had planned to wear the dress with a long-sleeve shirt underneath, but she had plans for her bare shoulders today. Dean would see her all dressed up, she'd shiver from the cold, and he'd gallantly offer her his sweater or sweatshirt or something.

Audrey's car turned into the parking lot and Maggie waved as her friend, her friend's boyfriend, her friend's boyfriend's brother, and Dean all piled out of the vehicle. This time she and Dean were crashing Audrey and Cal's date, but miniature golf had been too good an idea to pass up. There were so many ways romance novels could turn this activity into a winner, and Maggie was determined not to let them slip away. She was zero for two on classic tropes, but this time things had to go in her favor. Right?

"You look amazing!" Audrey said into her ear as she wrapped Maggie up in her standard greeting hug. "I love the dress."

She looked around Audrey's slender body to wave at Cal and Mac. The brothers stood shoulder to shoulder, dark hair gleaming under the sun. Dean glowed next to them.

"Hi guys," Maggie waved.

Both Mac and Cal raised a hand in greeting. Dean waved and wrapped her in a hug.

"I like the kitties, Babs." Dean slipped his index finger under the thick strap crossing her shoulder. Cross stitch style cats covered the dress. Maggie kept running her fingers over the little bumps of their noses. Her breath caught when Dean's finger touched her skin. He looked her over from head to toe and smiled. "Very cute."

Maggie blushed. "Thank you,"

"I hope you brought a sweater," Mac said.

The breeze was chilly and under normal circumstances, she absolutely would have brought layers. Maggie felt her body flinch when Audrey whirled on Mac, eyes flashing. Cal dropped his head into his hands.

"What is wrong with you?" Audrey said through her clenched teeth.

"What?" Mac asked.

"Dude," Cal said, his voice low enough that Maggie almost missed it. "We talked about this."

Dean frowned, lines creasing the skin between his brows. He wrapped an arm around Maggie's shoulders and pulled her into his warm chest.

"Ignore him," Dean said, "You look great."

The men paid the entrance fee while Audrey and Maggie assigned colored balls to each player and grabbed putters. Audrey picked pink and grabbed a blue ball for Cal. Maggie grabbed a bright yellow ball, her favorite color, but also easier to see if it winged somewhere out of sight, for herself and for Dean, a deep green ball the color of his eyes.

"Mac can have the black ball," Audrey said and pocketed one for him. "It's the color of his soul."

"Just the other day, you said he was sweet," Maggie said, and Audrey scoffed.

"That was before he was rude."

Mac hadn't been rude, just honest. The temperature today was in the sixties. She was definitely going to be chilly. Especially with so much of the green shaded by big, leafy trees. Mac had been looking out for her, not criticizing her. But she also wasn't complaining about Dean's protective reaction, so she'd let Mac take one for the team, and she'd pretend to be offended.

"We should play in teams," Audrey said when they reached hole number one.

"We're not an even number." Maggie busied herself handing out golf balls.

"Mac, buddy, you've got to bring a date to these things." Dean said with his signature smile.

THE TROPE

It was Maggie's turn to frown at that. Mac with a date? Who would he bring? Probably someone sophisticated and educated. Someone with multiple degrees they could hang on their office walls in big, wooden frames. Although if he dated someone like that, he'd probably stop coming on silly little dates like the county fair or mini golf. Maggie held out Mac's golf ball and he took it, their fingers brushing. She felt electricity zing through her fingers at the contact. Mac pulled his hand back as though he felt the same.

"Ignore him," she said to Mac, "What was it you said to me? Pick someone who you want and who wants you? That was brilliant advice. It worked out well for me." Maggie turned her smile on Dean, who was sizing up the first hole.

"Did it?" Mac asked, his voice pitched for Maggie's ears alone. Louder, he added, "Flip a coin."

"Heads," Cal said, "you join the menfolk because we have multiple heads. Tails, you join the ladies since they're a piece of..."

"Don't even think about finishing that sentence," Audrey told her boyfriend. "Heads, Mac joins me and Maggie, since we clearly have all the brains. Tails, he joins you since you're an ass."

"Deal," Cal said, and pulled a quarter out of his pocket.

"Wait a minute." Mac snatched the coin from his brother's hand. "If it's my fate, then I'm flipping it."

Mac tossed the coin into the air, and it flipped end over end, glinting silver in the sunlight. It landed in his palm and Mac flipped it over onto the back of his opposite arm.

"Heads," Maggie said before Mac moved his hand.

"You don't need to call it. He already decided what each side meant," Dean said.

"I know," Maggie said, feeling an embarrassed blush stain her cheeks. "I just like to guess."

"Heads it is." Mac handed the quarter back to his brother and Cal shoved it deep into the pocket of his cargo shorts. "Can we play now?"

"Since we're down a player, we'll average the scores for each team. Ladies first." Dean gestured to the putting square for the first hole.

Audrey hefted her putter and said, "Don't mind if I do." She lined up her pink ball and tapped it down the green.

The first hole was simple enough, a straight shot to the flag with a slight bump in the middle of the green to divert the balls. Maggie wasn't an expert miniature golfer, but even she got her ball in on par. Maggie didn't worry about setting her plan in motion until hole three. The third hole had a pipe that ran under a fake pond feature. Maggie purposefully shot her ball wide, missing the pipe. One by one, her friends dropped their balls under the water and down to the next part of the hole, but Maggie missed twice more before finally dropping her ball down the PVC and into the hole at the other end. Audrey shot her a small frown but said nothing.

THE TROPE

Two holes later, karma was mad at Maggie for purposefully missing shots, and now she was almost ten strokes behind her teammates as she missed putt after putt. She'd quit trying to miss ten shots ago, but she couldn't seem to focus enough to get the angle and strength of her putts right. The breeze had picked up too and the goosebumps along her arms and collarbones were spreading faster than before. Ever the competitor, Audrey pursed her lips a little tighter each time Maggie missed another easy shot. After the fourth time Mac rescued her ball from the water or the rough, Maggie started tapping her ball along until she was close enough to sink it into the hole. The result was a high-as-a-kite score, but the edges of Mac's pants were finally drying out.

"You okay?" Audrey asked.

Maggie swallowed back the flutter of nerves. She hated feeling like a weak link, but the payout would be worth it. Totally romance novel-worthy.

"I don't know why I'm struggling. Am I lining up wrong?" She chanced a look at Dean, her attention skating over Mac as she did so. The corners of his mouth were threatening to tip up into what might have been a smile.

As they approached the sixth hole, Maggie blanched at the S curve of it and the rocks dotting the green.

"I'll help you with that, babe," Dean offered.

"I should just be my own team. Mac and Audrey can soldier on without me sandbagging their score."

"Relax." Dean put his putter to the side. "I've got you."

That sounded lovely.

Dean placed Maggie's yellow ball on the small black square. Maggie moved up to stand in position, her hands holding the top of her putter. She was small enough that she could stay fairly upright as she lined up her shot. Dean had to bend almost in half as he wrapped his body around hers and placed his hands on the putter, too. Maggie released the stick and tried to step back, but she only pressed herself tighter into Dean's chest.

"Grab your putter, Babs." Dean's voice rumbled in her ear. Maggie moved her hands back into position. "See that far wall?" Dean nodded over her shoulder to the tiny cement curb ringing the green. "We're aiming to bounce our ball right off the wall there so it turns and heads down towards the hole. Understand?"

Maggie nodded, hoping he understood the movement. His chin was just about even with her temple. She did not know what he'd just told her to do. Her brain had stopped working when he'd stepped up behind her. She was a decent player when she wasn't throwing her own game and figured they were planning to bounce the ball into position.

"Repeat after me, Babs: 'I will not hit the ball as hard as I can.'"

"I will not hit the ball as hard as I can."

"'If I do that, my ball will sail off the green and land in the water, and Mac will have to fish it out again.'"

"I don't mind," Mac said, arms crossed over his chest.

Maggie repeated Dean's words back. Then, with her fake boyfriend wrapped around the back of her body, the heat from his chest licking up her shoulders and down her arms, she took aim and hit the ball with all of her might. It hit the wall, bounced off the green, and rolled into the water. Dean let go of Maggie to go retrieve her ball, reaching the water before Mac, and Maggie couldn't stop herself from shivering at the loss of his warmth. She spotted Audrey and Cal trading wet kisses on the bench set off of the green, but Mac's eyes stayed glued to her, and she resisted the urge to shiver again.

"Babs." Dean held her dripping yellow ball out to her, "We said we would not smack it into kingdom come. Let's try again. Set up."

Dean put the ball back on the black square and then stepped up behind Maggie, waiting for her to be ready. Maggie wrapped her hands around her putter but hesitated to press back against Dean. With a low chuckle, Dean looped his arm around her waist and pulled her flush against his body.

"I don't bite." He placed his hands below hers again. "Okay, once more, with less feeling, Babs. Less, do you hear me?"

Maggie nodded again and tapped her ball with less force. It rolled to the wall, bounced off and changed direction to roll down towards the flag and the hole.

"It worked!" She said and turned to throw her arms around Dean's neck.

He straightened, pulling Maggie up onto the tips of her toes, and she closed the distance between them to brush her mouth against his. It was a quick kiss, barely a peck, but when she pulled back, Dean was grinning down at her.

"See what happens when you listen to me?" He said, "Only good things, babe, only good things."

Maggie putted her ball in on the next stroke and waited as everyone else finished out their turns. They were standing in a particularly shaded part of the course, and a shiver tripped up her spine again. Maggie could have fought the wrenching movement, but she knew from experience that suppressing the tremors would mean her teeth would chatter, clacking together like castanets.

The seventh hole looked equally devilish. There was a bridge each ball had to roll over, avoiding the water below and the fountain it flowed into. When it was Maggie's turn, she set up her ball and waited for Dean to come wrap himself around her again. He put his putter down and started towards her when Cal threw an arm out.

"You can't keep helping her. She's on the opposite team."

"She's my girlfriend," Dean countered, throwing a wink in Maggie's direction.

"Yea, I know, big love fest," Cal said, "You can't help her beat us."

Goddamn Cal. He was going to single-handedly ruin everything. They'd been stuck together like atomic nuclei. He'd pulled her butt back against his thighs, cocooned her in his arms, warmed her up, and she'd gotten a kiss. Well, a peck. Now if Dean had just thought to bring an extra layer to offer her as her goosebumps multiplied, then everything would have been perfect.

"Her own team can help her out," Cal said. "You did your duty as a boyfriend. Now do your duty as a teammate."

Dean met Maggie's eyes and shrugged. "You okay without me, Babs?"

"I can help her," Mac said, and then turned to Maggie. "If you want me to."

It was possible that all wasn't totally lost. Dean had held her, just like in the romance novels, and now he could get jealous seeing someone else do the same. Playing games between men wasn't something Maggie had thought about or planned for, mostly because she was having a hard enough time handling her feelings for one man, and she did not have the patience or mental fortitude to handle two. Then again, Cal had thrown this opportunity into her lap.

"Thanks Mac," Maggie said, and she didn't have to force a smile. It was already there. "I could use all the help I can get."

Audrey and Cal took their turns, their pink and blue balls sailing easily over the bridge to the far side of the green. Maggie toed her ball into place and squared up to take a shot. Mac stepped up next to her. He ghosted his palm down her arm to help reposition her hands on her putter, and Maggie felt her goosebumps explode out of control. Her shivering was out of control as her body trembled next to his.

"You're freezing," Mac said.

"I'm fine."

She wiggled her hips as she prepared for her shot. Mac slid into the spot behind her. He wasn't as tall as Dean—few people were—but his lips were even with her ear as he curled around her. Mac helped her hands choke up on the putter so that she bent even further forward. Her hips pressed back against his. Mac used one foot to open her stance, gently kicking her feet apart until they were just wider than her shoulders. The ache started low in her belly and Maggie thought about slamming her thighs back together before realizing she'd trap Mac's jean-clad leg between hers. Mac pointed to a spot on the far wall, the same one she'd been eyeing for her ball's trajectory.

"Aim there," he said.

Mac stepped back and let her send the ball all on her own.

The yellow sphere sailed along the green, bounced off the spot she and Mac had both chosen, bumped its way over the wooden bridge, and rolled right into the hole marked by the orange flag. A hole in one.

Audrey grinned as Maggie crossed the bridge herself and gave her a thumbs up, marking the score on their paper. Dean's green ball sailed over the bridge next, and a few minutes later, Mac's black ball joined it, knocking the green ball out of position as it came to rest right by the hole.

"She did even better without you," Cal said, as Dean walked across the bridge and Audrey lined up her putt. "Maybe I should make you help her again."

"Maybe I should," Dean said, watching as Mac crossed the bridge too.

They still had two holes to go and miniature golf was already an unmitigated success. Maggie barely reined in the urge to jump up, fist held high in the air. She couldn't stop her smile. The breeze ruffled the leaves overhead, and Maggie flattened her hands along her biceps. So the freezing limbs weren't a success. She'd hoped Dean would offer her some of his clothes to wear and to warm her up. If that was the goal, Maggie probably should have clued him in to bring extra layers. Like Cal, Dean only wore a long-sleeved shirt and shorts.

Maggie watched as Cal lined up his shot, marveling at how he could go from complete buffoonery to complete concentration in under a minute. Next to her, Mac pulled his sweater over his head and held it in front of her, blocking her view of Cal and Dean as they argued about what Cal should have done differently to have a better shot. The sweater was a thick knit in navy blue with wide stripes of red, yellow, and hunter green. It was so colorful, and so unlike Mac's normal, dark knits, that Maggie froze with it inches from her face.

"Take it," Mac said, his voice a low growl much closer than she'd realized.

"I'm fine," she said.

Mac growled.

"Has anyone ever told you you're basically one full moon away from being a werewolf?"

"What?" Mac asked, frowning down at her, with his dark eyes and dark hair and darker scowl.

"With the growling, and the frowning, and the hair." Maggie motioned towards his beard.

Mac ignored her.

"You're freezing. The amount of goosebumps you have is alarming. Your body is almost convulsing as you try to hold in your shivers, and your lips are turning blue."

"They are not turning blue," Maggie turned to face Mac. His gaze dropped to her mouth, and her lips parted.

Maggie stared up into Mac's eyes, his sweater between them. He couldn't seem to keep his eyes off her mouth, and even Maggie recognized the flash of heat in the dark depths. That stubborn muscle in his jaw ticked and his brows pinched so close together than they were almost a single unibrow. Maggie had the intense urge to run her fingers along the thick hairs there, and then to move her hand down to his beard. He stood close enough that Maggie could see a faint tinge of pink cross his cheeks. Was Mac blushing? He shifted restlessly from foot to foot and held the sweater closer to Maggie with a little shake.

"Please, Maggie." Mac said, "Just take the damn sweater."

It was the "please," that changed her mind.

She pulled the cotton over her head. It was big enough that Mac had to cuff the wrists for her, and it fell to only a few inches above the hem of her dress. It was soft against her skin, warm from Mac's body, blanketing her in his unique scent. Mac left the quarter zip undone and Maggie turned her nose into the collar, letting the smell of her friend's boyfriend's brother wash over her like the ebbing waves of the tide. Mac watched her, chest heaving, in a cream colored Henley. Maggie licked her lips and shivered again, but this time it wasn't from the cold.

There was no saving Maggie's team—her score was truly abysmal—but Maggie still felt like a winner when the game ended. This had been a date. Dean wrapped his arms and body around her, squared up her shots, and she was pretty sure he'd been flirting with her. Especially when Mac looked their way. Was Dean jealous of Mac?

He didn't need to be. Mac was a nice guy. He'd helped her. He'd protected her. He always seemed to pay attention to what she said and what she needed. He was fun to talk to, and with his shrewd eyes, glowering mouth, and bulging forearms, he was definitely fun to look at. Not that she was attracted to Mac. Maggie needed a foundational relationship in order to feel the stirring of arousal and, to be honest, Dean had occupied that section in her brain for as long as she could remember. There wasn't room for anyone else. It was nice that Dean was getting protective of their faux liaison, but Mac wasn't a threat. Maggie was never attracted to people she didn't know.

You do know Mac, her brain singsonged, the words ricocheting off of the crevices in her mind like bouncy balls dropped from a second-story balcony. *And what you know, you like.* Maggie pushed the thoughts away. They didn't matter. Not when she was finally making headway with the man of her dreams.

Dean reached for Maggie's club and she handed it to him. He walked to the welcome booth to turn them both in, and Maggie glanced down at the yellow ball she still held in her hand. She probably should have given it to Dean, but she hadn't thought of it. Everyone else's ball dropped into the PVC pipe buried under the last hole, but Maggie had missed again, shocker, and she'd slipped the ball into her fist instead of playing through.

"Are you okay?" Mac's voice said from over her shoulder, and Maggie turned to look at him, her smile automatically spreading across her face. Mac shoved his hands deep into his pockets as he watched Dean chat with Cal and Audrey by the entrance.

"Why?" Maggie wanted to know. Of course she was fine. She'd had an amazing day. No screw-ups, no throw up. What was Mac seeing that she wasn't?

"You threw your game," he said, finally tipping his chin down to look at her.

Mac had never played mini golf with Maggie. She and Audrey had played before, Cal, too, but never her and Mac. There was no way he should have known that she was faking her bad shots. Even Audrey hadn't picked up on her fumbling. Maggie frowned, rolling her golf ball from one hand to the other.

"How did you—"

"You lined up each shot perfectly, and then right before each hole you'd shift your weight back and swing just a little off. Every single time." Mac crossed his arms over his chest and raised an eyebrow at Maggie, as if challenging her to deny his claim.

"I'm great," she told him instead. "It was worth it. Besides, I noticed you cheated on the coin toss. You never checked heads or tails, so I guess we both played our own game today."

"It was worth it," Mac repeated her words. This time when his lips twitched, Maggie was sure he was smiling. There was a flash of straight white teeth, and then Mac reached over Maggie's shoulder and snagged her yellow game ball.

"I have to turn that in." Maggie said, but she made no move to grab the ball. It looked positively tiny in Mac's hands as he carefully cradled it against his palm.

"I'll do it," He curled his fingers over the rough surface and shoved the ball into the front pocket of his dark jeans.

"Don't forget your sweater," Maggie said and reached for the hem.

Mac's eyes flicked to Dean. He and Audrey and Cal were making their way back to the green. "Keep it," his deep voice said, and Maggie dropped her hands.

"I can't just keep your sweater, Mac," Maggie said, turning to face him because her neck was getting a crick. Not because he looked solid and strong in the sun's light, wind ruffling his hair.

"Okay," Mac said. He met her gaze head on. "I'll get it back someday." Mac reached out a hand and traced her hair clip. "I like the books, Maggie. They're perfect on you."

CHAPTER ELEVEN

When the next weekend came, Maggie was ready. She and Dean were about halfway through their faux entanglement, and while their dates had been fun and Dean had played the role of her boyfriend in spectacular fashion, Maggie still felt like they were right where they started. Her crush on her best friend's brother still flattened her daily, and while he was allowing her closer and closer, it was almost impossible for Maggie to know if he was playacting the dutiful partner or if his feelings were changing to mirror hers.

Maggie had been reading a lot more than she'd been writing over the last few weeks. She spent about half of her time buried in books to find new date ideas, and the other half trying to calm her meandering brain. She had exhausted most of her sweeter, more tender romance novels already, thumbing through well-read and dog-eared pages to find the moments where the hero and heroine finally recognized their chemistry and love.

She'd been devouring the scenes where they turned to each other, passion and love clear in each movement of their bodies and each shudder of their breaths. She felt the tingling start of some of those emotions, and some of the breathless tension, but she hadn't yet experienced the moment where her mind went crystalline lake calm, and the words tumbled out with absolute certainty.

Maybe instead of inspiring Dean's emotional response, Maggie should focus on a physical one? She could graduate to some of her steamier romance novels, the ones that made her blush but kept her turning page after page as her heart pounded in her chest and the place between her thighs went slick, pulsing to the words that flowed over her like thick honey. Maybe it was time to leave Romcom territory behind and plan a date that would remind Dean she wasn't the terrified kid he'd had to shepherd on and off the school bus.

"I'm going out," Maggie said to Audrey, after work. "I'm going to dress up and get a drink and remind myself that I'm an adult."

"Do you want me and Cal to tag along?" Audrey spread her body back over Maggie's striped comforter.

"No." Maggie ran a brush through her damp hair. "I've got a place in mind that isn't quite either of your scenes."

"I'm not sure you should go out drinking alone. I don't think anybody should."

"I'm meeting Shay there." Maggie pulled a small pleather skirt out of her closet. It was short enough to just cover what it needed to, and Maggie knew it would hug her hips. She reached into the top drawer of her bureau and pulled out a loose cropped shirt covered in neon dinosaurs.

Audrey eyed the shirt, "And here I thought we were going for adult."

"I'm not meeting Dean," Maggie added, and flushed because she was hoping to end the night with Dean even if he wasn't going to the bar with her. "I just thought it was time to leave PG-land behind and remember that I'm twenty-five and can go out and grab a drink with a friend if I want to."

"I've been enjoying PG-land," Audrey said. "Cal and I keep reminiscing about high school. We role-play that he's the quarterback and I'm the innocent honors student tasked with bringing up his grade-point average, but really I'm bringing up his—"

"Stop." Maggie pretended to gag. "There will not be enough bleach in the world to clean my brain if you finish that sentence."

While she might not want the mental image of Audrey and her boyfriend *en flagrante*, their nostalgia was a reasonable explanation for Dean's lack of advances. They'd been going on sweet, innocent, tell-your-granny-about-them dates. The kind that probably cemented Maggie's status as a kid sister in Dean's mind. She'd suspected as much, but hearing Audrey confirm what it was doing for her and Cal was the conclusive proof she needed. It was time to club Dean over the head with her innate sexuality—Maggie tried not to giggle just thinking that—or at least her adult status.

"Make safe choices tonight," Audrey said, "And text me or Cal if you need a ride."

"I'll text my boyfriend first."

"Fake boyfriend."

Maggie sighed, shoulders hunching inward. "I know."

♡

The Dark Side had been open about a year, but Maggie had never set foot inside. The arcade and bar were pretty popular. The town's two technical colleges provided patrons and the weekend gaming tournaments provided entertainment. With over seventy arcade games, a row of glowing pinball machines, and a room for Skee-Ball, air hockey, and more, it was a gamer's paradise. A roar from the back room sounded the end of a round on the Super Smash Bros tournament.

Maggie cozied up to the big wooden bar and laughed as she saw the cocktail menu broken down into fandoms. She scanned the list, debating between a Hufflepuff-themed drink and something from the Pokémon section. She settled on a Metroid-inspired drink and watched as the bartender poured vibrant green Midori and coconut rum into a stainless steel shaker. As a final garnish, three strawberries floated on the top of the neon liquid. The effect was so close to the actual Metroid larva that Maggie almost regretted drinking it. The strawberries were the best part, each one clearly steeped in the coconut rum until they burst with a sweet heat on her tongue.

"Hey." Shay leaned in for an armless hug, hands wrapped around two shot glasses, one with orange liquid and the other with a bright blue. Portal shots. "I was wondering if you'd make it tonight."

"I wouldn't bail on you." Maggie glanced around the filling room. "Well, not without a fantastic, fake excuse texted at the absolute last minute."

Shay threw their head back and laughed. "You are a refreshing delight, Maggie."

"Let's see if you still think that after I crush you at Pac Man." Maggie downed the rest of her drink, tried to hide her wince at the alcohol, and slipped off the stool she'd perched on.

"Where's your boy toy?" Shay asked. "He didn't want to keep an eye on you tonight?"

Maggie shook her head. "This isn't really his kind of place. I'll call him if I need him." She looped her arm through Shay's. "Tonight is about you and me playing outside of work."

"Really? I'd have thought this was exactly the kind of place Mac would love."

"What?" Maggie turned her head to stare at her friend. Why was Shay talking about him? Surely Maggie had shared that she was dating Dean. Right?

"Gary's here," Shay said. "Does that still count as outside of work?"

"We aren't on the clock, so yes," Maggie said, trying to shake her thoughts back into place. "We'll just avoid him, anyway."

One rousing game of air hockey later, which Shay won by a landslide, and back-to-back rounds at Street Fighter, Maggie excused herself for a quick run to the bathroom. On her way back, she poked her head into the tournament room to see how things were going. Several large television screens projected the eight different mashups, and sixteen players sat with their backs to their milling audience. In true gamer fashion, most of the participants and viewers were men, but one head drew Maggie's eyes like a magnet pulling cobalt or nickel.

Thick hair, a deep purple Henley, dark jeans, and a scruffy beard. Maggie watched Mac's blunt fingers fly over the controller cradled against his palms. He wasn't the biggest guy there, but the plastic looked positively tiny in his hands. She didn't have to see his face to know he was frowning at the screen in front of him. Meta Knight, the little gray and black ball he controlled, flashed his knives and flew across the screen as a blue fox tried to out-kick and outmaneuver him.

Maggie rubbed the palm of her hands down the faux leather of her skirt and dragged in a shaking breath. Mac had pushed the sleeves of his sweater up to his elbows, and she could see his forearms flexing as he hit buttons and circled the joystick. She couldn't help but imagine how those movements would translate to the bedroom. Maggie took a step back towards the door, needing to put some distance between herself and the wrong man.

On the big screen, Meta Knight took the win, and Mac turned his head. Their eyes caught and Maggie forced herself to give him a thumbs up through a wave of heat. Mac dipped his chin in a nod. He looked devilish sitting there, ignoring the tournament proctor announcing his victory. The next round would start any minute. Maggie backed out of the room, Mac's eyes fixed on her.

Maggie made her way back to the bar and grabbed another drink. She couldn't focus long enough to remember what she'd ordered, but there was a bite of cinnamon and whiskey. The plan was to get pleasantly buzzed, but this drink also meant she could blame the heat crashing through her body on alcohol and not on Mac's corded forearms and dexterous fingers.

Dean. She was supposed to call Dean and let him come collect her and cart her back home. Her short skirt, combined with the high percentage of male patrons, should get things back on track like they had been at mini golf. If she was going to break out of her comfort zone and frequent a bar, at least this one was nerdvana. And the drink menu was an adult version of spiked Kool-Aid and root beer floats.

The crowd was thickening, a press of bodies moving towards the bar. Maggie debated the merits of ordering her last drink while she still had a spot to stand. Three was the perfect number to get her just tipsy enough to convince Dean she needed a rescue, but not so drunk that she was unsafe. Not that she would actually *be* unsafe. She had Shay.

Someone bumped up against Maggie's back. She turned to ask for a little space, only to come smack up against a familiar chest.

"Mac." She stared at a spot between his pectoral muscles.

"Sorry I bumped you."

"It's crowded here." Someone jostled into Mac again, sending him a fraction of an inch closer.

Mac raised his arm to steady himself on the bar, his hand almost touching the sliver of skin above her skirt as he brought it past her waist to cage her in.

"I just wanted—" He shook his head, dislodging the correct words. "I didn't know you'd be here tonight, but once I saw you—I just needed—"

Maggie tilted her head to snag the eye contact he was avoiding. "Did you come over here just to check on me?"

He looked away.

"Thank you," Maggie said and laid her hand on the forearm next to her. His skin was warm beneath her fingertips. Even over the din of the bar, Maggie heard Mac suck in a sharp inhale. His arm shifted under her touch until it pressed against her waist, his fingers still wrapped around the curved edge of the bar.

"I'm here if you need me. I mean anything. If you need anything. I just wanted you to know."

Maggie smiled up at Mac. Underneath the facial hair and the scowl, he was probably the sweetest man she'd ever known.

"I'm sorry about the tournament."

Mac frowned, confusion wrinkling his forehead.

"I know they don't really take breaks, just keep playing, so you must've lost a round if you can be out here with me," Maggie explained.

"It's fine." Mac pushed his body back from the bar. The arm he'd been leaning on skated along her side, his hand squeezing her hip before he dropped it the rest of the way.

"I'll let you get back to it," Maggie said and smiled up into his handsome face.

He motioned towards the bartender.

"I'll have a Coke," Mac told him before turning his focus back on Maggie. The bartender looked at her, too.

"Oh. A Rainbow Road." Maggie smiled. "Thank you."

The bartender returned with a fountain drink and a martini glass layer with a rainbow of colored liquors. This was definitely going to be Maggie's last one for the night. Mac fished his wallet out of his back pocket and handed his credit card to the man behind the bar.

"You didn't have to pay for my drink," Maggie said.

"I've got you. Just find me if you need me, yeah?" Mac said and then he took his soda and headed back into the cheering and booing from the tournament room.

Maggie slipped away from the bar to find Shay at one of the pinball machines. Her friend was practically a pinball professional. They hit buttons and levers that kept the little ball in play and the lights flashing while

Maggie sipped the sweet drink in her hand. Pulling her phone from her tiny backpack, Maggie decided it was time to text Dean. The blood in her veins felt bubbly, like someone had popped a champagne bottle into her circulatory system, and she was fighting back the urge to smile at almost everything.

> **Maggie:**
> *Hey Babbyyy, What are you up to?*

Shit, were those too many letters? Who cared? The point got across. A minute went by with no answer. Not even the three little dots to show that Dean was typing anything back. She could give him a few more minutes. Shay's ball dropped and their game ended.

> **Maggie:**
> *Shay and I are at The Dark Side having funnnnn.*

Thirty minutes later, Maggie had another brightly colored drink clutched in her hand and she still hadn't heard from her fake boyfriend. She supposed it wasn't his fault. She hadn't given him any sort of warning that she'd need him tonight. To be honest, she had just assumed he'd be free since dating other people was off the table until their tryst resolved itself. The drink from Shay had a name Maggie couldn't remember, not even the fandom it belonged to, but there was cotton candy in it. It tasted like pure sugar, and she was enjoying each sip.

Shay had found a friend, so Maggie was finishing up her drink and swaying to the early 2000s punk music the sound system pumped out over the small dance space. Maggie let her hips rock with the beat, and she mouthed the familiar words into her drink. She checked her phone again, but still no message from her elusive fake boyfriend. Her last message shone back up at her. No dots, no reply, and probably no Dean riding in to rescue her like Gandalf leading the Riders of Rohan into the Battle of Helm's Deep.

> **Maggie:**
> *If you can, please come get me.*

She threw back the last of her drink and blindly slung the glass onto the bar before moving towards the small but well-enjoyed dance floor. Maggie wasn't the best dancer, but she could move what little assets she had, and the drinks she'd consumed during the night certainly helped her not give a damn what anyone might think of her. The song segued into another one of her nostalgic favorites, and Maggie brought her hands up over her head as she shouted the words out with the rest of the people on the dance floor. This was fun. She should do this more often, have a few drinks, dance to good music, play a few games, and spend some time enjoying life.

A pair of large hands gripped her hips hard.

Maggie turned to tell Mac he was squeezing her too tight, frowning because she would have put money on the fact that Mac would never hurt her. But the man behind her wasn't Mac. He wasn't Dean either. He was a complete stranger. A complete stranger built like Andre the Giant and who could most likely deadlift double her weight with ease. He halted her turn and spun her away so he could plaster her back up against his front.

"I'm not interested." Maggie tried to step out of his grasp, but he dug his fingers in and pulled her back even harder. "I have a boyfriend," Maggie said, but she didn't pull away this time. Unless he wanted to let go of her, she was stuck. He was stronger than she was, and her drinks had made her a little lightheaded. The man rubbed his groin against her ass, and Maggie felt like dry-heaving.

"I don't see him around," the man said. "I doubt he'd mind you dancing with me."

"He'd mind." Maggie looked around the dance floor to see if she could catch someone's eye and get an assist. If not, she'd stomp his foot, but she really didn't want to cause a scene and ruin Shay's night. Her chest felt tight at just the thought. Funny how being manhandled didn't rouse her anxiety, but the thought of causing a scene did. Maggie and her brain needed to have a long chat about priorities.

"Relax, doll." The man said and swiveled his hips against her while trying to use his hands to tip her forward. Maggie slid her right foot forward and widened her stance to put her in prime damage position.

"Stop," she said again, prepared to stomp his foot and elbow his junk as he dropped, but the weight of his body vanished.

Mac had his hands wrapped around the other man's biceps, and the look in his eyes said he'd rather it was around the sleaze's throat. It didn't matter that Handsy was easily six inches taller than Mac and broader than a mountain. Mac muscled him away from Maggie without even breaking a sweat. His strength was fueled by anger alone.

Had she ever seen Mac this mad before? Grumpy, sure. The man always had his brows pinched together, always had a furrow between them. He always bit his words off a little too abruptly, and his jaw clenched tight. When assholes misused Shay's pronouns he'd been furious then. This was different. The threat rolling off Mac's body was enough to send a shudder down Maggie's spine. Even the other day in the store had been nothing like this.

Mac zeroed in on her. If possible, he looked even angrier, his chest heaving as he wrestled with himself. Maggie was pretty sure Mac wasn't mad at *her*, but her pulse still tripped away in an uneven beat, and she felt the overwhelming urge to turn and run from the dance floor. She couldn't do that, though. Mac was enraged *for* her. She couldn't leave him alone to deal with the fallout.

"She was into it, man," the rat bastard said, and Mac took a deep, steadying breath.

Had she been considering retreat? Her anger burned that desire away like dry brush in the path of a wildfire. "No, I wasn't. I was pretty damn clear."

"I know," Mac said, his voice the growl of an angered bear. "She has a damn boyfriend."

"I get it," the guy squeaked, hands coming up to placate Mac or ward him off, Maggie wasn't entirely sure. It almost looked like he thought Mac would hit him. Mac might. "I didn't see you there. I thought she was fair game."

Mac growled.

"You have to see she's hot."

Mac released him so abruptly the jerk fell on his ass. "Go away."

"Yup, leaving." He scrambled to his feet and away from the crowd of spectators now openly ogling Mac and Maggie.

Mac was still panting, his breaths leaving him in audible punches. He reached his hands out for Maggie and then looked at them, horrified, and dropped them back to his side, fists clenched. Almost as if he were afraid to touch her.

That wouldn't do. Maggie stepped into his body and ran both her hands up his chest, over his firm pectorals, to rest against the sides of his neck. Mac's eyes drooped closed, and Maggie watched, fascinated, as he tried to pull himself back under control. She moved her right hand and guided his left to her hip, and repeated the gesture on the other side. She brought her arms back up to loop around his neck and stepped into his body, the warmth of his chest blanketing her.

"I shouldn't do this." Mac's fingers jerked against the pleather on her hips.

"It's okay," Maggie said. "I'm okay."

Mac leaned down to press their foreheads together and finally, finally, opened his eyes to look down into hers.

"You're okay." His voice was still raspy, like someone had rubbed sandpaper over his vocal cords. His breath was evening out, though the pounding of his heart matched hers.

"I was about to stomp his foot into tiny pieces."

The corner of Mac's mouth tipped up into his smile. "I'm sorry I ruined that for you. You didn't need me at all, sweet girl."

"I did, though," Maggie said, and it took effort to disguise the crack in her voice. She'd been prepared to stomp his feet and run, but he'd been a big guy, and she'd been more than a little bit afraid he wouldn't let go. "I needed you. I'm so glad you were here, Mac."

At the wobble in her voice, Mac's hands flexed on her hips. "I want to hug you."

"Please do."

Mac moved, wrapping his arms around her back and plastering her to his front. Maggie let her arms squeeze him back. She tucked her face into the warmth of his chest and let out a deep breath. Maggie felt the tension slowly seep out of Mac's shoulders as she sagged into his body, letting him hold her entire weight. They stood together on the dance floor through two more songs. As the third started, Maggie squared their bodies, pressing their hips together and Mac froze, muscles stone solid once more.

Mac let her go by degrees. His arms unwound from the small of her back and resettled on her waist. He pushed her hips back from his, letting her chest still rest against the soft purple of his sweater. It almost felt like Mac nuzzled his nose and chin against the top of her head before he pulled completely out of her grip, her arms falling back to her sides as she stared up at him. Maggie swayed towards him.

"I'll take you home," Mac said. "Tell Shay."

Maggie pulled her phone out to send a message to her friend and saw a new one waiting in her notifications.

> **Dean:**
> *Sounds like a perfect night out. I can be there in ten if you still need a getaway driver.*

Maggie looked up at Mac as he shamelessly read the text over her shoulder. He winced when he noticed her eyes on him.

"I'm sorry," he said.

"Don't be." And for reasons she couldn't quite articulate, Maggie made sure Mac was watching when she wrote back.

> **Maggie:**
> *I'm good. Mac has me.*

CHAPTER TWELVE

Mac handed Maggie into the front seat of his SUV in silence. His eyes dropped to her thighs, and she smoothed down her skirt, a blush staining her cheeks and throat. His gaze stuck for a moment before he shook himself, his hair catching the light from the street lamps. Mac shut the door before Maggie could say a word, and she watched through the windshield as he jogged around the car to the driver's door. He didn't look at her as he slid into his seat. Maggie turned to look out her window at the doors of The Dark Side.

Shay knew Maggie planned for a ride home with Dean, but she sent them a quick message about heading out, trying not to stare at the man sitting next to her. She'd touched Mac plenty of times, had been alone in the same room as him, but this was different, more intimate. The atmosphere was charged like the air during a lightning storm. The car rumbled to life under her seat, and Maggie slid her phone away. Even if they rode the entire way home without saying a single word to each other, it felt rude to be on her phone.

Mac wasn't a talker. It was kind of refreshing, actually. Maggie was comfortable talking with a tiny set of people, mostly because she took so long trying to figure out what to say that the conversation had either died or moved on by the time she got her words together. Mac used short, straightforward responses—they took a lot less brain power for Maggie to de-code—and didn't rush her to answer.

The sound of denim shifting over the upholstery dragged Maggie out of her thoughts as Mac leaned into her body. For a moment, Maggie froze. He was so much closer than he'd been a minute ago, and his body was so much bigger than hers. With the seat at her back, there was nowhere that she could go. Mac froze too, his glare deepening, and then with a harshly muttered "fuck," he reached for her seatbelt and dragged it across her chest and clicked it into place.

"I'm sorry," Maggie said, her voice barely audible over the sound of the engine.

Mac sat back against his seat and braced his hands on the wheel. "Don't apologize to me, Maggie. I shouldn't have invaded your space like that."

Maggie reached out and put her hand on his arm. Mac's biceps were rock-solid with tension. Her apology hadn't been for flinching—Maggie had once startled over a rock—but because she'd seen the hurt in his eyes when she had. She'd apologized because once she'd seen that it was Mac leaning into her space, Mac caging her body against the seat, she'd been relieved. Mac would never hurt her. She knew that. He'd gone out of his way more than once to make sure that she felt safe and in control of her own body.

"I trust you, Mac." Under her hand, Mac's muscles relaxed by minute degrees. "I wasn't paying attention, and you surprised me, but I know you. I said 'I'm sorry' because I thought—" This was ridiculous. There was no way her reaction had actually hurt him.

Mac turned to face her, his eyes zigzagging back and forth between her own, brows still pulled together as though her words didn't compute.

"Thought what?" he asked.

Maggie sucked in air, the scent of pine and iron making her dizzy. She forced herself to look into his whiskey eyes and, for a moment, they both sat there suspended. As if moving a single muscle would break whatever tiny ties were slowly knotting between them.

"I thought maybe I'd hurt you. Your feelings, I mean."

Mac closed his eyes and leaned his head back against his seat. Maggie felt those tiny ties pulling her into him.

"I would never hurt you, Maggie." Mac's voice was low and gravely, like ten miles of bad road. "I would rather—I'd never hurt you."

Maggie unclipped her seatbelt and leaned across the car, letting her right arm come across the front of Mac's chest. The left looped around the back of his neck. A bottle of water dug into her hip, and she had to be careful not to knock the gear shift with her knee, but hugging Mac was more important. He didn't turn and hug her back, but his hands looped over the arm she'd laid across his front and he held on to her, too.

"I know," Maggie said against his ear, his body relaxing into hers. "I know, I know, I know."

Mac eventually dropped his hands and Maggie pulled back to sit in the passenger seat. She clipped her own seatbelt, but kept her body angled towards Mac. There was something in his face, his eyes, that had Maggie's heart pounding in her chest. The urge to ground him, the way he kept doing for her, was overwhelming.

This was what friends did for one another. They stepped in. They showed up. They supported each other without question. Mac was good at all three. Maggie could return the favor. Wanted to return the favor. She needed to give him back what he gave to her over and over and over again.

"I'm glad you were here tonight, Mac," she said, her nerves making her breathless.

"Anyone would have done what I did." Mac didn't take his eyes off the road as he pulled out onto the empty street. "Anyone decent."

"If you hadn't been there—"

"If I'm not there, you call me. Or Cal." Mac's throat constricted as he swallowed. "Or Dean."

"If you hadn't been there," Maggie repeated, "I would have called you."

"But your boyfriend—" Mac shook his head, eyes pinging between her own and the quiet street. "You'd have called him first."

Maggie thought of the time it took Dean to respond to her texts. Of the times he'd used his fists to defend her or Audrey in middle and high school. Then she thought of Mac's hand slamming down on the counter at The Tattered Cover as he demanded that an angry customer treat her with respect. The way Mac's fingers dug into the biceps of the creep in the bar, but how he'd ultimately let him go. It was one of her favorite things to read, men turning feral to protect the women they loved, but the reality was less lusty and more terrifying. She loved Dean, but…

"I'd have called you."

Mac must have tapped the brakes because the car lurched sideways before he re-corrected. The street was empty, and Mac's reflexes had kicked in before they had been in any danger, but she watched his hands clench around the steering wheel until his knuckles turned white under his tan skin. A thin sheen of sweat beaded along his forehead and a single drop rolled down his temple. She wanted to reach out and brush it away, but touching Mac could make everything worse.

"Talk to me," Maggie said, leaning back against the passenger door so she could watch him as he drove. Mac's eyes darted to hers.

"I'm driving, Maggie. I almost just—" His breath heaved in and out of his chest.

Maggie knew what this felt like. The panic eating away at the corners of Mac's sanity. The thought of what could have been playing on an endless loop in his brain until it was no longer the worst-case scenario, but had bypassed it a million times over. How the deep breaths didn't seem to get deep enough, how each limb locked until they ached.

"But you didn't," Maggie said, keeping her voice low and firm. The soothing bullshit never quite broke through when things started spiraling. "Do you know why?"

Mac shook his head. It was such a slight gesture that Maggie would have missed it if she hadn't been staring right at him, cataloging his every move.

"Because you'd never hurt me, right Mac?" His shoulders dropped a fraction of an inch, and Maggie pushed on. "Your brain is playing tricks on you. I'm fine. You're fine. But I think you could use the distraction, so talk to me. Tell me how you started making knives."

"Blades, Maggie. I make blades. Not just knives." His breathing had slowed down to a more normal pitch, and while Maggie could still see the skin pulled taut over the backs of his hands, his knuckles weren't bone white anymore.

"How did you start making blades?" she parroted, grateful when he finally sank back against his seat.

"My gram had a collection," Mac said, and Maggie bit her lip to stop the delighted laugh from seeping out of her.

"Your gram? The one who left you and Cal the house?"

Mac nodded, "My grandfather was a blacksmith, he worked mostly with horses,"

"So your grandfather made the weapons, but it was your gram who inspired you?" Maggie watched as Mac relaxed his arms enough to bend his elbows again.

"I didn't know my grandfather, not really. He died when I was four. Cal hadn't been born yet. There's this old movie, *Seven Samurai*. It came out in the mid-fifties. Some of the best sword footage on film, even to this day. Gram and I used to watch it together." Mac dropped one hand off of the wheel to rest on his thigh. "She loved the fight scenes and wanted to learn, but where was a housewife going to find an *ōdachi*? That's the sword Kikuchiyo carried in the film. They were long swords with curved, single-edged blades. To qualify as an *ōdachi* they had to be almost 3 feet long. They were popular in the Kamakura period, about 1185 to 1333, and carried mostly by Samurai. The swords were so big and heavy that most Samurai carried them sheathed at their sides, and needed an assistant to help draw them for battle. Historians believe they were used to cut down charging cavalry."

"He made her one," Maggie said, a bubbly warmth starting somewhere behind her belly button and spreading out through her arteries to the farthest reaches of her body.

Mac looked at her now, an actual grin curving the corners of his mouth, and Maggie grinned right back at him. Mac was always magnetic, but right now, explaining something he was passionate about, his voice deep and strong, he was magnificent.

"It was awful." Mac said, "I have it at the forge. Gram left it to me when she died." His smile slipped, brows knitting together in his customary frown.

"Why was it awful?" Maggie wanted that smile back. "He made it with love."

"Apart from the fact that he'd never made a sword before? He had no idea how to forge a traditional Japanese blade. They're tough even for people who know what they're doing. The length makes heat treatment more difficult too. It's harder to bring the whole thing up to the same temperature in order for the metal to harden before quenching or rapidly cooling it back down. If you don't quench the whole thing evenly, the blade can warp and twist. The first one my grandfather made was warped to hell and back. It had no edge and weighed close to thirty pounds. That's a lot of steel. The first time she tried to swing it, she fell over." Mac was smiling again as he slowed the car to take a left turn. "My grandfather got better. He made her a few more swords, some daggers, and an ax."

"I bet she loved that first *ōdachi*." Maggie tested the word on her tongue, trying to recreate the syllables the way Mac had. "I bet it was her favorite. And now you make blades just like he did because they meant something very important to someone you love."

The tips of Mac's ears flamed pink. Mac glanced over at her again. He had fully relaxed now, limbs loose, hand draped carelessly over the top of the wheel. Maggie had never felt safer.

"I'm sorry," he said. "I must have bored you to tears. You don't pay me to lecture you."

"I like listening to you talk, Mac." Maggie laced her fingers together before she did something stupid like reach for his free hand. "I like what you have to say."

"I usually don't talk much," Mac said, cupping the back of his neck with his palm.

"I know, but you looked like you could use a distraction. I figured your brain was sending you some intrusive thoughts, and I know what that's like."

"I kept seeing us clip the curb and then flip into the brick buildings. Everything was on fire and I couldn't get you out." Mac tensed up for a moment and swallowed hard before dropping his hand. "I needed to get you out."

"We barely swerved a foot," Maggie said. "You were in complete control the entire time."

Mac pulled his car into a free spot in front of Maggie's apartment and killed the engine, but made no move to get out. He turned his body to face hers, and Maggie's stomach turned over. She sucked in a breath at the intensity in Mac's eyes as she felt his gaze move from the top of her head down to her knees. She resisted the urge to shift her hips on the seat.

"You de-nerved me," Mac said. His voice had dropped lower, rasping out into the car and over her skin.

"You've done the same for me." This time, she reached forward and touched the back of his hand. Mac's skin was hot under her fingertips. She stroked gently until he turned his hand over and let their palms slide together.

"You're something, Maggie." He squeezed her hand in his. "Something wonderful, and intelligent, and kind. Something magical, and I am lucky to spend even a moment in your presence."

Maggie leaned in until the seatbelt tightened across her front and stopped her momentum. She let her thumb rub along the side of his. His gaze dropped to where they touched. Sitting here with Mac, helping him through his own bout of anxiety, left her feeling magical and wonderful and kind. It was like all her own panic attacks had been worth something if she could help someone else come out on the other side of one.

"I like those moments," she said. Sure she would float away if the seatbelt and Mac's hand weren't holding her in place.

CHAPTER THIRTEEN

By the second time Maggie opened her fridge and stared into the empty abyss, she was ready to admit she was in way over her head. The problem wasn't the dinner invitation she'd sent to Dean. She'd told him she wanted to thank him for helping her out, and he'd agreed with the effortless charm and smile he always had for her. It wasn't even her lack of culinary skills because, given enough time and YouTube tutorials, she was certain she could put something together. The problem was that Maggie had zero idea what she was supposed to make.

You should have figured that out before texting him, Maggie thought as she pushed aside a half empty egg carton and a cup of lime yogurt.

She had bread, pasta, cereal, and enough dairy products to make any Midwesterner proud. She had fruit, some baby carrots, and enough frozen soy products to keep her vegetarian heart fed and happy. And Maggie was almost positive Dean would eat none of it except the bag of shredded cheddar. A quick Google search confirmed that Dean's keto diet meant no to the fruit, the carbs, and even the carrots. A few more Google searches and Maggie realized she was going to need to cook some meat if she wanted to satisfy her fake boyfriend.

Two hours, ten bookmarked recipes, and a trip to the grocery store later, Maggie stared into her now full fridge and was still as nauseated as she had been before the shopping trip. She'd had to go to three separate grocery stores to find the specialty sweetener the recipe called for, and then the tiny jar of agave cost more than the rest of the ingredients combined. But it was okay. She'd settled on a recipe that said it was foolproof and would take about twenty minutes. The only part standing in her way now was the hunk of raw chicken breast that stared up at her from the clear bottom shelf. Dammit, she should have bought gloves.

Her phone rang while Maggie was contemplating how to begin.

"How do you cook chicken?" Maggie said as she put her phone on speaker and set it on the counter.

"You don't," Audrey said. "You're a vegetarian."

"That's why I asked how *you* cook it," Maggie said. She pulled the wrapped package out with her pinched forefinger and thumb and threw it on the counter as though it might bite her.

"Don't you remember living with me? We starved because neither of us has any skills in the kitchen." That was true.

Maggie thought back to the time she and Audrey had tried to make eggplant Parmesan to impress Audrey's study group partner. They'd remembered to cover the vegetable slices with a thick coating of kosher salt, but they hadn't let them sit and drain, nor had they wiped off any of the excess salt. Audrey's date had been nice about it, but the finished dish had been inedible. All three of them had nibbled on pieces of untouched pasta, trying to fight past the burn of too much sodium and the tingling urge to cough.

"Is this for something you're writing? I can get Mac. He cooks everything Cal and I eat."

"No," Maggie's stomach was still a little pitchy thinking about Mac's hands bracketing her hips and his chest pressed to her cheek, a feral anger burning in his dark eyes. Standing that close to him had left her so unbalanced that she'd let Mac bring her home, ignoring her carefully laid plans to have Dean rescue her. There had been no question about it either. His muscles had been solid under her hands. He'd winced when he'd read her message, and Maggie had known she was going to turn down Dean's offer.

"It's not for a book. I'm cooking dinner."

"Chicken," Audrey said.

"And zucchini and other veggies and Thai peanut sauce."

Those parts of the recipe seemed a lot more manageable.

"And the chicken is for—"

"Dean," Maggie closed her eyes as if that would stop her best friend from reacting. "I invited him over to say thanks for all the help. Besides, this is cute romance novel type stuff, cooking for your significant other. At the very least, it will be a memorable experience."

Audrey was quiet long enough that Maggie double checked that the call was still connected. It was.

"Maggie." Audrey was using her soothing voice, "Dean knows you're a vegetarian. He won't expect you to make something you can't eat."

"He knows I don't eat meat?"

"Of course. You've been a vegetarian since middle school. I'm pretty sure he knows you can't cook, either."

"But he eats meat. I have to feed him something."

"So order takeout," Audrey said. "Dean will not care if you cooked the meal or not. I don't think he cooks much either. It's a Crandall family trait."

This wasn't just a thank you meal. The purpose of dinner was to be impressive. To show Dean that she cared through an act of service. She was going to cook him something he would eat. Something delicious. What was that age-old saying? "The best way to a man's heart was through his stomach." So she would not order takeout. She would pull up her big girl panties and face the stove, and the raw meat, head on.

"I'm sure it will be great," Audrey said. "Or at least edible."

"Thank you. That's the support I need."

"I'm always supportive. Is there anything else I can do to help?"

Maggie shoved her head into one of her lower cabinets, staring at her toaster and waffle iron. "Do you have a food processor?"

"I think we have a blender. Will that work?"

"I don't know. My recipe says 'food processor.'"

"I'll ask Mac," Audrey said, and the line clicked as she hung up the phone.

"I can do this," Maggie said out loud and stared down at the chicken. "Later."

She reached for the zucchini instead.

Forty minutes later, the squash still wasn't spiralized. Maggie had sliced her finger, and she still hadn't touched the chicken. She was thinking of taking a break and starting the sauce, but that required the food processor, and Audrey hadn't called her back. If she didn't hear from her soon, she'd have to go knock on Mrs. Weller's door and hope the tiny, ancient woman had one. Except Mrs. Weller was visiting her son in Alberta this week. This dinner plan had seemed a lot more doable before she'd gotten started.

When the knock on her door came, Maggie let out a sigh of relief. That had to be Audrey with the food processor. Maggie rushed to the door.

"I love you," she said as she threw the door open.

"What the fuck happened to your hand?" Mac's face was thunderous, but beneath the anger was something that looked strangely like panic.

"My hand?" Maggie looked down at the paper towel she'd wrapped around her thumb after cutting it on the blade of the spiralizer. She was fisting her fingers to put pressure on the cut and stop the bleeding. There was barely any blood, and Maggie was pretty sure it had already clotted. The tiny slice stung more than anything else, but Mac looked like a cornered animal as he shifted his focus from her makeshift bandage to the tiny drops of blood she'd left on the counter and back.

Mac pushed his way into the kitchen. He dumped the food processor onto the counter and reached for Maggie's hand. His own trembled as he peeled back and uncurled her fingers.

"I'm okay," Maggie said, but despite his glare, his fingers were gentle, and she let him look for himself. "It's just a cut on my thumb."

Mac looked at the pad of her finger, turning it left and right to see the damage. His fingers and palms were rough with calluses and small scars, but the way he swept those same fingers over her hand was soothing. Her limbs grew heavier the longer he touched her.

"You need a Band-Aid. Did you clean this?" Mac's gaze flicked to hers. He almost blocked the light out of her kitchen as he stood with his head bent over hers.

"I don't have a Band-Aid," Maggie said, "Hence the paper towel."

Mac closed his eyes and lifted a hand to pinch the bridge of his nose. He let out a long sigh.

"I have one in my car. Wash that off. I'll go get it."

Before she could blink, he was out the door, heavy footsteps pounding down the stairs. It was a wonder she hadn't heard him approach the first time. He sounded like a parade of elephants wearing ankle weights.

When Mac battered his way back up the stairs and into her apartment, she asked, "Why do you have Band-Aids in your car?"

"First aid kit." He walked straight to her sink. "I told you to wash that off."

"What?" Maggie said and Mac reached for her, making eye contact and waiting for her nod before he wrapped his hand around her wrist. "It's fine Mac, just a little cut."

"Humor me," he said and stuck her hand under the running faucet. "I keep a first aid kit in my car because sometimes I cut myself working and don't notice until later."

"You keep first aid kits everywhere, don't you." Maggie tried to pull her hand away as Mac reached for the soap. "I bet you have one in your office and offer Band-Aids to all your students during office hours."

"You'd have to come to my office hours to find out." Mac rubbed some soap along the pad of her thumb, avoiding the actual cut. It was laughably small, considering the lengths he was going to clean it. Mac stuck her hand back under the water, waiting until the stream ran clear.

"I just might."

Mac reached for a clean paper towel and blotted Maggie's hand, collecting water droplets on the soft white surface. He lifted her hand and blew across her skin. Maggie shivered.

As the tremble raced through Maggie's limbs, Mac's eyes grabbed hers and held. His body seemed to lock down, tension knotting his muscles, even as he bent forward to see her face. His pupils almost swallowed the umber irises, and Maggie watched them expand as his gaze tracked along her face. Goosebumps raced up Maggie's arms, and another shiver wracked her body.

Maggie let her lashes flutter closed and when she opened her eyes again, Mac was even closer. She didn't know which one of them had moved, but his breath fanned over her lips. Unlike the cool air he'd exhaled over her thumb, the sharp breaths that broke across her mouth bathed her in heat. Without conscious thought, Maggie's tongue swept out to wet her lips. Mac groaned and pressed his forehead to hers.

"I should back off," Mac said, but he didn't move. His mouth ghosted against hers with each of his words.

"Please," Maggie heard herself say, the word raspy and choked.

Her body was on fire, lust pounding through her veins. His hands still held hers, their mouths the only other part of their bodies that touched. She wanted to press up against him. Mac let his eyes drift closed once more and Maggie tilted her head. He was so close, so warm, so caring. She sucked in another breath. Her body swayed towards him.

And Mac stepped back.

He had a bandage wrapped around Maggie's thumb before she could process what had almost happened.

"I'm sorry," Mac said at the same time Maggie said, "Thank you."

"Don't thank me, Maggie, Jesus." Mac pulled a hand through his hair, and Maggie tried not to be charmed by the strands standing straight up. "Audrey asked me about the food processor, and I offered to bring it over, and I saw the blood. I'm sorry."

"If you get to tell me not to say 'thank you,' then I get to tell you not to say 'sorry.'"

Mac squeezed his eyes shut. He looked like he'd been run through with one of his blades. "I know you have a boyfriend. I won't put you in that position again."

A lead weight sat heavy in the pit of her stomach. She'd thought Mac was being a gallant idiot, pulling back when she was begging him to come closer. Dean hadn't even crossed her mind. Standing in her kitchen with Mac, cleaning a cut she'd gotten preparing a meal for Dean, she'd forgotten all about her fake boyfriend. Maggie could feel the grooves working their way in between her eyebrows and she went dizzy as the blood drained from her face. Was it cheating if her boyfriend was fake? Was she unfaithful?

"I'm sorry," Maggie said.

"That's even worse," Mac said.

"Thank you for the food processor and for giving me a Band-Aid. I'm sorry I—"

He shushed her, head shaking back and forth incredulously. Maggie was still lightheaded. She could hear her own heartbeat in her ears. Mac yanked his hands back through his hair again, then scrubbed them down his face.

"I'm the one who was inappropriate," Mac said. "I've been acting inappropriately for a while now. That's not on you, that's on me. So now I'm going to make it up to you. Talk to me about this dinner you're making. You've already cut yourself. Should we discuss knife safety? I can't believe I gave you a blade, and we didn't discuss knife safety."

"I cut myself on the spiralizer." Maggie said, and her world righted itself when Mac's lips twitched.

"I don't know what that is." Mac said, and Maggie pointed to the plastic kitchen gadget with a zucchini wedged in between a handle and a blade. "I still don't know what that is."

"It cuts veggies into noodles." Maggie twisted her fingers to show how the squash was supposed to curl.

"Why do you have chicken breasts?" Mac pointed to the package of poultry Maggie was working up the courage to tackle.

"I'm making dinner for someone. They eat chicken."

"You don't mind handling and cooking it?"

Maggie's face must have given her away, because Mac's frown deepened and he cursed. "If Dean knew how you felt about it, I'm sure he wouldn't want you to do it."

"I didn't say it was for Dean." Maggie jammed her hands onto her hips, but her face flushed.

"It's not for Dean?"

"I want to make something he'll like, and this seemed the easiest option. I just have to get over my aversion towards touching it, and I'll be fine." Maggie glared at the raw chicken again and breathed through the sudden pitch of her stomach. "The internet seemed divided. Do I wash it first?"

"Sweet girl," Mac said, pinching the bridge of his nose again. "Never wash raw chicken. You'll just splatter the germs all over your kitchen."

"Oh." Maggie nodded. "That was my only question, but maybe you should talk me through the rest of the cooking process. Just to be safe."

"What time is your," Mac swallowed hard, "date?"

Maggie blinked, searching her small kitchen for a clock. She settled for the one on her microwave. She had an hour. When did that happen? She was still in a pair of leggings and a t-shirt. She hadn't showered yet. She hadn't shaved.

"Go get ready, Maggie." Mac said and pulled open one of her drawers. "I've got you."

His eyes met hers, and Maggie wondered if he was thinking of the message she'd sent her fake boyfriend just the night before. She couldn't let Mac cook for her date. Not with everything else getting all mixed up in her brain.

"Mac?"

He looked up from where he was washing his hands at her sink.

"I need to do this." She held his gaze for long moments, the silence settling around them like a fresh-laundered sheet snapped over a mattress.

"Okay," Mac said. "I'll get it all ready for you, and then I'll talk you through the cooking part. But let me help make sure you don't have to touch any of it raw. Okay?"

Maggie nodded, and smiled, and headed for her shower.

Dean arrived fifteen minutes after he was supposed to and five minutes after Mac had left. True to his word, Mac had left the actual cooking for Maggie. He'd cut the raw chicken, helped her choose the proper seasonings, and then showed her how to set the heat on her sauté pan—she'd been calling it a frying pan for the last two years—and cook the pieces until there was no pink left.

The zucchini noodles, bell peppers, broccoli, and asparagus spears all mixed in a sweet and spicy peanut sauce were damn impressive, but Maggie was even more proud of the poultry on Dean's plate, especially when he closed his mouth around the tines of his fork and groaned out his appreciation.

"This is incredible, Babs." Dean took another bite. "Thank you for inviting me over and putting so much thought into the menu. I want to tell you, you didn't have to cook meat, but I don't want you to think I'm ungrateful."

Maggie smiled and took a sip of her Riesling—picked by Audrey—and smiled across her tiny dinette at her fake boyfriend.

"I'm glad you like it. Although I admit I had some help."

"Not from Audrey. I've tasted her cooking."

They shared a laugh. Dean let his left hand come down on top of her right one and he gave her fingers a gentle squeeze. Maggie's stomach flipped at the contact.

"You're right," she said and then she gazed up at him from under her lashes, trying to gauge his response to her next words. "Mac helped."

Dean pulled his hand back and reclined in his chair. Maggie's palm was cold without the contact, and she found herself nervous about what Dean was going to say.

"Mac, huh?" Dean tapped his knuckles against his wide mouth. "That was nice of him."

Maggie nodded and studied the expression on Dean's face. His nostrils flared under her scrutiny, and Maggie looked away.

"He's a friend." She flushed, thinking about how close their bodies had been in her tiny kitchen.

"Babs," Dean put his fork down and steepled his fingers. "Do you want to be all done? With me?"

Maggie's heart clattered against her ribcage. "No," she said, the refusal automatic. "Not yet."

Dean smiled.

"Okay," he said, and picked up his fork to finish the rest of his meal.

CHAPTER FOURTEEN

The car curved around another bend in the road, and Maggie was again grateful that Dean had offered to drive. He'd asked to plan the entire date, and so far he was being secretive about the details. He'd told her to dress in comfortable clothes and to be prepared for a day-long hike, so Maggie was wearing the purple running pants Audrey had picked out a few weeks back and the strappy sports bra she'd caved and gone back for. It was much easier to get on and off than she'd assumed. She looked every bit the part of the athletic girlfriend.

They were climbing in elevation, the typical leafy trees and green lawns of the residential neighborhoods giving way to open meadows and towering pine trees. The fresh scent of the mountains filled the car. It reminded her of Christmas morning: cedar, and pine, and crisp, clean air. Maggie wanted to roll down the window and stick her head out of the car to enjoy it. Unable to resist the urge any longer, Maggie tapped her window button and shivered as the air rushed into the car and over her heated skin. Dean glanced at her and grinned.

"I knew you'd get cold." He reached into the backseat to grab a big gray sweatshirt. He took another turn with an easy hand draped over the steering wheel.

Instead of pulling the layer on, Maggie cuddled underneath it like a blanket, her nose tipped up to the fresh breeze.

"I know you aren't the biggest fan of hiking and running, but I wanted you to see this place, and after our run the other day I thought you might be open to it," Dean said.

Maggie's pulse skittered at the unknown, but she smiled at Dean. Apparently, she was a brilliant actress because she must have sold herself on that run. Either that, or Dean had mistaken her joy at spending time with him for the enjoyment of physical activity. Damn.

It was their last weekend of their fake relationship, and Maggie had hoped to plan something epic and wonderful. Something to set the tone so that Dean would fall to his knees and wrap his arms around her waist and confess that he loved her just as much as she loved him. Without knowing Dean's plans, she couldn't set things in motion. She'd just have to trust things would fall into place. A month ago, that lack of control would have terrified Maggie, but now she was just excited to spend a day with Dean, no matter how it ended. Strange how that had changed over the last few weeks. Especially since her love for Audrey's brother hadn't diminished at all.

Dean pulled his car into a dirt lot set in front of a long wooden cabin with a bright red door. The sign out front said "Wayfinder Inn & Restaurant." She looked out her open window at the trailhead glinting back at her.

"I knew you'd like this trail," Dean said, stepping out of the car and pulling a giant backpack out of the trunk. "It's long, but it's worth it."

"I'm not much of a hiker," Maggie said as Dean plunked a baseball hat on her head. She took it off to look at the logo and laughed when she saw their old high school mascot staring back at her.

"It's about seven miles to do the loop." Dean slid a matching hat onto his own head. "But less than a thousand feet of elevation gain." At Maggie's confused expression, he said, "It'll take us about four hours, depending on how fast we move and how many stops we make. I figured we'd come back and grab lunch at the restaurant before we head back, but we can turn back at any point."

"Let's do it," Maggie said and smiled up at Dean. She didn't want to admit it, but with the fresh air, the towering trees, and the quaint inn, she was actually excited about this.

Dean grinned as he shouldered the backpack. "I have water, snacks, rain gear, and some other stuff in here. Just let me know if you need anything."

They walked to the trailhead, and Dean used his phone to snap a photo of the map, then slid it back into his pocket and gestured ahead of him down the dirt trail. The path was neatly tended and wide enough that they could walk side by side. Trees lined each side of the trail, reaching long boughs up to the azure sky, and the sun filtered through their branches and down over them as they walked, stepping over the occasional rock or tree root.

The trail sloped upward at a manageable incline. After the first twenty minutes, sweat pooled in the small of Maggie's back and she stopped to strip Dean's sweatshirt over her head. He offered to roll it into the backpack, but Maggie declined, wrapping it around her waist. When the trail narrowed, Dean took the lead. He turned back and gave Maggie his hand as they navigated over a boulder blocking the path. Maggie paused on top of the large rock to tilt her head up to the sun, raising her arms overhead.

"You look like a goddess standing there." Dean's smile was wide and warm. "All kickass and golden in the sunlight."

Dean looked golden in the sunlight, too.

"I like it out here," she said, surprised to find that it was true.

She liked the smell of the trees, and the kiss of the air, and the crunch of the pine needles under her feet. Being short only bothered Maggie when people commented on her size, but she didn't mind how tiny she was under the shadow of the reaching pines or next to the rock formations bracketing the trail. There was something freeing about knowing she was such a small part of her surroundings. That she could do or say almost anything while she was up here, and it wouldn't matter.

"I do too." Dean said, giving her his hand to help her off the boulder. "I feel so powerful out here. Like everything I do is an important part of life and the mountain. You know?"

Maggie started to nod in agreement but stopped herself. "Actually, I feel the opposite. It's a relief to not have to worry about every little thing I do. Maybe I should be worried about falling off a cliff, or encountering a mountain lion, but honestly, I just feel so peaceful out here. My mind is usually a mess of nerves and self-doubt." Maggie shoved her shoulder against Dean when he didn't refute her statement. He laughed and slung his arm over her shoulder. "Out here, some of that has gone quiet."

She tilted her face up to look into Dean's and her heart stuttered at the affection in his eyes.

"This may be the first time you've ever disagreed with me, Babs." His smile was thoughtful and small, but no less real. "I like that."

"I like you," Maggie said and started back down the path.

They continued along the trail, this time Maggie leading the way. A chittering squirrel followed them for another half hour, scolding them as they stopped to talk back to it. During one of their breaks, Dean produced a water bottle from the backpack. He took a healthy swig and handed it to Maggie. She pressed the bottle to her lips and let the cool water coat her throat. It occurred to her, the second time they passed the bottle between them, that her mouth was covering the same piece of plastic that Dean's had. She smiled as she took another drink.

The trees thinned out as they rounded another bend in the trail, and an expanse of tall grass greeted them. The trail cut through the center of the meadow like a snake, winding in and around the yellowing tufts of plants and the vibrant clusters of wildflowers. To their right, the meadow rolled into a birch forest. Thick with green, rustling leaves. To their left, the ground dropped off into a steep decline. Out over the chasm, distant peaks rose towards the sky. Snow still capped the summits and Maggie tried to commit the scene to memory.

They left the grass behind, plunging back into a pine forest, and trekked along the larger incline of the trail until a small clearing opened up with a sheer rock face at its back. Maggie had heard the gurgle of water, but nothing could have prepared for the sixty-foot falls thundering over the rocks. Water tumbled from a natural ledge at the top of the rock wall, gathering into a small, crystal pool before bleeding out into a creek that ran back through the forest, perpendicular to their trail.

"Wow." Maggie froze in her tracks, hypnotized by the cascade. She turned towards Dean, heart pounding in her chest. "This is incredible."

He nodded and found a spot to sit on a large, flat rock.

"This place reminds me of you, Babs," he said, eyes trained on the waterfall. "Every time I think of you, I think of falling in love. That's what you write about, right? The story leads two people together. To that magic moment where they let themselves fall." Dean rested his forearms on his raised knees. "I've always imagined falling in love is like standing at the bottom of a waterfall. Water pounding down on you, ready to drown you under its relentless pressure. But also enjoying being carried over the edge and down to the rocks below. Falling with no guarantee of a soft landing, just a hope that you reach the bottom."

Maggie's heart turned over at Dean's words and she couldn't stop herself from slipping into a spot next to him on the cool rock. "Your version of love is a force of nature, Dean."

"My version?" He turned his face towards Maggie, but his usual smile was lacking. "You don't believe love is powerful?"

"Powerful, yes, but not as terrifying as you make it sound."

"Love is terrifying. You don't come out the same after falling in love."

"The water at the top of the waterfall is the same water at the bottom," Maggie said.

Dean leaned back, his hands braced against the surface of the rock. "But not entirely the same."

Dean was wrong, Maggie mused, as she sat back on the rock too, tilting her face up to the sun. Falling in love with him had been remarkably easy. The feelings had slid right in under the history they shared until one day she opened her eyes and realized that having Dean around made her happy. He cared for her, kept her safe, and made her smile. She had been the same Maggie before loving Dean and she'd been the same Maggie after. As though she'd loved him forever.

"How is your book coming along?" Dean laid his body flat against the stone. "Have our dates been helping?"

"Yes," Maggie said, and honesty made her add, "And no. Some things have been helping, but I'm still struggling with making the connections. I have a lot of work left to make the chemistry believable."

"We don't have to end things after today," Dean said. His hand found Maggie's, and he squeezed her fingers with his. "We can keep this going as long as you need."

Maggie squeezed back, the response caught in her throat.

"Thank you," she managed to say, but a loud *boom* drowned out her words and echoed through the clearing. The sky opened up over them, rain pouring down as if the waterfall had extended to the sky.

Dean wrestled two raincoats out of the backpack, but it was too late. Drenched to the bone, they carefully slipped off the rock. Maggie pushed her hair back out of her face and secured it with an elastic. They were a good two hours away from the car with rain blowing sideways.

"Should we head back?" Maggie asked, her eyes on the trail as the dirt turned from solid ground to muddy sludge.

"I don't think we should stay by the waterfall," Dean said, and held his hand out for her to take. "We'll just do the best we can."

THE TROPE

It occurred to Maggie, as they stumbled blindly down the trail towards the distant inn, that she couldn't have fabricated a better romance scenario if she had tried. They'd gone on a hike and drowned in a monsoon, only after some illuminating discussion of romance and love, and now Dean was clutching her hand in his as he navigated them back to relative safety. He'd also asked to extend their relationship. It was everything she could have asked for. The only thing left would be for her to sprain an ankle and have Dean carry her the rest of the way.

After half an hour of trudging through the rain, Maggie shivered, daydreaming about hot cocoa and sunburns and wondering why romance novels made this seem like this was the best scenario in the history of love. She'd pulled Dean's sweatshirt on and they'd donned the raincoats, despite already being soaked clear through. At least it stopped the bite of the wind. Dean's cheeks were pink from its nip, and despite how miserable the weather and the cold were, he still wore his wide grin, flashing white teeth at Maggie as they ducked their heads and kept moving.

They'd made it through the clearing, the storm completely blocking the views of the distant snow-capped mountains, when it happened. Like a zombie hand breaking the surface of a grave, a tree root came out of the ground, snagging her around the ankle. Maggie would admit she was a powerful manifestor.

Dean caught her before she added a mud bath to her list of morning activities, but there was a wrench, and a pop, and a slice of burning pain shooting through the bone at the side of her ankle. She shrieked in agony. Dean held her pressed against his soggy chest while she kept her injured ankle hefted into the air. Maggie pressed her forehead against the slick of his raincoat, so focused on breathing through the pain that she couldn't enjoy how close she was to the man she'd loved her whole life.

"It hurts," she cried.

"I know it does, Babs." He shifted her off of his body and looked down at her foot as though he could see it through her shoes and socks and seeing it would tell him how to fix it.

"Can you walk at all?"

Maggie tried to put her foot down and limp forward. Searing pain knifed through her ankle and up her calf. She sucked in a breath, swallowed her shriek, and ducked her head back into Dean's chest.

"That would be a no." He tightened his arms around her. "Good thing you're tiny, Babs."

Even though she knew what Dean was planning, Maggie still gasped as he hefted her up into his arms.

"In the movies this always looks so romantic," Dean admitted, ducking his head to whisper the words against Maggie's ear. "But honestly, I didn't think it was possible to feel worse out here until picking you up plastered both our wet clothes up against me."

"I imagined body heat and racing pulses," Maggie agreed. She tipped her face until she and Dean were close enough to share breaths. "But the shooting pain ruins the fun."

"No offense, Babs, but if my pulse is racing, it's because I'm about to carry you down a mountain in a hurricane."

"Don't exaggerate. The trail is basically flat."

"Seriously?" Dean grinned and rubbed their noses together. "No accolades from my fair lady for my heroic feats?"

"Ask me again when we get out of this rain." Maggie turned her face into his chest as Dean laughed.

The rest of the hike took longer than the trek out, but Dean didn't complain. She talked him through parts of her book, and he detailed the foods they were going to order the minute the restaurant was in sight. The rain still hadn't calmed when the trail head became visible. Dean had carried her all the way down a mountain, and she hadn't spent a single moment contemplating the solid mass of his chest or the strength of his arms. Maggie would have kicked herself if her ankle didn't hurt so damn bad.

"Food?" Dean asked, and Maggie nodded.

With Dean still holding her, Maggie pulled open the heavy front door of the Wayfarer Inn and they staggered into the dimly lit entrance. The front desk sat next to the entrance to the café with a snow-haired woman reading behind the counter.

"Two for lunch," Dean jostled Maggie to reposition her in arms that must've been screaming.

"I'm glad you made it back, dearies." The elderly woman didn't look up from her book. "The storm's closed the roads, so you won't be able to get out of here anytime soon. Things might open again tomorrow morning." She turned a page in her book. "This happens a lot up here. Trees fall, the road washes out. They don't want anyone skidding off the mountain."

"I suppose we'll take two rooms then, too." Dean said.

"Only have one left." The lady said, turning another page.

"One room then," Dean said and to Maggie he added, "If that's okay with you?"

And if it wasn't, would he offer to sleep in his car? Maggie tried to control her giggle, but she was sure Dean could feel the hitch of her shoulders.

"As long as you're okay with the fact that there will only be one bed," Maggie said.

"Why do you say that?"

"Because there's always only one bed, Dean. That's just how these things go."

CHAPTER FIFTEEN

She had been right, of course. The room had only one bed. That wasn't a total surprise, not in such an old building, but everything was clean, the bed neatly made, and the bathroom scented with cleaning solution. The window overlooked the pine forest with the distant peaks. Maggie couldn't have written a better scene for a romance novel if she'd tried.

Dean set her on top of the wide, cherry wood dresser. Water from their sodden clothes dripped into twin pools on the bureau's top and onto the hardwood floor. He dropped the backpack on the floor and unzipped his raincoat before he kneeled in front of Maggie and unlaced her sneaker with cautious fingers.

"I can do that," she said.

Dean glanced up at her with an incredulous look. He dropped the muddy sneaker to the floor and peeled down her sock.

Maggie's ankle was purple and puffy, although the dull throb had subsided into an almost tingling sensation. That was almost worse, because the lack of pain kept lulling her into the stupid belief that she could move her foot.

"Stop trying to wiggle your toes." Dean unwrapped the bandage and the cold pack the lady at the front desk had given them. "It hurts just watching you." He reached for the towel he'd grabbed from the bathroom and dried her ankle with careful circles before wrapping the bandage around the arch of her foot and looping it up around her ankle.

"You've done this before." The stretchy bandage was tight against Maggie's joint, and at least it was helping with the reminder to stay still.

"I can't remember the last time I wrapped someone else's ankles, but I've wrapped my own more times than I can count." Dean secured the Velcro and lifted his head up to meet Maggie's gaze. "I'm sorry. I brought you here for a beautiful hike and instead you're injured, soaking wet, and trapped in a hotel room with me."

"It's not all bad." Maggie smiled down into his handsome face. "This is literally a scene from a romance novel."

"One of yours?"

"More like every novel ever written, Dean."

"How is this like a romance novel?"

She pushed a lock of his hair off his forehead. The rainwater darkened it from its golden color to a slick of dark brown that reminded Maggie of a different man.

"Going for a hike, getting caught in a downpour, even twisting my ankle. Then coming back to a hotel for refuge and having to share a room. A room with a single bed." Maggie pointed to the bed in the center of the room. "Classic tropes, Dean."

"Trope."

"A recurring theme or motif. In this case, reoccurring across multiple novels in a genre."

"And what would my role be in this trope?" Dean asked, the corners of his green eyes crinkling with his smile.

"Obviously to fall adoringly at my feet as you confess your love." Maggie tilted her head. "It seems you're already at my feet."

"Look at that. I guess I am." Dean stood up. "We can wring as much water out of our clothes as possible, take a warm shower," he eyed her foot, "or a bath, and order room service."

Dean reached one hand over his head and pulled off his long-sleeved shirt and his undershirt. His muscles rippled in the low light from the floor lamp. Dean, shirtless, looked like a Greek statue. Eight defined bumps ridged the muscles along his stomach and a deep slanted V shape disappeared under the waistband of his pants. His skin was a sun gold everywhere except for his dark nipples, a tan Maggie knew came from spending every second he could shirtless.

Dean's hands went to his belt and undid the buckle, letting the leather rest in the loops. He popped the button on the front and his pants slipped a few inches lower. Dean helped them the rest of the way until they hit the floor with a wet slap. He straightened, a pair of dark boxer briefs plastered to his body. Romance novel Maggie would have snuck a peek at the front of Dean's underwear. Real-life Maggie kept her eyes above the belly button. The last time he'd stripped in front of her, she had run away and hid. At least she was making progress. Although she couldn't exactly run very far with a swollen ankle.

"Your turn," Dean said. "Give me your clothes and I'll wring as much out as I can while you snag a—" He looked down at her foot again. "Bath."

"Don't look," Maggie said.

"Don't worry about me, Babs."

She dropped his soggy sweatshirt with a wet thud and then peeled off her shirt. Sitting on the dresser made removing her pants difficult. Maggie got one side of the waistband down and then almost fell off the edge of the dresser. She righted herself, but not before her ankle slammed into the solid wood, and she let out a pained hiss.

Two large hands steadied her hips.

"Let me help."

Big fingers dipped into the stretchy purple fabric. Dean's skin was soft and tickled against her and Maggie sucked in a breath, determined not to giggle. With Dean tugging her pants down, Maggie used her arms to help shift her weight. The wet spandex clung to her thighs and Dean had to adjust his grip, his thumbs skating across the cold skin of her legs. Her old cotton leggings wouldn't have given her this much trouble. When they were dry, her pants felt slick under her hands, but soaking wet they stuck to her like tacky peanut butter. Dean went slow, inch by slow inch, pulling the leggings over her wrapped ankle and tossing them in the pile of both their clothes.

Maggie had always assumed that if she were to sit in front of Dean in her underwear, all her shivering would have been lust-induced. She had been wrong. The shivers wracking her body were definitely a product of the frigid temperatures in the hotel room. Dean's hands were warm on her skin, but his touch hadn't produced the expected tingles she had dreamed of. She blamed her lack of response on her sprained ankle and the beginning stages of hypothermia.

Dean stood and disappeared into the attached bathroom. Maggie heard the pipes groan as the water started. Against her better judgment, she slid off the surface of the bureau and tried to hobble the short distance to the bathroom. If she moved at the speed of a glacier, and only put weight on the outside edge of her heel, then she could move. The promise of pain made her lock her knee as well, and when Dean came back out of the bathroom, she was sure she looked like an off-balance stool tipping its way across the floor.

"I was coming to get you." Dean scooped her up.

With a shriek at the sudden movement, Maggie wrapped her arms around his thick neck.

"I was walking just fine," she said and stuck her nose into the air.

"You didn't mind me carrying you on the trail."

Maggie was aware of every place their skin brushed together. She still wore her sports bra and underwear, and Dean had his boxer briefs on. They were about as dressed as they might have been at a pool, but it had been years since they'd gone swimming together. Even longer since they'd played any sort of games that would have put their naked bodies into incidental contact.

"We weren't half naked then," Maggie said.

Dean set her down on the closed lid of the toilet and then backed out of the bathroom. Maggie peeled the rest of her clothes off and levered herself into the tub. The water was heavenly on her freezing body. Hot enough to turn her pink, but not enough to scald her skin from her bones. She dipped her head back and let her hair fan out around her, slicking it away from her face as she reached for the tiny bottle of complimentary 2-in-1 shampoo and conditioner.

What was she doing? She was naked in a bathtub while the man she'd loved forever stood just outside the door wearing nothing but his underwear. The same man who she'd been fake dating for a month now and who just offered to extend their agreement. The same one who carried her down a mountain, bandaged her foot, and stripped her to her underwear before carrying her to a warm bath. And she was in here washing her hair.

Her favorite romance heroines would roll over in the pages of their books, watching her. She hadn't batted her eyelashes. She hadn't chewed on her lower lip. She hadn't even ogled him. Dean had stripped down to his briefs, and she'd looked away. On purpose. He'd held her in his arms on the soggy mountain path, and she'd been thinking about how her clothes stuck to her like dry ice. They'd booked a single room with one undersized bed, and Maggie worried about when the road home would open back up. He'd said he loved her, and she hadn't jumped him.

Maggie rinsed the suds out of her long hair and tried to sit up. It was no easy feat while also trying to keep her foot and ankle propped on the tub's edge.

"You don't come out the same after falling in love." Maggie repeated Dean's words back to herself. Hadn't she though?

Maggie had fallen in love with Dean as a child. Now, as an adult, she was no stranger to the technicalities of sex, but her fantasies about Dean hadn't changed. She imagined him holding her hand. She imagined chaste kisses pressed to her cheeks and lips. She imagined whispering, 'I love you,' while sharing secret smiles and sweet laughter. She imagined sitting hip to hip while throwing corn to the ducks at the park. Her dreams of Dean were, by definition, childish. They were the dreams she'd conjured in elementary and middle school. They hadn't grown or changed in the last twenty years.

Maggie didn't write scenes like that. She didn't write books like that. She also didn't read them. She preferred books with passion and heat and sexual tension that left her own legs shaking. Could that be the reason everything felt so wrong? She'd built her whole idea of romance off two things: her feelings for Dean and the novels she banded around herself like armor. She was an expert in her field. What if she'd been wrong? Who would she be if she'd been wrong?

The bath water was turning cold, so Maggie pulled the plug—the real rubber kind on a length of chain. She used her limited arm strength to push herself out of the tub until she could sit on the edge, then she swung her legs over onto the worn bath mat. She grabbed one of the hanging towels and wrapped it around her slender body. The edges barely overlapped. Dean was going to be in big trouble unless he had a couple towels to work with. That thought passed through her brain the same way it would if she were thinking about Audrey or Cal. She'd give a slight smile, maybe a giggle at the odd picture they'd make trying to cover themselves with a hand towel. But nothing more.

Had she ever felt more?

Maggie closed her eyes and saw dark hair, a short beard, and a blue striped sweater. She could smell his molten metal and a hint of pine scent. She saw the frown he'd give to the tiny towel, and warmth bloomed in her belly. She imagined work-roughened fingertips, palms full of calluses and small scars, pushing down her purple leggings. The heat spread through her like a drop of water on tissue paper. She pressed her thighs together to relieve the ache. It didn't work. The heat blanketing her body, heat caused by thoughts of Mac, banished even the memory of being cold.

She dropped the towel, the rough terry cloth scraping over the sensitive points of her nipples, over the bones at her hips, and down the outside of her thighs. Maggie shuddered. Her fingers traced down the path of the towel. Her hands stopped at the dip of her hips before she slid them towards the center of her abdomen. They met in the middle and she let one hand slide up to cup her breast. She gasped at the light pressure, gently pinching at her nipple. Until now, she hadn't noticed her breasts ached to be touched. Her other hand dipped down over the coarse hair between her thighs.

Should she shave? Wax? Men liked that kind of thing. Would Mac like that kind of thing? The heat started to temper, and her hands stopped their perusing. What was she doing? Maggie faced her reflection in the mirror. Flushed cheeks. Glazed eyes. Goosebumps spread along her arms, and not because of the half-naked man in their shared hotel room, but because of grumpy and standoffish Tyler McCoy.

Maggie had felt sexual attraction before, although maybe not quite at this level, but it had never been centered around a specific person. She liked the idea of sex, and she liked the small orgasms she managed to wring out of herself, but choosing to get herself off was usually a conscious decision. Now it felt imperative.

Maggie closed her eyes and imagined climbing into the single bed and curling up underneath the worn comforter. It was Mac's arm she imagined circling her waist. It was Mac's breath warming the back of her neck. Mac's fingers trailing up with teasing touches to cup her breast. Her whole body shuddered at the thought, her core going slick and wet.

She needed to widen her stance, but she wasn't sure her ankle would hold. Maggie dropped her hand from her breast and let her weight fall forward as she braced herself on the bathroom counter. She raised her bad leg, propping her knee up on the counter. The throb in her ankle was nothing compared to the throb between her thighs. Maggie didn't care that there was another person just outside the door. She didn't care that she was in a dated hotel bathroom, standing under orange fluorescent lights. She didn't care that she was splayed wide open in front of a goddamn mirror. She brought her free hand between her legs and circled her entrance once, twice, three times before dipping two fingers into her wet heat.

A moan broke free from her mouth and she didn't care if Dean could hear her. She could barely hear the hum of the automatic fan over the pounding of her own pulse. She thrust her fingers deeper and felt the flutters start as her walls clamped down. They were Mac's fingers inside of her. It was the base of Mac's thumb that brushed against her clit and locked all her muscles down. It was the image of Mac's face, dark eyes and frown turning his lips, tattooed across her brain that tipped her over the edge and into the fastest, sweetest orgasm of her entire life.

"Need me to give you a hand?" Dean's voice broke through the lustful fog circulating through her brain.

That was the last thing she needed. Maggie dropped her knee from the counter and turned on the sink to splash water on her face. Her pulse was slowly evening out.

"I'm okay." Maggie called back, "I'll be right out."

When she finally emerged from the bathroom, Dean was sitting in the worn chair, his phone in his hands. Maggie could admit he looked like every romance hero come to life. He lounged back in the chair, legs spread out in front of him, as comfortable in his underwear as he was dressed. Maggie could only dream of having his confidence.

He'd spread the bulk of their clothes along the heater. The sweatshirt she'd been wearing and his fleece were both laid out on towels by the window. Everything was still damp, but at least the dripping had stopped.

"Shower is all yours," she said.

Dean lifted his head to look at her and she struggled to contain her blush.

"Phones are okay." He stood from the chair, stretching each of his carved muscles. Maggie waited for the rush that didn't come. "I just checked that yours would turn on. It's on the dresser."

He had to step in close to her on his way to the bathroom.

The heat from Dean's body seeped along her collarbones and down the tops of her thighs. She waited for a spark or a throb as Dean's green eyes met hers. Nothing.

Dean tugged the end of Maggie's towel. "These things are awfully tiny, Babs. I don't know if this will work for me."

"That sounds like a you problem," Maggie said and sat herself down on the edge of the one bed.

Dean's chuckle followed him into the bathroom. She heard the door click shut and the shower turn on. Maggie wondered if maybe, for the last twenty years, she'd been wrong about everything.

CHAPTER SIXTEEN

Stupid, stupid, stupid, Maggie told herself as she sipped her half hot chocolate and half coffee at a small round table in the Perk-u-later. The sweetness from her drink wasn't resetting her brain in quite the way she'd hoped it would. In fact, all the coffee was doing was scalding off her taste buds.

The shop was quiet—not abnormal for a Monday morning—and Gwen had already dropped some nibbles on the table with a promise to stop by for a real chat a little later. The whole café smelled of toasted coffee beans, warm chocolate, and melted butter. Despite the comfortable feelings those smells evoked in Maggie, she couldn't stop remembering the scent of pine trees and fresh rain and molten metal.

Even with fresh clothes, several warm showers, and a full night in her own bed, a chill still wracked Maggie's body. She'd assumed the twenty-four hours with a nearly naked Dean would have generated enough heat to blanket that chill out of existence, but it hadn't. She'd woken up on the left side of the bed, in still rain-damp underwear, Dean's back to her as he sprawled on the right side, and she'd been even colder. Dean was beautiful to look at, strong and capable as he lifted her into his muscled arms, and just flirty enough to keep her laughing, but the spark she'd always assumed would arc between them had been nowhere in that hotel room.

Maggie wanted to blame the weight of the heavy rainstorm for drowning their chemistry, but stripping down to their underwear and climbing into a bed barely big enough to fit one and a half adults should have brought the heat roaring up like an alcohol-drenched fire.

Maggie wasn't the most experienced or the most forward woman, but it hadn't been nerves that had stopped her from rolling right into Dean's body heat. It wasn't anything about Dean that stopped her from playing out the classic "one bed" trope with his broad body. It was the strange thought that settled deep into the recesses of her mind and wouldn't let go: that cuddling up to a naked Dean would hurt a man with dark hair and darker eyes.

The bell over the door jingled and Audrey rushed into the shop, hair flying. "Sorry." She slid into the seat across from Maggie. "I know I'm late."

"If this is a bad time, we can meet tomorrow." Would Maggie have preferred to talk about her jaunt to the woods with her best friend today? Yes. Would it kill her to wait? Probably not.

"No." Audrey put both her hands palm down on the wooden table. "I have so many questions about everything, and I need them answered. But first take this."

Maggie was of the opinion that her own questions were a bit more pressing, but Audrey wasn't really someone who could answer them for her. That was a journey Maggie needed to explore on her own. She took the small bag that her friend was shaking in her direction. Inside was a small pink pouch with a red heart and a familiar white cross on the front. Maggie unzipped it and laughed as she saw the instant freeze pack, a set of crayon-shaped Band-Aids, an elastic bandage, and some alcohol wipes. A fully-stocked, travel first aid kit. The other item in the bag was a neon yellow umbrella. Both were barely bigger than her phone.

"They seemed necessary, given your recent adventures." Audrey smiled at Gwen as she slid a steaming mug of tea in front of her. "So you and Dean got stuck on a mountain together."

"Sort of. The road was closed because of the storm, but there was a hotel, a heater, and room service, and the road was open by the next morning."

"That's literally a romance scene," Audrey sighed. "You couldn't have written it better if you tried."

Maggie took a sip of her coffee. "That's kind of the whole point of us dating. To help me write better scenes."

Audrey frowned and spun her tea bag into her ceramic mug. "Is it working?"

Dean had asked the same question, and this time Maggie had an answer. "No." She slumped back into her chair.

Maggie had barely written anything in the last four weeks. She'd tried to take notes on the physical reactions her body had had to Dean, the way his mouth curved when he smiled at her. She'd created the most perfect romance novel dates, and yet nothing was different now, after a month of them. How could her writing change if she wasn't different? Would extending their agreement change anything? Another week? A month? It didn't seem likely, not after her complete lack of reaction to a mostly naked Dean. Maggie didn't know if Dean was the wrong guy, or she was the wrong girl. Maybe she wasn't built for the kind of romance she read about.

"I'm just struggling with all of it." Maggie put her head into her hands. "I'm discovering that I know a lot less about love and romance than I thought I did."

"That's normal." Audrey sipped her tea. "Especially for someone who spent so much time reading that she forgot to date."

Maggie flushed. "I've dated. A little. Just nothing like what happens in books."

"That's because real life isn't like books," Audrey said. "It's still wonderful and thrilling and empowering, but it isn't the instant connection that happens between the covers of a novel. Just look at me and Cal."

Audrey and Cal had fallen in love the normal way. They'd crossed paths first at work and then through mutual friends. Their first several meetings happened in a group. Cal had scrounged up both Audrey's contact information and the confidence to use it. He'd taken her out to dinner at a tiny Italian restaurant that served mouthwatering salads and antipasti. Two days later, he'd called and asked her on another date. A month later, they were official. Six months later, Audrey's lease ended, and she moved in with Cal and Mac.

On paper, stories like that seemed unimaginative, but Maggie had watched her best friend experience each part of Cal's attention and interest. Maggie had watched them fall in love. Instead of directing her own narrative by faking a relationship, she should have just interviewed the happy couple. Even without a meet-cute and a series of perfect dates and challenges, Cal was in love with her friend, devoted, and Audrey was one hundred percent invested right back.

Maggie had known when Cal started ordering a Diet Coke with no ice and a separate glass full of water with lemon every time they went somewhere, because that's what Audrey ordered with all her meals. He didn't wait for her to ask him. Audrey often ran late for their dates, so he had things ready for her when she got there.

"I thought I knew what being in love looked like. I thought I'd lived it," Maggie said.

Audrey tipped her head to the side, blond ponytail swinging, as she studied her friend. Her eyes narrowed. "You don't mean—"

"I think I was wrong." Maggie said, "But I don't know if I was never actually in love at all, or if I just don't know what actual love is."

"Don't be ridiculous." Audrey shook her head. "You know love. You just need the right person." Audrey was a blur of activity. She fixed her ponytail, clenched her fists around the strap of her bag, stirred one, two, three sugars into her tea. Her eyes met Maggie's before skittering away. "You've been conflating love with being *in* love."

Maggie sat back in her chair. She lifted her cup to her mouth, letting the soothing sweetness of her coffee spread along her tongue. Audrey was probably right—she had a bad habit of being right—but until the right person came into Maggie's life, it would be hard to prove any of Audrey's statements.

"Maybe," Maggie watched as Audrey's frown bled away into an encouraging smile.

"Maybe that's why your reviewers didn't find the chemistry believable between your main couple. Because you've always settled for less than real chemistry without even realizing it. Or your reviewers are just wrong."

"They can't be both right, that my writing lacks chemistry because I have no personal experience with toe-curling chemistry, and wrong, because my book actually does have chemistry. You have to pick one." Maggie fought back a laugh.

"I don't have to pick one," Audrey said. "I'm your best friend. It's my job to be unreasonable."

Unreasonable. It was unreasonable to keep dating Dean when it wasn't helping her writing. He had offered to keep up the ruse as a favor, not out of a burning desire for her. It was unreasonable to believe this would work when it hadn't been working so far. She had no chemistry with Dean. She had tepid comfort and affection. Dean was handsome, but she couldn't remember the last time she'd wanted to press her mouth to his, not for the sake of writing about it, but because his lips had looked too kissable to ignore. It had been someone else's lips she had wanted to kiss, someone that she was struggling to ignore.

"How did you know you were in love with Cal?"

Audrey straightened in her chair, pushing her shoulders back under her cotton shirt. She took a sip of her tea and placed her cup down with a small clink. "It wasn't instalove like in most romance novels." Audrey said, "He was cute, and he was attractive. I wanted to drag him off to secret places to do nasty things to him, but it took longer to fall in love. It was how he looked at me, the little things he did to put me first, the way I didn't want to be with anyone but him."

"I get that part. I loved your brother for standing up to my bullies, for the special nicknames, for the smiles he always gave me, but what does *being* in love feel like?" Maggie leaned across the table to grab Audrey's hand. "What made you sure that he was the one?"

Audrey's brow furrowed, but she didn't pull her hand away. The sounds of the café had faded to a low hum as Maggie watched her best friend. Looking thoughtful, Audrey turned her face away from Maggie. "The first time I saw Cal, I couldn't look away from him." Audrey said, swinging her gaze back at her friend. "We were at a party, and it was like I could see him everywhere. I'd leave the room only to run into him again. I'd go to refill my drink and our eyes would catch and hold from across the room." Audrey smiled.

"Then the first time he got close enough for us to be introduced… it was like I couldn't breathe. My chest was tight, and my mouth was dry. Being around him was like swallowing a burning candle, this heat that started in my stomach and spread. I'd watch his hands, his mouth, his eyes. I could feel his presence when he entered the room. That was the initial attraction, and it didn't go away."

Maggie watched a flush diffuse along Audrey's cheeks as she twisted the end of her ponytail around her finger. Had Maggie ever experienced any of that with Dean? No. But she had with someone else.

Audrey's words resonated with Maggie. She'd had at least some of those feelings, just not on the same scale Audrey had for Cal. Maggie had felt those feelings for Cal's brother.

Maggie wasn't a virgin, but her former trysts hadn't been based on pure lust or even a committed relationship. They'd been good, old-fashioned, experimentation meant to help her explore some of the more fun parts of the books she read. Everything seemed so hot and desperate on paper. That never quite translated to in person.

Her few prior encounters had been fine. The men had been equally curious and appropriately respectful, but she wasn't missing out on too much when she went back to reading about sex instead of having it. There had been no urgency, no feeling that she'd crumble into nothing if their hands didn't skate up her ribs or notch their hips to hers.

Maggie had always assumed that was because she was waiting for Dean, until she'd started to feel some of those tingly things just from standing too close to Mac. Sitting across from Audrey, Maggie decided that if she had experienced half of what Audrey said, she probably would have been champing at the bit for more orgasms with other consenting adults.

"It wasn't just heat, and aches, and magnetic looks," Audrey said. "I started noticing that he was always on my mind. Sex, too, but also about whether he'd like the lunch I'd brought to work, or which pair of shoes he'd like better. Or I'd see something, and it would remind me of Cal, so I'd have to get it for him. We had so many things in common, stuff we liked to do, the way we saw the world, things we thought were important. He let me be myself and still pushed me to be better."

"Was it like becoming a different person?"

"Yes, and no," Audrey said. "I was still me, but I had a new frame of reference for me."

"You changed for a man."

"I wouldn't say I changed for him." Audrey looked up at the paneled ceiling of the café. "But he changed how I saw myself. Cal believes I'm beautiful. Cal knows I'm smart. Cal says I'm worthy. I love Cal, trust Cal, so I believe him. I recognized that I was in love with him the first time we had a big fight.

"It was over some stupid misunderstanding, but I remember standing in his apartment and calling him a jackass before storming out to my car. And in the driver's seat, I pulled out my phone and wanted to call Cal to complain about Cal. I trusted him to build me back up and have my back, even when he was the one I was furious with."

"He picked up takeout, and you were going to cook him dinner."

"What?" A laugh pushed through Audrey's words.

"That was your first big fight," Maggie said. "You called me from the car, and I had to suffer through your chicken Marsala."

"Oh yea," Audrey grinned, "Asshole."

"You hate cooking. He was sure he was helping." Maggie grinned back. "And he was trying to spare you both a truly horrific meal experience."

"See?" Audrey said. "Even then, he was thinking of me. He was misguided and horribly, stupidly, male, but he really was trying."

"I thought I was in love with your brother." Maggie said, "But I wasn't. Not really."

Audrey bit her lip. "Dean loves you."

"He does," Maggie said. "I love him too. We had all those moments where he built me up, where I looked for him, where he was the one I wanted to talk to. But I've never experienced the heat, or the tingles." She ignored the wince that Audrey tried to hide. "He's never had the ability to hurt me the way Cal hurt you by accidentally messing up your plans to poison him with home-cooked food, because I was never as invested as you were with Cal."

"Rude," Audrey said, but she was smiling.

"I don't think I really know your brother," Maggie said. "I know ten-year-old Dean, and I know the Dean I made him into in my mind. But we're actually really different."

"My brother is a good guy," Audrey said, her hands clenching and unclenching on the tabletop.

"Just not my guy," Maggie said, and Audrey shook her head.

"I'm sorry," Audrey's voice was quiet and her eyes solemn.

"You did nothing wrong."

"I could have just supported you."

Maggie frowned at her best friend. "You did, Audrey. You didn't stop me from giving it a shot. You didn't tell me it was a stupid idea or that it wouldn't work. You let me figure it out on my own with no judgment. I'll forever be grateful for that."

"You'll always be my sister, just not through Dean." Audrey said.

The silence fell between them, punctuated by the whir of the bean grinder and the hiss of the espresso machine.

"You need a new guy," Audrey said, sipping the last of her tea. "One that makes your lady parts ache and tingle and burn."

"That sounds like a problem I'd need to see my gynecologist for," Maggie said. Audrey snorted into her tea.

The bell over the café door jangled and a group of two men and one woman entered the shop. From their table, Maggie couldn't see their faces, but that didn't stop the hitch in her chest or the way her heart pounded against her ribs. The man in the middle of the three had dark, tousled hair, the edges just brushing the collar of his gray sweater.

He'd pushed his sleeves up to his elbows, and Maggie felt her gaze drawn to the sinewy muscles cording his forearms. He'd shoved his hands into the front pockets of his blue jeans, and he was looking up at the chalkboard menu above the counter, but Maggie knew what those eyes looked like. She'd felt those eyes pour over her every time they were in the same space.

The woman with him said something, and Maggie felt her skin heat as his husky laugh seeped across the café and beaded over her skin like water. Her lips parted and Maggie let her tongue sweep out to wet them. Audrey's words banged through her brain like a ping-pong ball made of lead. He wasn't even looking at her yet, and she needed to be doused in a bucket of ice water. The woman, with her dark glossy waves and fitted pencil skirt, put her hand on his arm and Maggie felt her stomach turn over.

"I'll have Cal invite some of his friends over. We'll find you someone you have explosive chemistry with." Audrey said. She pulled out her phone, fingers tapping away as she texted her boyfriend.

Maggie didn't hear her friend over the sound of her pulse pounding in her ears. She nodded, no idea what she was agreeing to, and watched as Mac shrugged off the other woman's touch. That movement settled the wild buzzing that had been thrumming beneath her breastbone. Audrey grinned into her cup of tea, but Maggie didn't notice. Her focus was on the man at the coffee counter. He turned, dark eyes finding hers immediately. The corner of his mouth hitched up, and Maggie sucked in a quick breath. Mac didn't look away.

CHAPTER SEVENTEEN

The door was unlocked, so Maggie let herself into her friends' living room. She didn't see Audrey, but Cal sat on the overstuffed loveseat with three other men Maggie didn't recognize. The oak coffee table overflowed with bowls of popcorn, chips, and pretzels. There were also a few smaller dip containers along with a bevy of glasses. Maggie raised her hand in greeting, and Cal raised his in return.

This was not the way movie nights typically started. Not with three strangers crashing the festivities. There was a vague memory of Audrey saying she'd invite some of Cal's friends over for Maggie to meet pinging in her brain, but she'd vetoed that idea, right? She didn't need a setup when she had Mac setting her on fire just by skipping through her brain. Although maybe she hadn't shut this situation down *because* Mac had been skipping through her brain. Dammit.

"Audrey's in the bathroom," Cal said, clearly interpreting her panicked face. "But come meet the boys."

Maggie forced a smile and walked around the back of the couch to see Cal's friend's head on. They were good looking—Audrey would have stressed the importance of chemistry and attraction to her boyfriend—and all three smiled at her. It was a little strange seeing them packed into the couch, but the social awkwardness put Maggie a little bit more at ease.

"Josh," the dark-skinned man smiled, showing straight white teeth gleaming behind full lips.

"Ryan," The man next to Josh had a smattering of freckles covering most of his pale face, each freckle the same copper as his hair.

"Ted," the last man, sitting on the far side of Cal, had a familiar mop of dark hair and a beard that gave Maggie a double-take.

"Nice to meet everyone," Maggie slipped her bag off her shoulder and propped it next to one of the squashy beanbag chairs Maggie knew came from the spare room turned study.

"You can sit here." Cal stood up, leaving a spot between Ryan and Ted on the couch. "I'm going to snag Audrey, and we'll take the loveseat."

"It's no problem," Maggie eyed the size of the three men. "I can stick with the beanbag. It looks like you guys could use the extra elbow room."

"I don't mind a beanbag," Josh said and stood up, too. His gray sweatpants hugged muscular thighs about the size of Maggie's waist. "I can join you."

"Okay," Maggie gestured to the second, squashy chair.

The second beanbag chair was on the other side of the coffee table, so it wasn't like they'd be touching. Then Josh hefted the bag up with one hand and shifted it closer to its twin.

"I'll stick with you so you can tell me what's going on in the movie. I'll admit that I've never seen *Captain America* before, so I'll need some help."

"That's sacrilege," Maggie said, her mouth tipping up into a real smile. So far, no tingles and no heat for any of Cal's friends, but they seemed nice enough. There were also worse ways to spend an afternoon than engrossed in the Marvel universe. That didn't mean she wasn't going to plan sweet, slow revenge on Audrey. "I'm going to hit the bathroom before we start." Maggie said.

"You can use the upstairs one," Cal said. "Audrey was going to scrounge up snacks, so she's probably still downstairs."

The old Cape house had two bedrooms, one for Audrey and Cal and the other for Mac. Both were on the second floor, with a bathroom in the middle at the very top of the stairs. Maggie was just stepping onto the top stair when the bathroom door opened. She expected to see Audrey, but she came face to face with a glowering Mac.

On anyone else, the perpetual frown would have been intimidating as hell, but Maggie had seen the way Mac's eyes glittered when he found something funny and the way the corner of his mouth tipped up into a smile. She wondered how many people had backed off when faced with Mac's sparkling personality and how many stuck it out to see the heat and humor behind his dark eyes. His fiery gaze dropped from her face to her breasts and down to her hips before he looked away. It was enough for the tendrils of heat to form low in her belly and pulse outwards along her limbs.

"What are you doing here?"

"It's movie night," Maggie said. "Aren't you coming down to join us?"

Maggie wanted Mac downstairs. She wasn't interested in meeting or flirting with three new men, no matter how nice they probably were. Maggie wanted to sit and watch Captain America defeat the Nazis while the outside of her thigh pressed against Mac's and they lobbed covert glances back and forth. She should have just told Audrey she was into Mac, but it felt weird admitting a crush on Audrey's boyfriend's brother, right after ending a fake relationship and admitting her previous love for Audrey's brother.

"No." Mac moved towards his bedroom. He was a gruff person, but this was extra surly, even for Tyler McCoy. As he walked past her, she got a whiff of pine and metal. She swayed towards his body, and as though drawn by a magnetic force, Maggie followed him.

Mac sat in a computer chair facing a large wooden desk with a dual monitored screen. His bed butted up against the far wall, tidy and made with a solid green comforter and a set of beige sheets. He glanced at her out of the corner of his eye as she walked into his room, but he didn't tell her to leave. A set of floating shelves sat above his desk, and Maggie appreciated the memorabilia he had showcased. There was an intricate Lego R2D2, a Newton's Cradle, and a Galileo thermometer. A battered set of Tolkien's *Lord of the Rings* was stacked with their spines out. One book, *The Two Towers,* was missing from the set and a quick glance around the room showed the book on the small wooden nightstand next to Mac's bed. At the very end of the top shelf was a familiar black and green box with blocky yellow letters—the Megazord Maggie had sold to him—and next to that was a little yellow ball with bumpy edges, so bright that it scalded her retinas.

"You're in my room." Mac's words were a rumble of distant thunder. Maggie's bones vibrated with the impact.

"I am." She boosted herself up onto the edge of the desk. A taller woman would have been able to keep her feet touching the hardwoods, but Maggie's swung a few inches off the ground. That kind of ruined the confidence she was trying to exude, but she ignored it. She wasn't right in front of Mac, but she was close enough to him that his forearms could brush her thighs if he leaned forward. Maggie struggled to draw in enough air. She wanted him to lean forward.

"What are you doing here?" Mac's voice dropped lower, and he did what she wanted, leaning forward to brace his palms on the surface of his desk. He was wearing another Henley with the sleeves pushed up, and the heat from his forearms seeped through her thin black leggings. She flexed her thigh muscles, overwhelmed with the need to bring their bodies into fleeting contact.

"I don't know," she said. She was lying.

Mac had been his normal self, and she'd been unable to stay away once they made eye contact. And she didn't want to go downstairs and flirt with random men. She wanted Mac to come down with her so they could sit on the beanbags and pretend not to stare at each other.

Mac kept his eyes on his outstretched hands as the fingers clenched into fists and then released.

"I don't mean in my room. I mean, here at the house with Cal's friends." He let out a breath that sounded as shaky as Maggie felt. "You have a boyfriend, and those guys are under the impression that—"

"Oh, we broke up." Maggie didn't enjoy interrupting people, but she couldn't let him finish that sentence. "Cal actually invited his friends here to see if I had chemistry with any of them. Not that I—"

"You what?" Mac lifted his gaze to hers. "You and Dean—"

"Broke up."

This conversation, discussing the implosion of her relationship, should have embarrassed her a bit more. Maggie would deny it to almost anyone, but the more Mac's jaw clenched, and the more his hands fisted, and the more he mentioned the men waiting in the living room, the bigger the ache between Maggie's thighs became and the harder her heart pounded.

"Chemistry," Mac repeated, raising a hand to run it through his thick hair.

She nodded.

Maggie reached her foot out and ran her toe up Mac's calf. She wasn't sure what possessed her to do that. She only knew she might throw up or pass out if she didn't touch some part of his body with some part of hers. His jeans were rough against her sock-clad foot, but the warmth was there, along with an intense array of tingles that moved up one of her legs and settled into the warm, damp place between them. Maggie watched Mac's knuckles turn white against his skin.

"I love Dean," Maggie said. "I always will, but there wasn't any—I didn't feel—" Maggie stopped.

Mac didn't need to hear about the tingles and the heat and the aches. Except maybe he did. He was the one causing them. She should tell him and jump him and experience some of those magnetic intimacies Audrey had talked about. And orgasms. Mac looked very capable of giving her orgasms. Ones she wouldn't have to work for.

"Didn't feel what?" Mac asked.

His voice grated against her ear. He shifted his hands on his desk until his pinky finger was resting against the outside of her thigh. Mac's eyes were glued to the spot where they touched.

This! Maggie thought and opened her mouth to tell Mac, but the word stuck in her throat. Her whole being angled towards the spot where he touched her, all the neurons firing in her brain pinpointed the small contact. Maggie didn't break a sweat, which was surprising, given how her body burned. Her brain hiccupped, wanting him to wrap his hand around her thigh. To wrap his hands around both of her thighs and spread them wide. Maggie shifted her hips to relieve some of the pressure in her core. Mac moved his eyes from the roll of her pelvis up to her mouth.

She wanted to kiss him, but she still had the movie to get back to. Audrey would send out a search party if she didn't go downstairs soon. Not that the thought of being caught with Mac was embarrassing—she doubted Audrey would care—but when she finally tried to ease this need, she wanted enough time to do it the right way.

"I have to go back downstairs." Maggie said, her voice a ragged hum.

Come with me. Tell those other guys to go.

The words were on the tip of her tongue. She could taste the shape of them when Mac pulled his hands away. He leaned back in his desk chair. The furrow between his brow was back.

"Yeah," he said. "Go."

The heat that had been building in her bloodstream turned cold at his tone, but the ache was harder to ignore.

"What? No—"

"I said, 'go,'" Mac lifted his eyes to hers, his pupils blown wide, eclipsing the dark of his irises. They pinned her with a cold and unwelcoming glare.

"You're mad." Maggie said, which was ridiculous.

THE TROPE

Mac was always grumpy, but rarely angry. The few times she'd seen his temper, he had never directed it at her. But now, the clench of his jaw, the flare of his nostrils, the ridged grooves between his eyebrows, and the way his stare chilled Maggie like a polar plunge all pointed to the same thing.

"No," he said, but he dropped her gaze and stood from his chair, putting more space between them.

Maggie pushed herself off the desk. She needed to go back downstairs and join the movie. She'd deal with Mac's attitude later. Maggie turned towards the door, and her eye caught on the corner of the desk. She wasn't sure how she'd missed it before, but sitting next to his mouse pad was the tiny Lego set she'd found and given to him that night in his forge.

Mac had put all the pieces together so the tiny blacksmith stood in front of the little plastic anvil, protective hood covering his yellow head. Mac had placed one of the silver swords in his hands, the hammer in the other. The armor sat displayed on the tiny brick table. Her silly little gift. Set in a spot where he would see it every day. Butterflies started the rumba in her stomach.

"Come watch with us." Maggie said. *With me.*

Even when Mac was grumpy, she wanted to spend time with him. Even when he was snarling, she wanted to see him. Even when he was glowering, she wanted to go to him.

Mac shook his head. "You have three guys down there dying to get to know you. Dying to see what kind of *chemistry* you share." He let out a small, humorless chuckle. "I won't mess that up for you."

Why not? She wanted to ask.

Maggie liked the idea of him messing it all up. Especially if it involved more of his hands on her body or his eyes eating her up. He was looking at her now, his eyes devouring her like whipped cream, and she wanted to hand him a spoon.

"I want—" She let her words die because Mac was shaking his head again.

"I don't." He moved until he was standing beside his open door. "Go, Maggie."

Maggie shivered as Mac's words crested over her. He didn't want what? Had he known what she was going to say? He had his arms crossed across his chest and his eyes trained on a spot on the floor. From the open door, Maggie could hear the murmur of Audrey and Cal and their friends. She had to go downstairs. Mac didn't want to join them, and that was okay. It was unfortunate that she'd burned with heat for him, and now he was willing to send her off to meet someone else.

Maggie had been sure that Mac was drowning in the same attraction that had her, but she might have misread the whole situation. She might have misread him. Maybe heat was all he felt, and he wasn't interested in anything else. At any rate, it was time to back off, regroup, and then try a full-frontal attack. As if he could hear her thinking about him, Mac looked up and when their eyes met, a shiver ran down her spine. She ached. Well, at least she could tell Audrey that chemistry itself wasn't the problem.

THE TROPE

Cursing, Mac turned and pulled a sweater from the top drawer of his dresser. Before Maggie could blink, he'd dropped it over the top of her head and pulled it down around her neck. She raised her arms and pushed them through the soft gray knit. The quarter zip was open, and the sweater was long enough that it hit her mid-thigh. With trembling fingers, Mac let his hands slide around her waist. He walked her backwards out of his room. As she stood on the landing, wondering what was happening, Mac shut the door in her face.

Audrey, Cal, and the three other men all looked up as Maggie walked back into the living room. Audrey jumped up from her boyfriend's lap and came towards Maggie, a glass of something pink in her hand. Josh was smiling from his beanbag chair, and Ryan and Ted—was his name Ted?—gave her brief nods from the couch. Cal furrowed his brow as he looked at her, taking in the new addition to her wardrobe, and Maggie's cheeks heated. She worried Cal had some sort of sixth sense and knew what Maggie had been doing with his brother upstairs.

"Are we waiting on anything else?" Cal asked.

His eyes found Maggie's, and she knew he meant his brother. She tried to hide her wince. This movie marathon was exactly the kind of activity Mac would join them for. He was more of a Doctor Strange fan than a Captain America fan, but under normal circumstances he'd have sat on the same couch as Maggie, and they'd have debated the merits of each hero while Audrey and Cal played tonsil hockey.

"Nope," Maggie said.

Cal and Audrey shared a look before Audrey shrugged. "Start her up."

Cal pressed play on the remote, and the Marvel intro played, bathing the living room in a soft red glow. Maggie took her seat on the beanbag chair next to Josh. When she glanced back at the couch, Cal had his eyes trained on her. Maggie wanted to scream, sure she and Cal both knew she was the reason Mac hadn't come down the stairs. What he didn't know was that Maggie was ready to go back upstairs and join him.

CHAPTER EIGHTEEN

Maggie scrunched her body further into the blue vinyl and wondered how a two-hour movie could last an eternity. She liked the film—who wouldn't like to watch shirtless and sweet Chris Evans save the world—but she also felt twitchy in her own skin and unable to focus on the screen. Every time she shifted in the seat, Mac's scent wrapped around her, seeping off his sweater and teasing her nose with hints of pine and steel. She hadn't been cold when he'd pulled it over her head, but wearing it gave her the same tingles that his littlest finger had against her thigh.

The vodka and lemonade from Audrey had heated her belly nicely, but she'd declined a second glass. She wanted to be sure, when she next experienced tingles, that the heat was from chemistry and not alcohol. Not that she had any right now. Not from Josh sitting next to her, or from Ryan or Ted on the couch.

Cal had retreated to the loveseat with Audrey draped over his lap. The only time Maggie's body flushed and tingled was when she watched Cal's fingers brush the bare skin of her best friend's collarbones or the sliver of skin bared at her waist. She wasn't a voyeur, but the small touches immediately brought forth all the times Mac had pressed against her, and she had to press her thighs together to relieve the ache.

Josh leaned over from his beanbag chair, his smile blinding. "I'm really glad Cal set this up. I've wanted to meet you for a while."

"A while?" Maggie kept her voice low to avoid disrupting the movie. Not that anyone was watching. Ted was playing sudoku on his phone, and Audrey had her tongue down Cal's throat. Ryan might have been watching, but Maggie would have had to turn around to get a glimpse of him, and she wasn't about to do that.

"I was here the last time Cal and Audrey threw a party, maybe a month ago." Maggie had a vague memory of seeing someone who looked a bit like Josh in the press of bodies the night she'd finished her manuscript. "Cal also has a picture of you and Audrey in his cube. It's super cute, and I thought you looked pretty. Fun."

That was sweet. Josh was handsome, and his hand was warm as he reached for hers, but Maggie couldn't muster up any genuine interest.

"Thank you," Maggie said.

"But you have someone," Josh said. He squeezed her hand before letting go and pulling back onto his bean bag. "Cal mentioned you had been seeing someone. I suppose you're still into them."

Maggie thought of Mac's dark eyes and clenching jaw. "I am. Sorry."

"Don't apologize," Josh said. "We like who we like. I think you're nice, both to look at and to talk to, but I'm not looking to be a rebound or a quick hookup. I'm also not looking to mess with what you have."

"You're a good guy," Maggie said.

Josh turned his attention back to the movie.

Maggie realized she hadn't even considered Dean. He was the obvious person Cal had been referring to when he'd told his friend she was seeing someone. But what she'd said to Josh had been one hundred percent the truth. She was attracted to Mac. She was interested in Mac. She was pretty sure Mac was into her too, but something was getting in his way. Maggie had seen the heat in his eyes, felt the strength of his body against hers. She'd also seen him pull back each time they'd gotten close.

There were two options available. Maggie could either deny her attraction to Mac and focus her energy on finding another man she wanted to kiss and touch, or she could make the first unambiguous move and show Mac what she wanted, letting him decide whether to meet her halfway. Mac was a grumpy introvert, but he was respectful to a fault. If he thought she wasn't interested in anything physical with him, then he'd hold himself back. In his room they'd barely touched, though his small grazes were electric. Maggie thought Mac had felt it, too, but when she'd mentioned both Dean and the men in the living room, he'd shut down so fast it made her dizzy. Was that what made him angry?

If they'd had an intense moment, and Mac had mentioned other women, she would have gotten mad, too. He should have said something. Although, had the roles been reversed, she wouldn't have said anything either. She would have panicked, her brain shutting down her logic and reasoning skills until nothing but a sweating mess of thrumming nerves remained.

Maggie didn't think she was in love with Mac—she'd thought she was in love before, and she had been wrong—but she liked him a lot and she wanted to explore their chemistry. After the movie, she'd hunt him down and lay all her cards out on the table. And if she chickened out and kept her cards hidden, she could pretend she was there to return his sweater.

The credits scrolled across the scene and Maggie stood, ready to excuse herself from the living room.

"You okay?" Audrey stirred in Cal's lap.

"I have to get something." Maggie pointed towards the kitchen.

"You're going to miss the cut scene." Ryan shook his red hair out of his eyes. He paired that statement with a boyish grin. "Don't you want to see the teaser for *The Avengers*?"

"Does the teaser matter if we're just going to start the next movie?" Ted nudged his friend with his shoulder.

"Start the next one without me." Maggie took a step towards the kitchen entryway and the stairs to the second floor. Audrey was watching her, a smile playing with the corners of her full mouth.

"Take all the time you need, Maggie." Cal winked his left eye, a lazy blink she almost missed. "We'll get the next one started."

Maggie's cheeks heated with her blush. She was sure Cal was onto her mission, possibly Audrey, too. Maybe this was a good thing. Hopefully, they'd keep anyone from interrupting.

Maggie hit every creaky stair on her way to the second floor. Mac's door was closed—no surprise there. She raised her hand to knock, sucking in a fortifying breath as her fist hit the dark wood. The breath froze in her lungs as Mac pulled the door open, his body backlit by the lamp next to his bed. She couldn't see much of his face, not with the shadows covering him from forehead to chin, but she noticed the way his hand fisted against his doorjamb as he stared, Maggie assumed, down at her.

"Maggie." His voice was gravelly and low, thrumming over her ears and along her skin. "What's wrong?"

He reached out and placed his calloused hands on each of her shoulders, moving him into the light from the hall. Maggie watched as his eyes skipped from her face down to her feet.

"Nothing's wrong." Maggie said.

Mac continued to check her over with his eyes.

"I'm okay." She reached out and cupped his cheeks. He snapped his gaze to hers and Maggie dropped her hands. "Everything's okay,"

Mac let his hands fall from her shoulders and crossed his arms over his chest. She always forgot just how wide Mac's chest was. With his muscled arms banded across his front, the solid wall of his body drew her eyes in and wouldn't let go. Only a foot separated them, his heat rolling over her like a crashing wave.

Yeah, the chemistry was there. It may have taken Maggie longer than it should have to recognize it, but now that she had, she was one hundred and ten percent on board with exploring everything with Mac.

"What do you need?"

You, Maggie wanted to say, but he looked rattled, enough to close the door in her face again. She smiled instead. "I thought you might want to come down and join us for the next movie."

Maggie didn't think it was possible, but Mac's glower deepened.

"I'm good," he said. "You have enough *people* to entertain."

And there it was. Mac never said no to her, but something about movie night, about Cal's friends, was bothering him enough to turn her down. It was there in the flash of temper behind his eyes and the grind of his teeth. It was there in the way his gaze dipped to her mouth before his frown deepened. Maggie's heart raced at breakneck speed.

"I'd rather spend time with you."

Mac's eyes slammed into hers and her breath suspended in her lungs. He seemed closer than he had been a minute before, his arms falling away from his chest to hang at his sides. Maggie looked down to see his fists clenching and unclenching before she looked back up into his handsome face. She took a step forward, close enough that the very edge of her—his—sweater brushed the folds in his shirt.

"Why?"

Maggie didn't know which one of them moved. The tips of her nipples brushed against his firm torso.

"You know why." She slid her hand up to cradle the nape of his neck. "I like you, Mac."

His breathing grew shallow. He pressed his chest into hers with each ragged breath, but his hands remained clenched at his sides. Maggie thought they'd have come up to bracket her hips by now, sure he would have bent down to take her mouth. She was so sure that this would have been an easy sort of seduction, one where she just needed to get the ball rolling, and he'd take control for the rest of the run. Unless she'd read the whole situation wrong?

"I'm not Dean," Mac said.

Maggie smiled up at him.

"I know." She pressed her lips to the springy hair covering his jaw. His body trembled against her, a humbling thing to see in a man so solid. "I don't want Dean."

"You don't?" His nose touched the sensitive skin along her temple and his breath ruffled the wisps of hair that had escaped from her ponytail.

This was the moment of truth. The moment that had taken her weeks to recognize, but here she was. She was ready to take a chance and tell him the truth because the prospect of not having his hands on her again, not standing inches apart while they shared air, was incomprehensible. Mac wouldn't make a move without her permission, so it was time to send out the welcome wagon. Maggie shook her head, just a tiny movement, but she felt the sigh that escaped him.

"I want you, Mac." The words felt strange on her tongue, but that couldn't be right. Her body was burning up with just the possibility of him. "I want you, Tyler."

Finally, *finally*, his hands came up to bracket her hips and his head dipped as he fused his mouth to hers.

There was no restraint in Mac's kiss. His lips were firm against hers and he tilted his head to better align their mouths. He slid one hand up her back to cradle the nape of her neck and hold her to him. His tongue swept the soft crease of her lips. When she opened her mouth, he plunged inside, twisting around her tongue. Maggie moaned into his mouth, and the corners of his lips twitched against hers, smiling as he kissed her. She smiled too and kissed him back.

Using the hand on her hip, Mac pulled Maggie into his chest and stepped back into his room. As soon as the door closed behind her, Mac pressed her against it. He leaned his torso into hers, solid but not too heavy. Despite the way his lips and tongue plundered her mouth, his hands held her with a gentle strength. It surprised her. She couldn't have written a better juxtaposition.

Heat rolled through Maggie, spreading outward from every inch their bodies connected. Shudders followed in its wake until she was trembling against

Mac's hard form. She was wet. Her core clenched with a delicious ache. Maggie pushed up on her toes, her hips slotting against Mac's as she chased his mouth. He froze, a groan rumbling through him, then pushed his hips back into hers. *This* was heat. *This* was chemistry. *This* was everything that had been missing, not just with Dean, but with everyone.

"Slow." Mac wrenched his mouth from hers, brushing warm, wet kisses down her jaw and throat. "There's no rush. We take this slow."

Maggie didn't want slow. Her brain felt like it was melting, pouring out of her ears. Her body was losing shape, sinking into Mac's solid heat until they fit together like matched puzzle pieces. Maggie carded her fingers into Mac's hair and pulled his mouth back up to hers.

"Please."

She sipped from his full lips, raising her leg to drape her thigh over Mac's hip. He moved his hand to catch her behind the knee, pulling her leg higher. The movement brought the bulge under his jeans in direct contact with the ache between her thighs, and his groan poured into her waiting mouth.

"Fuck." He rolled his hips against hers, catching Maggie's breath.

Mac slid the hand holding her leg until her thigh rested on his powerful forearms. It left his hand free to grip her hips and tilt her pelvis into his. Maggie released his mouth, her head thudding back against the door as she panted.

"I was going to do this right," Mac said against her throat. The short hair from his beard both tickled and scratched against her sensitive skin. "I've thought of this for so long—I had plans, Maggie. I can't think when you're around—I can't—"

He sucked a bruise onto the column of her throat, right over her thundering pulse. He kissed the aching spot, his tongue swiping over the throb.

Maggie nodded, unable to make her voice work as he continued to rock their hips together. She'd had no plans. She had never even imagined this kind of heat, this kind of want, existed. Fast. He was right that they were moving fast, but the thought of stopping brought physical pain to her sensitized skin. She didn't want to stop. She never wanted to stop. Maggie had been sure this electric feeling of need only happened in the pages of books. She'd never been so happy to be wrong.

"Please." She forced her gaze to his, despite her heavy lids. "I need you."

Mac groaned again and dropped his forehead to her collarbones. She could see the light sheen of sweat gathering along his temples. He worked his free hand up under her sweater and gripped her hip, his thumb brushing against the sliver of skin between her t-shirt and her leggings along the way. She shuddered at the contact and his hips stuttered in their rocking rhythm. He picked up where he'd left off, driving against her with more force.

"You don't need to beg me, Maggie." Mac squeezed his eyes shut, panting. "Whatever you want, I'll give it to you. I'll give you everything."

"I only want you," she said.

Mac removed his hand from her skin long enough to hit the lock on his door. Scooping under her knee, he lifted her until she could wrap both her legs around his waist. He carried her to his bed and sat on the edge, pulling her tight against him as she straddled his lap. Maggie couldn't resist the urge to roll her hips against him. She didn't care if he could feel how wet she was, soaking through her leggings.

Mac reached over his head and pulled his shirt off, baring his chest. Dark hair curled along his pecs and down his stomach. It swirled around his belly button before arrowing down under his strained waistband. She wanted to press into him again, to roll her hips against his, but she wanted to be naked first.

"I'm sorry." Mac drew her eyes up to his. "I know I'm not all muscled. Not like—"

Maggie crossed her arms down her front, grabbed the hems of her borrowed sweater and the t-shirt underneath, and pulled them over her head. She dropped them on the floor next to Mac's Henley and pressed herself against him. Maggie could've sworn she heard a sizzle as their bodies came into contact. He might not have had the ridged ab muscles and defined "V" cut like Dean, but Maggie discovered she didn't care. He was hot under her hands and lips, and her body craved his. There was no one else she wanted to touch, wanted to be with.

"Shut up, Mac." Maggie pressed her mouth to his, tangling their tongues and lips together.

Their kisses made her wonderfully dizzy, disoriented, and she found herself on her back looking up into his darling, frowning face. He bent forward to suck her aching nipple, rolling the pebbled tip on his tongue. He bit down on her sensitive bud, teeth pressing into her enough to sting, but not hurt, and Maggie arched her back, whimpering.

"I'll slow down," Mac said, his hand sliding down her front, sending tingles through her belly. He dipped under the waistband of her leggings. "We can stop."

His lips trailed the path of his hands.

"Don't stop."

Maggie twined her hands into his hair and Mac paused. He looked up at her from over her hip bones, his pupils huge and his cheeks flushed. His tongue peeked out to wet his lips as his breath sawed out of his lungs. He looked as lust drunk as Maggie felt, like someone had taken a giant club and smacked them both upside the head with their attraction and hormones. Mac kept his eyes on her as he peeled her leggings down over her hips, spread her thighs wide, and shouldered his way in between them.

"Can I kiss you?" Mac asked and Maggie nodded, her head falling back against the dark blue comforter. "Words, Maggie."

"Yes. Please," she said, and he watched her as he laid a devastating kiss next to her belly button and slipped his fingertips under the waistband of her cotton panties. He continued watching her eyes as he pressed his mouth to the damp fabric covering her core. Maggie's eyes closed, breaking their connection, but she was sure his eyes were still on her face as he pulled her underwear to the side and licked into her center.

CHAPTER NINETEEN

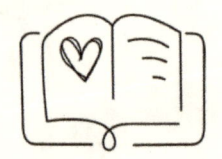

Mac had given her exactly what she wanted: an orgasm she didn't have to work for. Two, actually. And if it was chemistry that brought Maggie to her second orgasm before Mac got his pants off, then Maggie wanted to kick herself for not putting more stock into it earlier. Or she would just as soon as she found her bones.

The hand she had shoved into Mac's hair had gone from yanking to petting. The tremors that rocked her body were no longer tinged with desperation but with bone deep pleasure. Mac pushed himself up, bracing over her on his forearms. His mouth and chin were shiny and wet. His chest was heaving, which made sense, Maggie thought, since he was doing all the work. He wiped the back of his hand over his face and smiled down at her.

"Still with me?" he asked.

"Yes." Maggie smiled back.

Lifting his hand, Mac pushed her hair back from her sweaty forehead, eyes crinkling at the corners as he watched her. "I'll drive you home."

Maggie frowned. "I drove here. And besides, we aren't done." She gestured at the crotch of his pants. His erection was straining the dark denim.

Mac looked at it and then back at Maggie.

"Ignore him." His hand cupped her cheek, thumb sweeping over her flushed cheekbone. "I don't want to rush you with this. We have time."

Maggie pushed up on her elbows. It took more effort than she expected. Her muscles quivered like Jell-O. Mac straightened as her body pressed up towards his until he was kneeling between her spread thighs. Unable to resist touching, Maggie rested her hands on his stomach and slid them up towards his pecs, enjoying how the crisp curls of hair flattened under her palms. Mac's pulse pounded under her hand, and there was a slight tremor in his muscles. He didn't look as relaxed as she was. Maggie could fix that.

"I want this." She slid the hand not pressed over his heart down to the button of his jeans, unfastening it. "I want you to feel the way I do."

Mac lowered his forehead, pressing it against the top of her hair. His lashes above her painted dark half-moons on the tops of his reddened cheeks. From her angle, she didn't know if his eyes were closed or if he was watching her hand on the waistband of his pants. His hands shook against the dark denim covering his thighs.

"If you don't want to have sex, it's okay," Maggie said, her fingers dipping into the top of his underwear and brushing over the velvety head of his cock. With Herculean effort, she pulled back and rested her hands over the denim still clinging to his hips.

Mac covered her hands with his, bringing his forehead to hers. "You have no idea how much I want this. Want you. We're just moving fast. I don't want you to have any regrets, Maggie. None."

Maggie smiled and intertwined their fingers. She brought his hands with hers as she shoved his pants down his thighs. The hair around his cock was as dark and crisp against her palms.

"No regrets, Tyler. None."

At his name on her lips, Mac shuddered. He closed his eyes and bore her down to the bed, groaning as he fastened his mouth to hers. His lips sucked, pressed, and teased until she opened for him and took his tongue. A jet of white-hot need replaced the loose, sated warmth that had been soaking through her body. Maggie hitched her legs up around his waist, rocking into him with a sigh.

Mac's kisses moved to her jaw, down her throat, down her chest, lower still. His fingers dipped between her legs and circled her with just enough pressure to make her gasp. She rocked her hips up, and his fingers slipped into her wet core. Maggie moaned, and Mac answered with a muffled growl against her breast. He bit down gently, sucking the soft curve into his mouth. It would bruise later, but all it did for now was make her blood hotter. She liked the idea of Mac marking her body. More than that, she liked the idea of someone else seeing it and knowing who had put it there.

Maggie dragged his head back to hers and bit down on his lower lip. Mac's free hand came up to clutch the sheets next to her head. His other hand left her center and tilted her hips so that his hard cock was right at her entrance. All it would take would be a shift of his hips—or hers—and he'd slide right in.

His tongue stroked against her, trading deep, wet kisses as he held himself still against her. Funny how she didn't mind his tongue sliding against hers. She didn't mind the wet slip of saliva. She wasn't a bad kisser at all, she just needed to be kissing Mac. Maggie canted her hips, and they shared a groan as the tip of him slid into her wet heat.

"Fuck," Mac hissed and shifted his hips, pushing himself deeper. His voice was guttural, agonized with a hint of awe.

Maggie couldn't resist her smile spreading at his harsh word. She bit his shoulder and wiggled under him, hoping to goad him into action. Mac pushed the rest of the way in and then stilled as she tightened around his intrusion. Nothing had ever felt better.

"Fuck," he breathed.

"Yes, please." Maggie rolled her hips until his pelvis bumped against her clit. Her pussy clenched down around him again.

"Condom, baby," he said, hips stuttering against hers. "I can't believe I didn't—You feel so good—couldn't wait—"

Maggie dragged her brain back from the euphoric edge and palmed his cheek, forcing his eye to hers.

"Do you have one?"

Mac nodded. His hips ground against hers and both of their eyes rolled back, matching each other's moans.

"Get it."

With a shuddered breath, he pulled out and slammed around the drawer in his bedside table. He came up with a full cardboard box. Maggie watched through half-closed lids as Mac bypassed the perforated top and ripped it apart with his hands, tearing open one of the gold foil packets with his teeth. He pinched the tip of the condom and rolled it on as he took the two steps back to where she still lay, legs splayed out, wet and aching. He kneeled between her thighs, grinning down at her.

"Hold on to me, baby." Mac reached for her hands and brought them up and around his neck. He fisted his cock, lining himself up at her entrance. "I'll get you there. I promise." And then he slammed home.

Everything Maggie thought she knew about sex, Mac obliterated on the first shift of his hips. Maggie had expected a rough ride, given his entrance, but Mac favored slow thrusts that had her legs trembling over his thighs. Each time he pushed all the way to the hilt, Maggie felt the air forced out of her lungs. Mac lifted her hips off the bed as he changed their angle and the head of his cock hit something truly delicious. Maggie moaned and he bent his back to take her mouth with his, swallowing her sounds and giving her back one of his.

"Right there, baby." Another slow thrust and Maggie's vision started to white out around the edges. "We're riding that spot until you go over."

It wouldn't take long. Already tension was coiling in Maggie's abdomen, like a spring winding tighter and tighter. Any minute now she was going to snap. Any minute. Any minute. Mac looped an arm under Maggie's left thigh and lifted until her calf rested over his shoulder. The stretch helped him get impossibly deeper. His stomach rubbed against hers with each thrust, the dark hair a crisp scrape against her skin, and his pubic bone bumped her clit. He panted warm breaths over the top of her head. Maggie was losing her mind. She could feel her core clamping down around Mac as he kept his pace steady.

"Please," she moaned, head thrashing from side to side.

Right there. Right there.

There. There. There.

"I need—" Maggie gasped. Her whole body was so tight it almost hurt, her nerves skating the line between pleasure and pain. She wanted to squirm away from the colossal something bearing down on her, but she also wanted to charge it head on. It had never felt like this before. The throb. The heat. Not even by herself had she ever reached this height of need.

"I know." Mac's voice was so low she barely heard him over the sound of her pulse pounding in her ears. "I've got you." He dropped one hand between their bodies and let two fingers circle her clit once, twice.

On the third circle he thrust his hips hard and Maggie's body splintered outward.

She shuddered in Mac's arms, her core pulsing as he held still, buried in her core. He watched her with hungry, heavy-lidded eyes that sent a fresh wave of shudders through her sated body. His fists clutched handfuls of his comforter next to her head. Every muscle in his body strained with the effort to stay immobile, and it was automatic for Maggie to lift one arm—despite her muscles feeling like strands of cooked linguine—and stroke her hands up and over his quivering biceps.

"Thank you," she said when she had enough air back to talk. Mac was still seated deep inside her, the thin line of his control almost visible. At her words, he chuckled, and the movement shifted their hips, sending sparks flowing back through her bloodstream.

"Oh sweet girl," Mac dropped his head until he could drag the tip of his nose up the side of her cheek to her temple. He pressed a kiss there, the move completely at odds with the way their bodies interlocked. "We aren't done."

Maggie didn't have time to wonder what he'd meant before Mac rolled to his back and brought her with him. She braced her hands on the soft hair covering his chest and sat up, trying not to moan at the way he filled her from below. Mac was breathing hard through his nose, nostrils flaring. His cheeks hollowed out as he clenched his teeth. He shifted his hips under her, and Maggie's body shook.

"Yes, Maggie?"

She nodded and let instinct guide her hips in a small circle. Mac threw his head back on a groan.

"Take what you need baby, I'm not sure how long I've got," he said and his hands bracketed her hips, helping move her in a quick back-and-forth rock. Each slide ground her hips against the base of his erection and Maggie could feel the climb begin again at breakneck speed.

Maggie had slept with a few men, and she'd read enough toe-curling smut that she'd thought she'd understood sex. Mac was nothing like she'd ever imagined and she was a little worried that the fullness of him inside her, the rasp of his hands against her skin, and the pleasure that melted her organs like butter on a hot day, was fast becoming an addiction. She could want this every day. It wasn't just Mac's body and technique. He also paid attention to every move that made her shift, sigh, or smile. Then he repeated them. Frequently.

It was also the heat and affection that poured out of his dark eyes. The way his lips pressed soft kisses against any part of her he could reach. How he whispered curse words like prayers. By the time Mac slid his hand down to touch her, his thrusts deep and urgent, she was so ready that she splintered for the fourth time and dragged him over the edge with her.

He dropped to the bed beside her, panting. They lay there, catching their breath. Their arms pressed against each other, sticky with sweat. Maggie shivered against the side of Mac's body, and he turned to look at her, the corner of his mouth tipped up into a smile. It was a sweet look for Mac, one that made the tingles flare up again. Now that his hands weren't perusing her body, she was uncertain about what to do next.

"I should get going," Maggie said as Mac unrolled the condom and dropped it into the trash can by his desk.

"You don't have to." He was standing in front of her as she sat on the edge of the bed. He cupped her face in his hands and touched his forehead to hers. "You can stay."

Maggie was tempted to do just that. With him smiling down at her and his hands against her skin, the heat was back, and the lack of oxygen felt exciting. One of Mac's hands slid under her hair at her nape, his fingers massaging into her scalp. She wanted to crawl under the mussed sheets of his bed, breathe in his pine and iron scent from his pillow, and skip the talking parts that were coming next.

"I shouldn't." Maggie closed her eyes as her head flopped back into the steady pressure of Mac's hand. Even as she said the words, she was already thinking about the next time she could see him again.

"You're right," Mac dropped a sweet kiss onto her parted lips. "Too much, too soon. Next time."

Maggie kissed him back, her whole body flushing at the idea that Mac wanted to do this again.

"I don't want to scare you off." His next kiss brushed the column of her throat. "I also don't want you to think I would take advantage of you."

"I don't think that," Maggie said, "but I wasn't planning on an overnight. I have work tomorrow, and some edits I need to work on."

"I haven't asked," Mac said, frown reappearing. He picked up Maggie's discarded leggings and undies, helping her get dressed. "How's your book going? Make any headway on your characters?"

Maggie let Mac pull her shirt and his sweater over her head. Her bra hadn't been located, but if he wanted to keep it, that was kind of hot, and she wasn't complaining.

"It was slow going," she said, "but I think I'm getting somewhere now. Actually, I want to go home and write a little tonight."

"Really?" Mac let her stand, but pulled her into a firm hug the minute she was on her feet. Maggie nodded, head tipped back to look up at Mac's handsome face and kind eyes.

"I was struggling because I didn't understand real chemistry before, but I definitely get it now."

"We were so hot we're making it into your book?" Mac asked.

"Sort of. We assumed I struggled to write good relationships because I didn't understand them. I dated Dean, and I thought I'd understand since I thought I loved him for forever, but the chemistry wasn't there."

"We?"

"Audrey and me. She thought I should try for some white-hot attraction, and well..." She gestured between their bodies. "I think we both know how that ended." She grinned up at him, not embarrassed at all about how quickly he'd set her body on fire and how much she'd liked it. Liked him.

"So, this was planned research?"

Maggie studied Mac's face. His smile had dimmed, but he hadn't moved away from her, arms still wrapped around her waist.

"More like an opportunity I couldn't pass up. You're safe." She wanted to add, *You're sexy, and kind, and I think about you more than I should, and you're still safe because you won't ever hurt me.* "We're friends, and—"

"Friends," Mac said, with a nod.

To be honest, Maggie thought of Mac as much more than that. She'd planned on saying so before he cut her off. Maybe he wasn't ready for more yet. She could respect that. Love was a complicated and terrifying emotion. She thought she'd been in warm, comfortable love before, and she'd been so wrong it was almost laughable. It was almost inconceivable that she was sure she'd tumbled head over heels into the same scary emotion for Mac this quickly. So maybe he was right to protect them both and cut her off before she could finish. Because she was pretty sure she was in love with Mac, but she also knew she considered him one of her friends.

Maggie didn't have a lot of friends. She had Audrey, Dean, and Shay. It was only recently that she'd started seeing Mac as one of her them and not just the brother of a friend. She genuinely liked Mac. Genuinely cared for him. He'd snuck his way into her inner sanctum, and she now considered him part of her closest circle. Part of the small group that she'd go to hell and back for.

"...ank you," Maggie smiled up at him. "Tonight ...than I could have imagined, but I do have to get home so I can write while everything is fresh in my brain."

And because if she stayed any longer she'd slide tackle him back onto the bed, and she couldn't be greedy after three orgasms.

"I'll walk you down." Mac pulled on a pair of sweatpants and grabbed a t-shirt from his dresser.

Cal's friends had left when they made it down the stairs, but Audrey sat at the kitchen counter while Cal dug something out of the fridge. Maggie prepared herself for a public interrogation, but Audrey just smiled and sipped her drink.

"Thanks for joining us," Cal said, grin splitting his face. He was holding a Tupperware filled with rice and broccoli.

Maggie fought the blush and looked at Mac. His glare was back in place and trained on his younger brother.

"Don't." The sound of his voice sent shivers along Maggie's spine. She wanted to lean back into him and bask in the tiny flips her stomach wouldn't stop performing.

"I'm just saying Maggie disappeared for a long time. Then you come back together, both smiling..."

"How can you tell?" Audrey studied them.

"Tell what?" Cal asked.

"That Mac's smiling?"

"It's obvious. He's less growly, and his lips are all twitchy."

Audrey and Cal both stared at Mac as if he were on display.

It was time for Maggie to go, just to avoid the awkward stare down. Eventually Audrey would turn it on her, and what was she supposed to say? *Sorry I just got over my misinterpreted feelings for your brother and jumped into bed with your boyfriend's brother?* Was there a term for women who went after brothers? A fratophile? Was that a thing?

"Well," she said brightly, "thank you for everything, Mac. I'll see you soon."

Mac flinched, dropping his eyes to the floor.

"You better text me back," Audrey yelled as Maggie hightailed it to the front door and down the driveway to her car.

♡

The words flowed out of Maggie's fingertips almost faster than she could type them. She supposed it helped that she was exploding with feelings. Maggie could see the sparks igniting between Jenna and Luke on the page. When he pulled Jenna in for a kiss, Maggie could feel the touch of Mac's hands on her back and his lips against hers. Her heart pounded right along with her characters as she rewrote the first time their eyes met. She was excited about her fictional world and fictional people again. Mac had given her a gift even better than orgasms, and he'd given her those, too.

THE TROPE

Her skin flushed remembering Mac's eyes boring into her as if she were the most fascinating woman on the planet. Had they moved quickly? Yes. Did she regret it? No. She regretted not staying and seeing where the rest of the night would have taken them. Her phone buzzed on her desk, drawing her attention away from daydreams and memories hot enough to scald her internal organs.

Audrey:
Text me everything, bitch!

Audrey:
Right now.

Audrey:
Did you ride him during the entire Avengers movie? Because Ted, Ryan, and Josh didn't leave until the end and you stayed upstairs the whole time.

Audrey:
He looked much happier than he normally does.

Audrey:
Hello? Hello?!?!?!?

Maggie:
I'm not talking about this. Not tonight.

> **Audrey:**
> *Fine. We'll ask Mac.*

> **Maggie:**
> *Fine. Go for it.*

Maggie didn't wait for a response from Audrey. She doubted they'd actually pester Mac into sharing the details, but even if they did, Mac was a trustworthy guy. Her friends cared about them both. Nothing was going to dampen her good spirits tonight. She was too happy with how the night turned out. Too relaxed. Too satisfied.

"It was a good night," Maggie said to her Jane Austen duck, running her fingertips over the plastic wing and tiny book. She couldn't wipe the smile off her face, and she didn't particularly want to. With her nerve-endings buzzing, Maggie couldn't resist sending a quick message to Mac. She'd been texting him most evenings.

> **Maggie:**
> *Hey. Thank you again for tonight. And I'm sorry if Audrey and Cal drive you nuts.*

His response took over an hour to come through.

THE TROPE

Mac:
It's fine. What are friends for?

CHAPTER TWENTY

Maggie couldn't resist the pull of Mac's forge when she stopped by the house for girls' night. It had been five days since she'd seen him, and if she were being honest, the lack of his presence was starting to get to her. Usually they ran into each other at the shop, or she'd see him in the coffee shop.

He's just busy, she told herself as he sent her fifth call to voicemail and left her twelfth text unread. *He dropped off four blades yesterday after you left. That's a lot of time and effort, not to mention his classes. Aren't finals coming up?* Even with logical Maggie making an appearance, she couldn't shake the idea that something was very wrong.

She could hear the whine of the grinder as she parked her car. It was still early enough and light enough for Mac to work without disrupting the neighbors. Maggie closed her car door and speed walked around the back of the house. Her heart beat faster at just the prospect of seeing him again.

Mac's back was to her, the shed door open wide, and the flame from his forge splashing reds and oranges along his brawny forearms. Today's Henley was navy blue, and it fit his solid back and arms like a second skin. Her own skin tightened over her bones as she watched him work, especially when she let her gaze drift to the firm swell of his ass in the dark denim he always wore. He had on ear protection and a pair of clear goggles, and Maggie watched as he methodically drew the metal back and forth along the spinning sander. Sparks sizzled off the blade, and Maggie paused, heart in her throat. Mac didn't even flinch.

He held the blade out in front of him, nodded, and set it down on one of his tables. Mac turned, headphones still over his ears, and froze as his eyes met Maggie's. His gaze dropped to her mouth, and she watched as his pupils spread, almost covering his dark irises. His own lips parted, and Maggie couldn't stop the small smile that curved her own.

"Hi," she said as Mac pulled his headphones off.

She immediately wanted to plant her face in her hands. All she could come up with was "hi?" Had his butt fried her brain cells?

She tried again. "I haven't seen you in a few days and—" *I missed you? I want you again? I feel like you're avoiding me? I think I love you.* "I wanted to say—"

"Hi?"

Maggie nodded.

"Okay then," Mac said, his gaze still fixed on her mouth.

Mac wasn't exactly verbose, but something about this conversation felt off. Where was the little half smile that usually tipped up the corner of his lips? Where was the pink that tinged the skin of his cheeks? He used more words with Audrey, for god's sake.

"Do you need something?" Mac asked.

He turned off the grinder and Maggie watched his arms flex with the movement. He grabbed a towel and wiped the sweat from his forehead. She needed him to look at her. After sleeping together, Maggie hadn't thought they needed to define their relationship, especially after he'd cut her off, but maybe she'd been wrong. She'd assumed they were a couple. That they were together. She'd thought Mac knew her well enough to know that she wouldn't have just slept with him without her heart engaged at least a little. Maybe she'd been wrong.

"I missed you," Maggie said. "I know we haven't been hanging out that long, but I like seeing you and talking to you and—"

Maggie lost the rest of her thoughts and words as Mac leaned forward and pressed his mouth to hers. Her lips were already open, and his tongue pushed inside in a proprietary sweep before tangling with hers. One of his hands snaked around her waist and pulled her up against his chest before sliding down to grip her butt. His lips were firm and dry, and everything about him was hot from the forge, so the inside of his mouth was a cool caress in comparison.

Maggie lifted on her toes and pressed closer to him, catching his groan with her mouth as they traded slow, wet kisses back and forth. She could feel him hardening against her belly, and heat tripped through her veins as she wrapped her hands up and around his neck. She carded them through his hair, holding his face to hers.

His lips slid from her mouth and pressed little nips and suckles to her jaw, her neck, her exposed collarbone. She was damp and achy between her thighs. Maggie wasn't sure if wearing jeans had been a horrible idea, since there was an extra layer keeping Mac from pressing into her, or if they'd been a wonderful one because if she shifted her hips just right, the center seam pressed on all her good bits.

Maggie lifted her leg to wrap around Mac's waist. The toe of her sneaker snagged on a hammer he had on his workstation. It clattered to the ground, with a bang that echoed in the tiny forge.

Mac froze against her. For a heartbeat she thought he would kiss her again, that the interruption had been momentary, but Mac unwound her hands from his neck, and pushed her away from his body.

"This isn't a safe place for—this," Mac said. "I'm sorry. I got carried away."

Maggie's smile spread to the tips of her toes. He wasn't saying no, just not here. She could work with that. It wasn't a rejection.

"Audrey is going to be looking for you." Mac picked up the fallen tool. She didn't know what it was for, just that it looked heavy and solid in his hand.

"You'll want to go inside before she finds you and tries to drag you in by your hair."

"It's fine," Maggie said, although he was right. Audrey had a scheduled program of events, and until they'd finished their movies, pedicures, and face masks, she would not have time to talk to Mac, let alone put her whole being on the line.

"Fine," Mac said. "Have you met Audrey?"

"She knows we're—"

Maggie wasn't sure how to finish that sentence. *She knows we're dating? We're lovers? We're an item?* Mac was a very private person. He'd shut down when Cal and Audrey had ribbed them in the kitchen after the best sex of her life. She'd avoided discussing their relationship with anyone else because she knew he wouldn't like it. She defaulted to the last relationship definition he'd seemed comfortable with.

"She knows we're friends," Maggie said. "I didn't tell her anything, but she won't think it's weird that I came to say hi to you."

Mac's face had gone pale under his dark beard. His eyes were a cold flash beneath furrowed brows. "You did more than say hi," he said, and Maggie blushed. "And we aren't friends."

That was blatantly ridiculous. Poor, sweet, idiot. Of course they were friends. Possibly best friends. She loved Audrey, always would, but there were some things that she felt the most comfortable sharing with Mac. She trusted him to listen to her, to support her, to care about her. The fact that she was in love with him was a completely separate facet of their relationship. He didn't have to love her back, not yet, but they were both friends.

"I think we need to talk about what happened the other day." Maggie tried to catch Mac's eyes. "I think I made a mistake getting carried away the way I did, and I owe you an apology."

When his fingertips had been smoothing against her skin, she'd heard him say something about plans and waiting, and her libido had jumped the rails. He'd lit her up like a set of fireworks and Maggie had felt powerless against the pull of his hands and his mouth and his cock.

"Don't fucking apologize." Mac's voice snapped like a whip and Maggie flinched. "Fuck, Maggie."

Mac raked a hand through his hair and then reached for her. His fingers shook until he clenched them into a fist. Maggie slid her hand over his and squeezed.

"It's okay," she said, trying to keep her voice soothing and calm. "You've been working a lot. I saw the knives you dropped off at the store. You normally bring them when I'm there, so I know your schedule must be packed."

"I'm fine." Mac brought his arms up to wrap loosely around her waist, even as he continued to stare at a spot over her shoulder. "I'm sorry I yelled."

"Do you want to talk about it?" Maggie asked. "Friends support each other, so if there's anything I can—"

"No thank you," Mac said and dropped his hands, stepping away from her.

He still wouldn't look at her, and the burn of unshed tears stung the backs of her eyes.

If he'd shoved his bare hand into her chest cavity and ripped her heart out in his bloodied fist like Mola Ram in *The Temple of Doom*, it would have hurt less. Maggie bit back a sound she was certain would have been a sob and tried to blink the tears away, too. At the strangled sound, Mac's eyes shot to hers, concern bleeding through them before they went blank again.

"What?" she asked, keeping her voice steady through sheer force of will.

"I'm not your *friend*, Maggie." Mac's voice cracked, and his gaze couldn't stay on hers. "I don't want to be. I never will be, and I never wanted to be. Got it?"

The tears she was holding on to were teetering on the edge. Mac's eyes flitted back to her face as one broke free and slid over her cheek. Out of the corner of her eye, Maggie saw Mac clench his hands into white-knuckled fists. She wrapped her arms around her middle as a sort of armor. Another tear joined the first in tracking down her cheeks. Mac stepped closer to her. Maggie stepped back.

"I'm sorry. I wish I'd known how you felt before everything the other night. I wouldn't have—I thought we liked each other. I thought we were—I don't—" Maggie blinked back more rapidly forming tears. There was no more heat in her veins. Her blood was ice cold.

"I should have never touched you," Mac said, eyes closed to avoid looking at her.

THE TROPE

That was that, then. No need to stand around dripping tears onto his work boots. There was nothing to talk about, not that Maggie could breathe past the vice squeezing her ribs. Mac was looking at her now. He was saying something, but she couldn't hear him over the roaring in her ears. She tried to focus on his mouth to read his lips, but her vision swooped in a dizzying swirl. Her heart beat inside her chest in an aching staccato. Her entire chest hurt with each thud. She tried to swallow, and it was like a mass had lodged in her throat.

Mac turned away from her as if he were shouting something to someone else. Maggie fought through the pain radiating from her heart. Was she dying? This felt like a heart attack.

Audrey's blonde head appeared in her line of vision, her mouth moving too. Maggie tried to shut her eyes, anything to block out the panic. She felt a warm weight grip her wrist, and long fingers interlace with hers. Maggie lifted her head to look at her best friend.

"Five things you can see," Audrey said, voice firm, crouched in front of her. When had Maggie ended up on the floor?

One, Audrey's moss green eyes. Two, the dark spot on the concrete where one of her tears had fallen. Three, the red headphones, thrown over the top of a workbench. Four, the weathered wooden handle of a mallet that lay on the floor. Five, a crumpled yellow sticky note with Mac's dark handwriting just visible.

"Good girl," Audrey said. "Four you can feel."

One, the sweat beading on her bare arms. Two, the scratch of the tag at the neckline of her shirt. Three, the warmth of Audrey's fingers intertwined with hers. Four, the cool press of the floor against her bare legs.

"Three you can hear."

One, Audrey's calm and clear voice. Two, the sound of a car engine turning over. Three, a dog from a few houses down the block.

"You're doing great. Two things you can smell."

One, the lingering scent of propane and metal from Mac's forge. Two, the floral and woodsy musk of Audrey's perfume.

"One thing you can taste."

One, salt from a tear that caught on the edge of her lips. Suddenly she was mortified that her one thing she could taste was always tears, but the panic attacks always made her cry. Just another fun side effect to deal with.

"I'm okay," Maggie said, willing her pulse to even out. "Sorry."

"You never have to apologize for that," Audrey said and squeezed her hand tight.

Maggie looked around Mac's forge. She didn't remember sitting down, but she was crumpled on the floor, Audrey sprawled out next to her. Mac was gone. She took a deep breath and pushed down the stab of pain of realization. He'd left her on the floor while she fell apart.

"Let's get you up," Audrey said. She dusted off the legs of her jeans and offered Maggie a hand to lever her to her feet. "We'll go inside, grab some food, and watch that dating show we love. I'm pretty sure Will is going to pick Jane."

Audrey looped her arm in Maggie's and slowly pulled her out of the converted garage. She stopped to close the rolling door and then continued on to the back door of the house. A quick peek showed Mac's car was gone, and Maggie felt her tears prick against the backs of her eyes again. She'd been holding on to the hope that maybe he was in the house waiting for her.

"How'd you find me?" Maggie asked, anything to take her mind off of the implosion of her life.

"Oh, sweetie." Audrey pulled her in for a squeeze. "Mac got me."

Maggie couldn't stop the tears from flowing again.

Audrey pushed her hair back out of her face. "You can tell me whenever you're ready."

CHAPTER TWENTY-ONE

Two hours later, Maggie woke up on Audrey's couch, bathed in the gentle glow of the television screen. She blinked a few times, trying to remember how she'd made it inside, and felt the couch shift under her body. A soft knit blanket was wrapped around her shoulders and Maggie freed her hand as Audrey held out a glass of water.

"Eat," Audrey said, and traded the water glass for a chocolate chip cookie the size of Maggie's head. Maggie examined the cookie in her hand. "It's not poisoned. It's from Mac."

That brought Maggie's head up. Her last memory of Mac was cold, dead eyes, mouth set into a firm line as he told her that sleeping with her had been a mistake. As he told her they weren't friends. And still the thought of him, frosted over and untouchable, turned her heart over in her chest.

"Mac?" Maggie asked as Audrey guided her hand to her mouth.

"He left literal tire tracks in the driveway when he went to get it for you. He left it in the kitchen while you were sleeping."

"He's here?" If he was, Maggie should probably go.

Audrey shook her head. "He had to go stop by his office and finish grading some papers or something like that. I'm pretty sure he sleeps in his desk chair sometimes because some nights he doesn't come back. I'm surprised he left, actually. I don't think I've ever seen Mac so torn up."

"I messed up." Maggie's voice came out a whisper and Audrey leaned in to hear better. "Mac and I had sex," Maggie said, knowing it would get Audrey's attention. "It was fantastic and heart stopping, and I was looking for ways to set up a round two when he turned frosty."

"That doesn't sound right." A frown had replaced Audrey's smile. "Cal says he's besotted, enchanted, in love. The sex was a given—hello, you missed an entire movie behind a locked door—but I was sure you guys walked out of that room in a relationship. What happened right before he iced over?"

Aside from multiple orgasms? Aside from feeling her soul vibrate while he pushed into her body? Aside from the way his eyes softened as he'd pulled her pants up her legs?

"We were talking about my book, about the plan you and I had to help get the romance back on track."

Audrey closed her eyes and lay her head back against the couch cushions. She looked so much like Dean that, for a millisecond, Maggie lost track of where she was and which Crandall sibling she was talking to.

"Is it possible that he thought you only slept with him for research?" Audrey asked, eyes still shut. "That would be enough to piss off anyone."

"I told him it wasn't like that. That I'd wanted to sleep with him because he was safe and we were friends and—"

"And you used that word? Friend? Dammit, Maggie!" Audrey groaned and *thunked* her blonde head back against the couch several times.

Maggie frowned. Maybe if people would stop cutting her off, they'd know she was going to say friends *and*. Friends and more. Friends and lovers. Friends and soulmates.

"We are friends, Audrey." Maggie spoke slowly, enunciating each word.

"No you aren't," Audrey said back, just as slowly. Maggie opened her mouth to protest, but Audrey waved her hand through the air, stopping her. "You're not friends, Maggie, because Mac is in love with you."

Maggie felt like she'd been slapped in the face. She'd thought Mac cared about her, at least a little, but his performance today had really thrown a wrench into that assumption. Audrey had to be mistaken, too. If Mac loved her, why hadn't he said anything? He'd had more than enough opportunities.

"No," Maggie said. "He doesn't."

Audrey rolled her eyes, muttered something that sounded a lot like "fucking dumb ass," and excused herself to the kitchen. She returned with a bottle of butterscotch schnapps and two shot glasses. She also returned with Cal.

"I needed reinforcements," Audrey said and Cal nodded, taking a seat on the loveseat and cracking open the beer he'd brought with him. Audrey exaggerated the motion of looking from her boyfriend to her best friend, and back again. She cleared her throat.

Cal didn't seem to notice.

"Tell her," Audrey said as she poured two shots of honey-brown liquid and slid one in front of Maggie.

Maggie threw back the sugary sweet schnapps, the heat burning down to her stomach. Audrey immediately refilled her glass, but didn't pressure her to drink it.

"Mac told Cal about how wonderful you were the first day the two of you met," Audrey said. "We were moving, and you were carrying one of my boxes. You tripped, and Mac watched you slip right down the entire flight of stairs. When you got to the bottom, you first checked to make sure the box full of my stuff was okay, and then you laughed."

"He talked about your laugh for weeks," Cal said.

"He wanted to ask questions, but didn't want to come across as creepy. The day he unknowingly stumbled into Tattered Cover, he came home a completely different man."

"I thought you told him I worked there," Maggie said, and Audrey shook her head.

"I wouldn't do that. What if he'd been a stalker? No offense, baby." Audrey leaned over to pat Cal's hand.

He shrugged. "No, that was pure coincidence. He didn't ask about your schedule, but he was paying attention. He started dropping stuff off while you worked. He didn't ask about your favorite foods, but he started cooking vegetarian options after the second time you ate here. If I mentioned you were sick, Mac had a container of homemade veggie soup waiting for me to bring to you. If I mentioned you'd had a hard week, then he had a book I should drop off."

He must have thought of her almost constantly, and yet Audrey never let on.

"He asked me not to say anything," Audrey said. "He just wanted you taken care of, but he didn't want to scare you off. I thought it was sweet, and I thought it was possible he had a crush, but then the night you talked to Dean, Cal pulled me aside to tell me that Mac is in love with you."

"He was pissed that I was thinking of setting you up with my friends," Cal said. "He wanted me to be sure I picked people who would be respectful and would listen if you said 'no.' I wanted you to pick him."

"We both did," Audrey smiled reassuringly. "We both kept trying to push you two together."

"Without being obvious about it." Cal set his empty beer down on the coffee table.

"And then I started fake dating Dean."

Cal frowned, glancing between Audrey and Maggie. "Did you say fake?"

Audrey refused to meet Cal's eyes.

"So my brother has been ripping his own heart out, thinking she was in love with someone else when it was all just a joke?" Cal's voice was harsher than Maggie had ever heard.

Maggie didn't think it was a good time to mention that she'd thought she'd been in love too. It wasn't like she'd gone out of her way to hurt Mac. She'd barely known him. She hadn't known he was an option to date. She hadn't known he was interested. She wasn't sure it would have mattered.

"Nobody was playing a prank, Cal," Audrey hissed. "Grow up. It's not Maggie's fault that Mac didn't have the balls to say something to her."

Maggie felt like she couldn't breathe. Her stomach rolled, displeased with the cookie she'd offered it. A dull throb was starting in her temples. Having Mac's feelings laid bare in front of hers was a lot to process, and she was feeling a little guilty that it wasn't Mac who was telling her everything. It felt like an invasion of privacy. The stakes felt too high, like one misstep would send her spiraling down several flights of stairs into a deep, dark abyss.

"Why didn't he just say something?" Maggie asked, and immediately two sets of eyes flashed to her.

Cal leaned forward to pin her in place with his stare. It was so much like Mac's that she sucked in a breath. "Please understand that I wouldn't share this with anyone but you, and I'm only doing this because you love my brother. He's probably messing this up just as much as you are, and frankly, of the two of you, you're the only one I trust to listen to reason."

"I will." Maggie said quickly. "I want to fix this. I'm just scared there's nothing to fix." She took a deep breath. "He made it sound like I was a one-night-stand, not even worth friendship."

"What?" Audrey shot to her feet, anger pouring from her like steam. "That motherfu—"

Cal groaned and dropped his head to his hands. "My brother is a dumbass and apparently an asshole, but hopefully a forgivable one." He took Maggie's hands in his. "Mac is not now and never has been good in social situations. He just doesn't care what people think or say, and he has that scowl honed to perfection, so most people leave him alone. I only remember one other person who ever had him tied up in knots before you, and even she was small beans compared to you."

"I don't need to know." Maggie tried to pull her hands away. This was private. Mac would tell her if, and when, he was ready.

Cal shook his head.

"She friend-zoned him, Maggie." Cal said and when Audrey opened her mouth, frowning, he added. "I know that most guys in the friend-zone deserve it because men aren't entitled to anything from their female friends, but this was different. She let him do things for her, bring her gifts, drive her places, she let him take care of her. I was a freshman, and they were seniors, but I even heard the rumors about how into her he was.

"He asked her to prom, one of those big promposal things everyone did in the early two-thousands, because she said she needed a grand gesture. She turned him down flat in front of half the school. She said she'd never go to prom with someone who was just a friend. She needed to go with someone she was actually attracted to. Someone she could actually care about."

Maggie didn't want to hear more. How awful that must have been for Mac. He'd put himself out there in a way she knew was so anathema to him, only to have it thrown in his face in such a cruel way. She wanted to ring that bitch's neck. The similarities also weren't lost on her. Once again, Mac had been loving her, taking care of her, showing her through little acts of service from a distance, and everyone seemed to know. And what had she done? Told him they were friends. As if none of that other stuff mattered. As if she didn't love him back. He'd obviously seen his past staring him in the face, and had lashed out like a cornered animal.

Maggie supposed it didn't matter if she'd done it on purpose. Calling Mac her friend had ruined the tenuous relationship they'd been building. She could stomp her feet and cry about how he'd cut her off, how he'd stopped her from saying that they were friends and that she wanted to be more. At the end of the day, he'd been hurt, and he'd tried to protect himself.

And then when her world imploded, he'd gotten Audrey and gotten her a cookie, but hadn't trusted himself to be around her.

"Do you think of Mac as your friend, or as something more?" Cal asked.

That was the question of the hour, wasn't it?

Why did she have to pick one or the other?

Why couldn't it be both?

Why couldn't he be her friend, possibly her best friend, and...

"I'm in love with him." Maggie said, shifting her gaze from Cal to Audrey, and then to her own hands in her lap. "How do I fix this?"

"Tell him," Cal said, "and after you kiss and make up, make sure he apologizes to you, too. He acted like an ass, and I'll kick his if he doesn't make it right."

CHAPTER TWENTY-TWO

The only upside to the chasm that seeing Mac had left in its wake was the fact that Maggie's revisions were speeding forward. As an author, she would be the first to say that negative emotions were better than no emotions, but now that she was sitting with the ache in her chest, she had to admit she'd never experienced anything quite like this before. Every part of her wanted to repudiate the idea that Mac had only been after one thing. Cal had all but sworn that Mac hadn't meant what he'd said, but as a week passed without a message, a text, or a call, she had to admit her confidence was waning.

She raised her hand to rap on Dean's front door with her muddled thoughts swirling. Maggie had avoided his two calls a day, and she'd broken their deal to be exclusive. She definitely owed Dean an explanation. Probably a fruit basket, too. Or a cheese platter. She wasn't sure about the fruit, but he could at least eat cheese. Maybe a sampler of beef jerky.

Dean opened the door shirtless, rubbing a navy blue towel over his firm, smooth chest, and Maggie sighed as she realized not a single atom of her body tingled in response.

"Babs," Dean said, surprise pulling his brows together, but he was gentlemanly enough to step back and usher her into his apartment. "I called."

He shut the door behind her, and Maggie winced, glad he was standing at her back. "I know," she said. "I'm sorry."

Dean waved her off and tossed the towel up on his spotless countertops. "I was just worried about you. Even Audrey says she hasn't seen you this past week."

That was true. Avoiding Dean had been relatively easy if she didn't pick up his calls. They didn't frequent the same spaces. Blowing off her normal get-togethers with Audrey had been trickier and required a careful balance of avoidance and misdirection. She was still wracked with guilt about both. But she hadn't figured out how to talk to Mac yet, and until she did that she was avoiding Audrey and her game of twenty-questions.

Dean stepped into his bedroom and returned with a shirt. Maggie bit back a laugh as she recognized it from their soggy hike. The universe wouldn't even give her a break here, would it? He started his deluxe coffee maker and pulled two glass tumblers from his pristine overhead cabinets and set them on his marble countertops. Maggie couldn't comprehend how to start that machine if her life depended on it. Dean pressed the buttons without even looking.

"You look like you could use a pick-me-up," Dean said as he added tiny cubes of ice to each glass. "I figured you'd prefer one of your sweet coffee confections to alcohol, but if you want a drink, I've got a stocked bar."

Neither alcohol nor caffeine was particularly soothing, but Dean was right. She'd much prefer the coffee. She watched as he added almond milk to one glass along with a healthy dose of sweetener. He poured the fresh coffee into both glasses and mixed them with two metal straws. If he had to be fancy, at least he was environmentally conscious. Maggie reached for the milk-laden drink and Dean batted her hand away, reaching into his fridge for a silver canister and added a healthy dose of homemade whipped cream to the top of her drink.

"What, no chocolate shavings?" Maggie joked, but Dean grinned and added a handful of tiny chocolate pieces to her coffee even as he rolled his eyes.

"We should talk," she said.

He grabbed both of their drinks and brought her to the living room. "Sit down, before you fall down," he said. "I'm not mad at you, so I'm not sure why you look ten seconds from going out the window."

The window was a good idea, actually. She'd been calculating how long it would take to get to the front door, down the flights of stairs, and out to her car, and if she could do it before he caught her. She'd seen him run and was pretty sure it was a definite no.

"You can tell me anything." Dean smiled, his green eyes soft on her face. "You know I love you."

"Yeah." Maggie said. "That's kind of what I wanted to talk to you about."

Dean raised one of his golden eyebrows at her, but said nothing. Maggie took a deep breath. Her stomach was rolling, but the anxious pitch was easily distinguishable from the heated twist it so often did around Mac. This was the roil of nerves making themselves known. Maggie took a steadying breath.

"When I first asked you to fake date me, I had an ulterior motive."

"I figured as much," Dean said, but his voice was gentle. "Why don't you tell me about it?"

Maggie took a deep breath and a sip of her drink. The liquid was sweet on her tongue, which helped with her nerves.

"I kind of believed I was in love with you," she said with an exhale. "I thought while we were on all these dates, you'd realize you were in love with me too, and then we'd date for real. Just like in all the romance novels."

Dean put his tumbler on his coffee table and rested his elbows on his knees. He ran one of his hands over his face, eyes wide and staring at the floor. Twice he opened his mouth and twice he closed it again without saying a word. Maggie snuck glances at him out of the corner of her eye. If she looked at him full-on, she was sure her face would flame.

"It wasn't one of my smartest moments," Maggie said as Dean leaned back against the couch. He was fidgety, eyes still wide in his classically handsome face. "I'm sorry. I wasn't honest with you from the start. I'm sorry I asked you to fake a relationship with me, and I'm sorry I avoided you instead of telling you I don't want to continue that fake relationship."

Dean looked at her. "I have some things I'll need to say, but first I need to ask, why now? Why are you done pretending with me?"

That was probably the easiest and hardest answer of all.

"I don't think we should fake a date anymore because I'm actually not in love with you at all. I never was. I love you platonically, which is completely different, even if it took me an embarrassing amount of time to figure it out." Maggie studied her shoes against Dean's gleaming hardwood floors.

Dean stood from the couch and walked to his window. It had a view of downtown and the lights from all the other buildings winked like stars in the darkening evening. Dean's reflection frowned, and he brought his hand up to rub at his temples and his forehead.

"I'm so sorry Dean." Maggie said and watched as the reflected Dean shut his eyes and rested his forehead against the window.

"What changed?" he asked, eyes still closed. "How did you figure it out?"

"It was a bunch of things. The first was what you said at the waterfall. Your version of love sounded so beautiful and powerful. It sounded right, but it didn't describe what I felt for you. Even my version of love didn't describe what I felt for you. Not really."

"And the second reason?"

"I recognized that what you had said described the way I feel about someone else."

Dean pulled away from the window, turning to lean his shoulders back against it. He studied her as if he'd never seen her before. She waited for his anger and disapproval. His lips had twisted, and he worried the bottom one with his teeth. God, he was already mad at her, and she hadn't even told him the worst part yet.

"It's Mac, isn't it?" Dean said and pushed off the window to come back to the couch.

Maggie nodded.

"That's good," Dean said. "You deserve that."

Maggie wasn't sure what that meant. Wasn't he upset? She'd manipulated him, lied to him. Was this sarcasm? "Deserve what?"

"Everyone deserves someone who looks at them, the way that man looks at you."

Maggie's whole body flushed at the comment, and her mouth dried up. She chewed on her thumbnail. "How does he look at me?"

Dean wrapped his arm around the back of the couch, his fingers lightly touching her shoulder. He tugged on the ends of Maggie's hair. "He looks at you like you're a glass of cool, clear water, and he's been wandering through the desert for days."

"That actually sounds really nice." Maggie's eyes burned.

"I'm glad you found him." Dean said, pulling her into a full side hug. "I'm glad things finally fell into place."

Dean smelled good and his hug was nice. She'd felt weird about touching him while they were fake dating, as if there was too much expectation behind each brush of their bodies. Now she remembered how nice it was to have someone wrap her up and just hold her. It was good to have his arm be a warm and solid weight over her shoulders while they sat in silence.

"I'm glad you'd told me, Maggie. I just wish I'd known all this when you first asked."

"I know." Maggie's voice was a whisper. "It wasn't fair of me to have expectations you didn't know about."

Dean took a deep breath, the movement shifting her body right along with his. She patted his rock hard stomach and looked up into his worried green eyes.

"It would never have worked, Maggie."

"I know." Maggie said. "I should have known before, but you were safe, dependable, and your looks don't hurt."

Dean didn't even crack a smile at that. Maggie frowned.

"I'm shocked you don't know," Dean said. He was frowning again, staring out into nothing. "I was sure everyone did."

Maggie's brain started working double time. Dean had said he wasn't in a relationship. Had he lied to her? Had she ruined something for him? That was a horrid thought. True, he could have explained everything to his significant other, but who would be okay with that? With their boyfriend pretending to date someone else? Potentially kissing someone else? And to make matters worse, she'd been interested in turning their pretend relationship into a real one.

Audrey must have known. How could she have said nothing about another woman?

"Know what?" Maggie ran a soothing hand down Dean's forearm. The hair there was soft and downy, a perfect contrast to the coarse feel of Mac's.

Dean swallowed before turning to her with a soft smile. "I'm gay, Babs," he said.

"Oh," she said. "How did I miss that?" Maggie couldn't remember the last time Dean had had a girlfriend, but she'd thought that was a good sign that he wasn't a player. He'd lived with Dante for a year, but Maggie had been sure the two were just roommates. Was she really that clueless? Or had her misplaced crush on him changed her perceptions, the way tinted lenses could change the color of the world? Maggie laced her fingers with Dean's and squeezed them tightly.

"I don't know." He said and squeezed back. "I'm not exactly in the closet."

"Did you have a boyfriend?"

Dean shoved a hand through his hair and laughed, but the sound was low and self-deprecating. "I don't have a boyfriend. There was someone, but it wasn't anything official. I don't date a lot."

"Why agree to help me?" Maggie asked. Surely his decision to pretend to be in a relationship with her would have caused some confusion with Dean's someone.

"You're important to me, Babs." Dean said, "And to be honest, I wasn't ready to deal with how serious things were getting with him, so a fake relationship bought me some time. I was helping my little sister's best friend, so it was heroic. I also thought it might give Mac the kick in the butt he needed to ask you out. Although it took him a lot longer than I anticipated. And Kyle wasn't worried because you—"

"Don't have a penis?"

Dean winced. "Something like that."

"Why didn't Audrey say anything?" Maggie asked. "I could have handled knowing."

Dean sighed. "Audrey is…protective. It's easy to forget, since it happened so long ago, but I had some friends react badly after Audrey accidentally outed me to them. She's a firm believer in letting me share my own story. I'm sorry you got caught in the crosshairs."

"No, I'm sorry," Maggie said again. "Did I ruin everything for you two?"

Dean shook his head. "Actually, you helped us. I don't make time for dates, I don't put thought into romance or love or feelings mostly because I don't have time, but also because I really wasn't looking for a relationship. I'm just too busy. But you needed dates. You needed time." He sighed. "I'm so sorry, Maggie, but every time we had one of our dates, I thought about how nice it would be to share them with Kyle. How right it would be to ride a Ferris wheel together, although I could do without the barfing, and run together in the park, without the spilled coffee, or hike out to the waterfall…"

"Without the Biblical flood?" Maggie offered.

Dean laughed. "I was going to say without the sprained ankle."

"It was just a twist, thank you. I probably could have walked it off."

Dean groaned, and Maggie couldn't stop her laugh.

"That day at the waterfall, before you apparently conned me into carrying you back to base, I was working through some intense feelings. I didn't see Kyle at all while we were together, but he'd been out with a mutual friend the night before, and it really messed with me. I was jealous, and scared, and you still needed me, so I offered you more time."

"And Kyle?" Maggie asked, her heart aching for Dean.

"It had been a work dinner. When we got back to town, and you hadn't given me an answer, I showed up at his door. I was a desperate, jealous, thoroughly besotted mess, and he made sure I knew it."

"Dean. I'm so—"

"So I've been groveling. He's actually coming over for dinner tonight. He said he didn't want me if I was only interested because I was jealous. And he was right, so now it's my job to show him I love him without anything getting in the way."

Maggie almost wormed her way out of staying to meet Kyle, but she was glad she didn't. Kyle was wonderful. He was a middle school art teacher, and he showed up at Dean's house in paint-splattered jeans and a short sleeve button down. His dark skin gleamed under the hallway lights. His smile was kind, and his eyes were warm. He kissed both of her cheeks when Dean introduced them, and Maggie loved him instantly. The same warm, comfortable love she got from Dean.

"I'm so glad I had time to meet you," Kyle said. His voice had a lilt like the gentle rock of waves. "I have a lot to thank you for."

Dean sat both her and Kyle down on the couch while he went to the kitchen to finish preparing dinner. Maggie struggled not to laugh, remembering when she'd tried to feed him herself, and she hadn't even cooked his meal, Mac had. The laugh died at the thought of Mac.

"Please don't thank me," Maggie said. "I selfishly demanded help from your almost-boyfriend and caused a lot of extra drama for the two of you. Not to mention I completely assumed Dean's sexuality, and that isn't fair of me either. I swear I'm usually not so self-centered."

Kyle threw his head back, laughing.

"Oh Dean, she is just a doll," he said, and Maggie blinked rapidly, wondering how she went from selfish to a doll in seconds. "Maggie, Dean loves you. He wanted to help you, and I can't blame you for being blinded by his good looks and charm. Not only that, but spending time with you helped him figure out that he wanted me. I don't mean that the way it sounded."

This time, it was Maggie's turn to laugh. "I'm still sorry, even if everything turned out well for you two."

"Didn't you get a happily ever after too?" Kyle asked. "Dean mentioned a Mac person who thinks you've hung the moon. A Mac person who was supposed to be so overcome with jealousy that he swept you off your feet?"

"Totally smitten," Dean called from the kitchen as he opened the stove to remove a tray of roasted veggies. "But no sweeping. Either he's a good guy who didn't want to poach on her happiness, or he clocked me and knew I wasn't a threat. Although you should have heard the things he said when he found out I let her fall down a mountain and sprain an ankle."

Maggie froze. "Things?" Mac had known about that? She'd been back to normal by the next day, so she hadn't thought much of the fall. It was the rain that had been the most annoying.

"He has a sixth sense about you, Babs. I swear you fell and his eye started twitching in his office."

"Are we worried about this guy? That sounds a little creepy," Kyle asked, and Dean started laughing.

"No, Mac's good people. It's romance novel stuff. I was sure that call meant they were together, and he'd found a way to unleash all his jealousy from when Babs and I were *dating*."

"Tell me everything," Kyle said. "I love a good romance."

"We're working on it," Maggie said. She didn't need Kyle's sympathetic frown to know the hitch in her voice had been noticeable. "I made some mistakes, but I'm fixing them. I, uh, slept with him, and called him my friend, then he started avoiding me, and he told me he doesn't want to be my friend at all, and we haven't been able to talk since."

"You're such a little romance author," Kyle said with a kind grin. "This is a classic miscommunication trope."

"Can you break that down for those of us that don't read?" Dean asked.

"It's exactly what it sounds like: two people who aren't hearing what the other person is saying. 'I don't want to be friends' is usually followed by 'because I want to be more.'" Kyle said.

"I'm hearing what he said," Maggie said because she was now, after Cal and Audrey translated for her, "now I just need him to hear me. Why can't he be my boyfriend *and* my best friend, dammit?"

"He absolutely can. A lot of great relationships are founded on friendship. Maybe even all of them. Now come sit down with me," Kyle patted his hip, "and I'll help you plan. I've read so many novels I can practically guess the endings. That has to count for something."

CHAPTER TWENTY-THREE

The history building wasn't too difficult to navigate, even though Maggie had never been inside. It helped that both Cal and Audrey had given her directions, and she'd already asked two separate people for help once she had arrived. Cal had also come through with her scheduling questions, so assuming she didn't get too lost, she'd get to Mac's office at the perfect time.

Maggie stepped along the linoleum, her nerves leaving her bouncy and on edge. She'd chosen her outfit carefully: a pleated tennis skirt and the oversized sweater she'd never returned. It was her school-girl homage but in comfortable Maggie clothes. Her Keds squeaked on the floor and she turned down the last hallway on the left and started counting doors. She passed three rooms before stopping in front of the large wooden door with the name "T. McCoy" printed on a plaque on the adjacent wall. Underneath was his class schedule and office hours availability. Maggie checked her watch. Three... two... one... she knocked on the door.

"Come in," Mac's voice called from inside.

Maggie took a deep breath, tightened her hands around the straps of her backpack, and then reached out to push the door open. Mac was sitting behind a large wooden desk, head mostly obscured by a double computer monitor and a pile of old leather-bound books.

"Office hours just ended. Email me or come back tomorrow after one."

He didn't look up when she walked in, and she smiled. She loved him surly just as much as she loved him happy.

"Actually, Professor McCoy," Maggie said, and Mac froze in front of his computer. "I was wondering if you had a minute to talk."

Mac's head didn't whip in her direction, instead it rose by millimeters. Maggie's stomach pitched, but she recognized it as a combination of nerves and hope. The light from his screen bathed his face in a glow of blue light. He'd trimmed back his beard until it was short against his cheeks and chin. Maggie couldn't help the heat that traced her spine as she thought about how those coarse curls tickled against her inner thighs.

"Hi," she said when his eyes finally met hers. He was glowering. Not his normal frown, but a truly scary glare that gave her a moment of self-doubt.

"You shouldn't be here." Mac said and stood from his desk. He was wearing a black sweater today with his dark jeans, and Maggie couldn't stop the way her blood heated and her pulse tripped any more than she could stop needing oxygen.

"I think you're wrong." Maggie moved closer to plop herself into the seat across from Mac's desk. "Actually, I think you're wrong about quite a few things, but I also need your help, so here I am."

Mac's eyes shot to her bare thighs as she crossed her legs. "If you need help, then ask Cal, or Dean," Mac said, and Maggie had another dip in confidence.

If he was sending her to other men, then he was serious about pushing her away. Except Cal wasn't available, and even if Mac hadn't been aware of Dean's sexuality, he knew Maggie wasn't interested in him. She'd told him so. Mac was trying to throw her at men who weren't romantic options. Whether or not it was on purpose, it still meant something important, and she was going to make sure she grabbed on with both hands.

"I don't need Cal or Dean, or any other guy. It has to be you." Maggie willed her confidence back on track.

Maggie knew she looked good. She'd brushed mascara over her lashes and glossed over her lips. Her skirt was just on this side of too short and showed off her smooth thighs. Mac's sweater did little for her figure, but she hoped the combination of wearing his clothes and the school-girl references would distract him, anyway.

"What do you need?" He finally grated out, sinking back into his desk chair with a long, drawn-out sigh.

"I'm working on a paper, and I need help organizing my thoughts as I get them all out." Maggie said.

"You aren't a student here, Maggie,"

"Just hear me out."

Mac shook his head, but said, "Okay, tell me."

"I'm exploring the differences between platonic love and romantic love. My thesis is that the two not only *can* coexist, but *should* coexist." She leaned forward and toyed with the small nameplate he had on his desk. It matched the one on the door. Maggie traced the lines of the gold T.

"What are you doing?" Mac leaned forward too, his hands less than a foot from hers.

"What kind of evidence would I need to best support my argument?" Maggie asked, "What would be the most compelling?"

"Maggie." Mac swallowed, his regular frown lines furrowing between his eyebrows.

"Professor McCoy," Maggie tried to hide her smile.

He hadn't thrown her out yet, but he also didn't seem to understand what she was saying. "I teach history," Mac said, "Not writing."

"Your students write papers."

"On weapons and battles. Not love."

Maggie looked at his darling face, lips, and forehead creased in his perpetual frown. This was her last chance to get through to him, mostly because Maggie wasn't sure if she could handle another rejection. She was putting all of her faith in Cal, Audrey, and even Dean. She was also putting faith in herself.

Mac mattered to her, mattered enough to try one more time to help him understand. Maggie wasn't the type to form attractions or romantic relationships with anyone she wasn't already comfortable with. The only chance she and Mac had was because they'd become friends.

Not the friend-zone.

Not friends-with-benefits.

Friendship *and*.

Friendship and intimacy.

Friendship and respect.

Friendship and love.

If she watched him long enough, the brief hints of heat were obvious even as he shut them down with ruthless force. For a man who said little, his body was easy to read if she just paid attention. The clenched fists. The tick in his jaw. The heave of his chest. Her body could read his, too. Certain gestures, facial expressions, the tiny half smile, the crinkled eyes, and she went liquid and hot.

"The basis of my argument is this," Maggie laid her hand palm up on his desk. "I've never had romantic feelings or attraction for someone I wasn't friends with. I cannot separate the two. And I think there are other people like that too."

Mac refused to look at her. He pushed his sleeves up to his elbows and then pulled them back down. He straightened a row of pens on the top of his desk, then opened the top drawer and shoved them inside. His shoulders moved with the telltale heave of his panting breaths.

"For a long time, I thought I was in love with my best friend's older brother. He took care of me. He was kind to me. I felt special when he was around. I knew I loved him, but it took me a long time to realize I wasn't in love with him."

Maggie paused, wanting to plan her words carefully. She needed to lay the foundation and let Mac fill in the cracks all on his own. Maggie looked around Mac's office, as though all the answers would be hiding among his file cabinets or hanging with the photos on the walls.

"How did you figure it out?" Mac asked, and Maggie jolted in her seat.

She hadn't expected his question. "Oh," Maggie said, "I met someone else."

Before her eyes, Mac shut down. It wasn't the anger and harsh lines from the last time she'd misstepped. This time his body went completely still, as though he was trying to avoid being seen by her. The heaving of his chest stopped. It didn't look like he was breathing at all, and the color drained from his face. His gaze seemed trained on her face, but his eyes weren't moving, even as she bobbed slightly from side to side. He was staring right through her.

"It was actually easy to notice the differences once I paid attention. Both men made me feel loved and cared for, but only one turned me on and made me want him. Made me want only him. There was only one man I ached to see and talk to every day." Maggie tried to catch his eye again, but couldn't. She had to finish this, though, had to get it out. "It was obvious in my book, too. My original characters were falling flat because I'd based their love and their feelings off my relationship with Dean. I couldn't figure out why no one was connecting with their romance, but I realized my mistake. The love I was basing my novel on wasn't real. It wasn't romantic love. I couldn't see it because I was so sure that I knew my own heart. But now? Now my characters sizzle on the page, their love is palpable, and I swear it's because this new man, this love that I didn't see before, is so real that it's universal. Even the least romantic person on the planet can see what they have. What I have."

Mac swallowed, the bobbing of his jaw the only movement of his body. "Does he treat you well?" he asked.

Maggie nodded. "Like I'm the most important person in his life. It took me a while to recognize his love language. He's an action man, showing his love through what he does. He's the guy who always puts me first, even if it hurts him. I promised myself I'd take better care of him, too."

Mac looked like he'd swallowed one of his swords. He'd shifted his gaze down to the top of his desk, fingers slowly tracing a small divot in the wood. There were white lines bracketing the sides of his mouth, a muscle in his jaw popping as he clenched his teeth.

"One time," Maggie said, trying to keep her voice breezy and light, as though her heart weren't hammering through the front wall of her chest, "he bribed a teenage Ferris wheel operator to make sure my car would get stuck at the top of the ride. All because I told him I wanted that perfect ending. On my date with someone else."

The fingers stopped their tracing.

"Another time he spent an exorbitant amount of money on an action figure for a fandom he doesn't even like, all because I'd refused to sell it to a bigot, and he didn't want me to get in trouble."

Mac's hand clenched into a fist.

"He forfeited his place in a video game tournament just to make sure I knew I wasn't alone. Even though he'd won his round and was headed for the quarterfinals. He walked away like it was nothing, so I wouldn't feel stuck or stranded in a bar by myself. And when I did end up needing him, he came. No questions asked. And that's not counting all the gifts. The first aid kit and my umbrella go everywhere I go. The duck sits on my desk and helps me write. And the clip..." Maggie reached a hand up to touch the tiny books holding back her long hair.

"Who told you?" Mac asked.

Maggie smiled. "Is that really what you want to ask?"

"Learning those things that he'd done. That's when you knew?" Mac let his pinky brush the side of Maggie's fingers. He lifted his gaze to meet hers.

"No," Maggie said. "I knew I was in love with him when his brother and my best friend shared those stories with me, and he was the first person I wanted to share it with. I knew I was in love with him when I made the biggest mistake of my life and thought he'd never want to see me again."

She traced the T on his nameplate one more time before she pulled her hands back to her lap and stood from her chair. "I'm going to go. I'm sure you have actual students to work with."

Maggie was at the door before Mac could stand up. He was still sitting in his desk chair, eyes on the spot she'd just vacated as she pushed his door open. He was staring straight ahead as she walked out. And he didn't move when the door slammed shut behind her. Maggie didn't see what he did after that because she was too busy trying to navigate back to the parking lot while blinded by unshed tears.

Making it to her car before the first tear fell was a tremendous accomplishment. Making it home in one piece, despite the snot and sobs, was a miracle. Maggie pulled into her parking spot. She wanted to curl up under her covers and cry until the memory of Mac, sitting stone-faced and immovable, was completely forgotten under the weight of fresh thoughts and feelings.

Somehow her feet got confused and led her into the Perk-u-Later instead. Thankfully, the café was empty. Gwen stood behind the counter, wiping down the glass tops with a clean blue rag. She took one look at Maggie silhouetted in the doorway, tears stuck to her cheeks like glitter, and dropped everything.

As Gwen enveloped her in a crushing hug, drawing Maggie's face to her chest, Maggie understood why her feet had overridden her brain. She wholeheartedly approved of the decision when Gwen procured a chocolate muffin and shoved her into a large velvet chair. Instead of heading back behind the counter, Gwen took the seat opposite Maggie and reached across the small table for her hands.

"Heartbreak," Gwen said, her thumbs gently brushing Maggie's skin, "is the worst kind of agony, but it's one of the few losses that you can recover from and be even stronger in the end."

Maggie sniffled, more tears brewing at the inner corners of her eyes. She didn't know if it was heartbreak. Not yet. Mac hadn't outright rejected her, but the release of weeks' worth of intense feelings was finally catching up to her. Maggie hadn't realized just how exhausting it was, trying to navigate someone else's emotions while also exploring her own. Her plan had always involved laying her feelings down for Mac and then letting him sit with them and soak them in. Mac was a planner. He was logical, methodical. Love was complicated and messy and would definitely throw him off his axis. Maggie hadn't realized how much she'd wanted him to take her into his arms and kiss her until he hadn't done it.

"I'm okay," she said when she finally hit a break in her crying. "It wasn't what I wanted to hear, but it wasn't a 'no' either." She'd been pushing him long enough. It was time to let Mac figure some things out and take a chance putting his heart on the line, too.

"I was worried you wouldn't figure it out yourself," Gwen said. "Give Mac a little time to get there, too."

Maggie frowned. The last time she and Gwen had talked about boys, Maggie had been fake dating Dean. Maggie studied the older woman, gaze moving from her red hair pulled into two round buns to her brown clogs. This was not the first time in their history of friendship that Maggie had wondered if Gwen was clairvoyant.

"Oh, honey," Gwen said, reading Maggie's confused frown. "It's been Mac for months now, probably longer, even if you only just figured it all out."

"I think I might need another muffin." Maggie took a huge bite of the chocolate confection sitting in front of her. "If anything is going to make me feel better right now, it's sugar and chocolate all mixed together."

Gwen left the table and grabbed another plate, but this one had a plain croissant. Maggie frowned. She couldn't complain about free food, but croissants weren't exactly her favorite. Chocolate croissants would work in a pinch, but they definitely didn't outrank a double chocolate muffin bursting with giant chocolate chips and sprinkled with crunchy gems of sugar.

"Thank you," Maggie said around another bite of her muffin, and Gwen just laughed.

"It's not for you, darling," she said. Behind her, Maggie heard the café door slam open.

The tingle of awareness started at the back of Maggie's neck and spread down into her chest and deeper into her belly. She didn't need Gwen's wink to know who'd walked into the Perk-u-Later. She didn't even have to turn around. Maggie's heart started pounding like a bass drum.

Maggie kept her gaze trained on her table and her baked treat until a pair of gray boots came into view. She recognized the threadbare laces and the edge of dark denim, and she swallowed past a lump in her throat. Her delicious muffin sat like a lead weight in her stomach, and for a moment she felt the café swoop into and out of focus. It was a good thing she was sitting, or she might have fallen over.

"Maggie," he said from above her, "look at me, please."

An enormous hand came down on her little round table, palm up, as though asking for something. Maggie let her gaze roam from his open hand marked with pale calluses, up his muscled forearm with soft dark hair and tan skin, over his bicep that curved from the time he spent swinging a heavy hammer against glowing hot metal, over his smooth throat just begging for her lips, to rest on his beautiful, frowning face.

"Am I too late?" Anguish pitched his voice to a low rumble.

Maggie directed her head to shake 'no,' but her body didn't move.

"I love you," Mac said, and Maggie's tears welled up again. "I've been in love with you since the first day we met. There isn't a minute of my day that passes without you in it. There isn't a single thing I hear that I don't immediately want to share with you. I've spent so long believing that you'd never want me back, never love me back, that I took what you offered the very minute you glanced my way. I owe you an apology for that. I took everything you were willing to give, and then I was upset with you for not understanding what I wanted. For wanting something different. You said you wanted to be my friend, and Maggie, I couldn't—" He ran a shaking hand through his hair, and Maggie couldn't help but smile as it stood on end. "I couldn't be your friend, Maggie. I wanted to be more than that. I *needed* to be more than that."

"I never meant for you to think we were only friends," Maggie said. She slid her hand over his palm, letting her fingers trace the bumps of calluses and the smooth bands of scar tissue.

"I've got that now." Mac's fingers flexed as he squeezed her hand with his. "What you said in my office? It was every dream I'd never let myself have. It took me a moment to realize that you were really there, and then you were out the door and down the hall and I could have kicked myself for not catching on sooner. Please tell me I'm not too late to fix this."

Maggie shook her head.

"Words, Maggie."

"Not too late." The words felt wrenched from her very soul.

"Thank fuck," Mac breathed.

Maggie didn't know which one of them moved first, but she found her lips against Mac's in the sweetest, gentlest kiss of her life. She was still holding his face in her hands, and his palms had moved to her hips, cupping her with soft intimacy.

"I love you," Maggie whispered against his mouth. "I'm sorry it took me so long."

"I love you, too," Mac whispered back. "I'd have waited forever if I needed to."

He pulled back from the kiss, but didn't let her step away from his body.

"I want to tell you it's all smooth sailing from here, but it probably won't be," he said and pressed his forehead to hers. "I'm not great at talking about things like feelings, and I don't like many people."

"I have a lot of anxiety, and I spend hours talking to characters in my head. And I often miss things that are right in front of me." Maggie added.

"I have some hang-ups about friendships and about trusting my relationships, but I promise that they have nothing to do with you. I think you might be my best friend, Maggie. And I'd like to keep you."

"I'd like that, too." Maggie pulled his head down for another kiss.

The End

Maggie and Mac's story is over for now. If you'd like a little insight into Mac's thoughts and experiences during their journey to Happily Ever After, including the story of how they met, sign up for my newsletter at www.authorstellastevenson.com.

STELLA STEVENSON

Maggie's book—the one she wrote about Dean—is coming soon. Read on for a sneak peek of BLIND LUCK, featuring untrusting boudoir photographer Jenna, her golden construction foreman Luke, and a blind date that goes completely off the rails

Acknowledgments

There is something uniquely thrilling about being able to put your thoughts and words to the page. There is also something uniquely terrifying about sharing that story with others. This story gripped me one night with manic glee, and didn't rest until I had the first sloppy draft written and no idea what to do next. Enter a group of the most supportive, honest, and truly wonderful human beings I could ever ask for. This book would not be in this form, and I would likely still be curled up on my kitchen floor agonizing over it, without their guidance.

My first thank you is to my mother. She may prefer the classics and less romance, but that has never stopped her from reading and enjoying my work. Thank you for every phone call to detail plot, every email for basic proofreading, and for every hour you spent entertaining my kiddos so I could write. Thank you also for skimming the parts I warned you to skim and never mentioning chapters 8, 15, 18, and 19. Ever.

To my husband, I know that I basically spend all my limited free-time parked in front of a word processor, but thank you for giving me the time and space to devote to this project. I know you aren't a reader, and the idea of doing what I do sounds like the ultimate form of torture, and all that just makes It so much more meaningful when you watch the kids so I can write, talk to me about plot holes, check out 50 million cover iterations, and try not to heave when I tell you how much publishing costs. I love you beyond compare, and Mac wouldn't exist without you to inspire him.

Thank you to my brilliant critique partners Bailey and Stellina. Thank you for believing in Maggie, adoring Mac, and helping me find all the places my book could be stronger. Bailey, this book would be much shorter, a lot tamer, and significantly more boring without you. Thank you for kicking my butt when I needed you to, and for pushing me to dig deeper with my characters, my plot, and my story. Also, my life. I don't know how I would have gotten through this process without you. Stellina, your advice on fandoms, your adoration of Mac's nerdy side, and your insights into Dean, Audrey, and Cal were invaluable. I cannot express how wonderful it was to wake up to new comments and suggestions from you!

To my beta readers Stephanie, River, Sierra, Markie, Jeneane, and Tiffany, who both hyped me up and found all the little holes that needed fixing. Thank you for taking the time to read my story and help make it the best it could be. To Casey and Gen, I will never not send you my novels. Your feedback is thorough and constructive, and your love and support are uplifting.

To my editor E, thank you for not only making my words and story stronger and smoother, but for mentoring me through so much of this process. Your support and kindness went above and beyond and I feel so much more confident putting my book out into the world with your guidance.

And a special thank you to the authortok community. I cannot imagine a more supportive group. No matter what the question, someone on there has an answer that they are willing to share with the newbies like me.

Blind Luck: Sneak Peek

Even before her date arrived, Jenna Andrews knew her third blind setup of the year was going to be the worst one yet. First, she had already caught her cashmere sweater on the exposed brick wall to her left. Second, the barista had asked her to repeat herself twice when she ordered a rooibos tea with honey and she'd had to settle for green. Third, it was only the second week in January and she was preparing to make odious small talk with a relative stranger. Again.

It was probably time to tell Clem that she wasn't interested in meeting anyone right now, but Jenna's friend had found love and it was now their mission in life to make sure everyone else found it, too. Jenna tucked her slick dark hair behind her ears and tapped her blunt fingernails on the lacquered top of the cafe table. According to her watch, the one she synced to the NIST-F1 atomic clock in Boulder, her date was already five minutes late. That alone was enough to darken her mood. She didn't need to factor in the slush coating the streets, slicking the sidewalks, and soaking through her nicer pair of black boots.

"Green tea for Jen," the barista called, holding up her paper cup.

Jenna snorted a breath out through her nose, lips pursed together. She'd even spelled her name out when she placed her order. When no one else stood to take the cup, Jenna pushed her chair back and slid her legs out from under the table. Her black tights snagged on a splinter at the side of her wooden chair and she could feel the run up the back of her left thigh. Well, that was just great. She would grab her tea and go back home. This was karmic justice for allowing Clem and Frankie to play matchmaker when she wasn't interested in another relationship. Jenna ran her hands down her black suede skirt, smoothing the nonexistent wrinkles.

The cafe was straining at capacity. Between the bass line of conversation, the melody of "Frankie's Greatest Hits" playing over the speakers, and the harmony as the bell dinged every time the door slammed open and shut, Jenna didn't hear someone walk up behind her.

"So you're Jenna." The man leaning against the counter had sandy blonde hair and laughing eyes the same color as his hoodie sweatshirt.

"Lucky?"

His smile was lopsided, favoring the right where a deep dimple creased his stubble-covered cheek. He looked down at the emerald green sweatshirt where peeling white vinyl letters spelled out LUCKY HILL CONSTRUCTION.

"Luca." He held a hand out for Jenna to shake. "Luke."

Luke's hand was broad, with long blunt fingers tipped with short nails. Small round calluses marked the fleshy part where his fingers met his palm. She'd been staring too long. Luke pulled his hand back and wiped it down the front of his sweatshirt.

"Sorry." His grin showed straight white teeth.

Luke extended his hand again and Jenna slipped hers into his. She aimed for an air kiss of a handshake, the kind where she'd already been pulling back before he managed to get a real grip, but his hand was warm and his palm was dry and her own hand looked tiny wrapped in his even though Jenna was not a tiny woman. Her fingers flexed against his and the calluses she'd seen before rasped against her skin, sending a small shiver down the back of her neck.

Small lines appeared at the corner of Luke's eyes and Jenna pulled her hand back.

"I have a table over here," she said and turned on her heel, not caring if he followed her.

"Thanks," Luke said, keeping pace as she walked across the cafe. "I was a little late, I know, but it looks like you've been having fun without me."

"Excuse me?" Jenna glanced at him over her shoulder.

"You've got a hole in your tights. I assume you got it by hopping a fence or playing red rover while waiting on me."

"No," Jenna said and slid into her seat. She forgot about the sharp edge and snagged her tights again. There was not enough tea in the world to drop her heart rate.

Luke dropped into the seat across from her, his denim-clad legs stretched out on either side of the table. He wasn't invading her space, but it was impossible to ignore him sitting across from her. Luke still had his grin fixed in place. Something about his amiable smile had her feeling like a cornered cat. Spitting mad and ready to strike. That was probably a sign that she was...

"Prickly, aren't you?" Luke said as he took a sip of his drink. Jenna was sure it was black coffee overflowing with caffeine.

Jenna stiffened. She wasn't prickly. She was careful. She was on a blind date with a complete stranger. A stranger that her best friend had led her to believe was a woman. Luke, with his laughing eyes, and strong hands, and fun-poking, was very, very male. And Jenna was barely on the market for a relationship. She was decidedly off the market for a relationship with a man.

"It's okay, you know," Luke said, despite the table in front of him. He cradled his drink in his lap, carefully held between his two strong hands.

Jenna frowned.

"To be nervous on a date. Frankie didn't tell me much about you, just your name and that you'd probably be wearing black, so we're basically strangers, but I'm game to give this a shot if you are."

Jenna stopped her fingers from tapping on the table and forced her eyes to meet Luke's green ones.

"That's all Clem told you?" *She didn't mention that I said I was done with men?*

"Clem? No, Frankie set this up. She said your name was Jen, and you dressed like the Grim Reaper."

Frankie was a pain in the ass. Jenna felt her blood actually boil. There was no way Clem's fiancee called her Jen, but the grim reaper? Black was classic. Black didn't show stains. Black went with every outfit. Black was the perfect color for a photographer who was used to staying out of the limelight. And her boots were Sam Edelman, dammit.

"At least I put on something stain-free." Jenna stared pointedly at a brown stain on the front pocket of Luke's sweatshirt.

He shrugged, his shoulders rolling one after the other, just a hair out of sync. "Touché."

Jenna sipped her tea and studied Luke across the table. Even the messy clothes couldn't detract from the fact that he was a gorgeous man. A strong square jaw covered in light stubble couldn't hide his dimple or the slight cleft in his chin. His hair was longer than most of the men Jenna spent time with, falling in soft waves around his head. The color moved from a dark blonde at the roots to a naturally gold highlight at the edges. Jenna knew that color came from good-old-fashioned work under the sun, not a salon. His straight nose ended above a set of full lips, the kinds that people paid a lot of money for. Small lines bracketed the sides of his grinning mouth because this man clearly spent most of his time smiling. Jenna spent most of her time not smiling….

STELLA STEVENSON

Thank you,
Stella ★

Printed in the USA
CPSIA information can be obtained
at www.ICGtesting.com
LVHW040946070524
779566LV00002B/367